SAVING *Paige*

A DARK IRISH MAFIA ROMANCE

ISBN: 979-8-9906039-1-2

Cover Art by Kaite M.
Editing by Maggie Smith-Weller
www.maggieswedits.wixsite.com

Author Note

Saving Paige is a dark mafia romance that is not suitable for readers under the age of 18. The nature of this book is **very dark** and contains content that may be triggering to some readers.

All content labeled as graphic is *graphic,* so please take special consideration before continuing.

If you have no triggers and/or wish to go in blind, please continue to the prologue.

If you have any questions or concerns, or if any triggers were missed, please email me at kaitemauthor@gmail.com

Please remember that this is a work of fiction and is for entertainment purposes only.

For a full content/trigger list please scan QR code.

To the girls who have been broken and rose from the ashes.

This one is for you.

Prolouge

Paige

(age 15)

The muscles in my body tighten as I hear the door to my bedroom creak open. Cold sweats and dread overwhelm me. My never-ending nightmare continues yet again.

It's been two years since these visits began and they've started becoming more frequent as I've grown older, and my body's development continued.

Once my body started drawing the attention of the men my mom brought around, she made a deal. They could have their way with me as long as she was able to get her fix.

That's what happens when you're the daughter of a drug addict without a soul. I'm nothing more than a form of payment she can use at her disposal.

Working to keep my breathing steady becomes nearly impossible as heavy footsteps advance toward me. My heart beats uncontrollably. I'm sure at any moment it's going to burst from my chest and leave me to suffer alone. I feel the foot of my bed dip with his body weight, and I bite down on my fist to avoid whimpering. The blankets scorch my skin as they slide away from my body.

My insides begin to churn at the level my panic has reached. You'd think with the number of times my body has been used, I wouldn't feel this way. But I keep holding on to hope that maybe... just maybe, my life can somehow change. That someone out there could save me.

"Wake up, Paige," Mark says shifting my body, so I'm now lying on my back. His darkened silhouette fills my vision, and I can't control the tremor that escapes me.

"I'm on my period, Mark," I cannot hide the shaking in my voice. It's never stopped him before, but wishful thinking and all that bullshit.

"Well, then I guess it's a good thing you have other holes I can use." Forcing my legs to part, he places his fat and sweaty body between my thighs and grinds his pelvis on my center.

His cheap cologne, that smells of rubbing alcohol, is so potent that my eyes burn.

"Please," I beg. "Can't I have at least this one night? I don't feel good, and I have school in the morning."

He grabs my throat tightly before bringing his face to mine. The smell of his rancid breath, cheap beer, and cigarettes fills my senses and I choke down my bile.

"I don't give a flying fuck how you feel. I need a tight pussy to sink myself in, and you're mine," he growls.

I whimper and work to clear my mind. If I let myself think then I'll feel, and the disgust of my entire situation is already too much.

When I don't respond, he releases my throat before working to lower my sleep shorts. The frigid air touches my skin and I shudder.

He releases his small cock from his jeans and strokes himself, then he hovers over me like a soul-sucking dementor. His mere presence sucks the light of everything in his vicinity.

"Now hold still. This ass is mine tonight." He whispers before bending my legs upward – fully exposing me. My breaths become shallow as my chest constricts, I'm surprised it hasn't caved in yet. My throat closes as the lump inside grows.

My eyes burn and my vision blurs with unshed tears. The room closes in and I'm suffocating. The crushing weight of what is about to happen presses down on me. I feel him line himself up with my back entrance and those tears begin to fall. The sensation of them rolling down my cheeks and falling into my hair feels like acid.

"Fuck, baby, you know how I love to see you cry," he pushes himself into me. Stretching me. Hurting me. *Staring blankly at the corner of the room, I let myself fall into an emotionless void.*

Chapter 1

Paige

(age 21)

"Let's go get our party on, bitch!" my best friend, Sarah, shouts from the front door of our shared two-bedroom apartment.

Appearing at the door of my room, she scowls when she spots me lying in my bed. This is one of the very few places I find comfort anymore. It's not the room or home Mark has tainted or where my mother has beaten me. It's a place that is mine and Sarah's.

"I don't think I'm feeling up to going out tonight, Sarah. Can't we just have a night in? Or like, not do anything at all?" My begging is useless.

"Oh no, it's your twenty-first birthday and you can FINALLY go into the clubs and bars with me. So, get your sexy ass up and get ready."

"Remind me again why you're my best friend. I must have been under the influence of something because I cannot think of a good reason for it," I mutter, trying to cocoon myself further into my mountain of blankets.

"Because babe, you needed my award-winning personality to help you out of your shell." She muses as she makes her way to me and rips my warm safety net away.

"Sure, we'll go with that," teasing sarcastically. I get up and stride toward my closet. The truth is, Sarah is my lifeline. Without her, I wouldn't be here. Would I have been in a better place? There's no telling. But for the past three years, Sarah has helped me build a life I'm beginning to actually *like*. And considering the life I've lived, that's saying something.

Satisfied that I'm going to make good on her demands, she leaves my room to ready herself.

Sorting through my clothes, I decide to wear my best pair of whitewashed high-waisted jeans with tears on the thighs and a black lace corset top that accentuates my trim waist and B-cup breasts. I'm a petite person with little curves to my body, so this helps make me feel more feminine without drawing too much attention.

"Don't forget to shave your legs and vagina!" Sarah sings from down the hall.

Fucking lunatic.

Sarah has the libido of a succubus. I will never understand how she can be like this *all the fucking time.*

"I will shave my legs where the holes are and don't worry about my vagina. It's out of commission, remember?"

Sarah appears in my doorway again dressed to the nines in a white-lace bodysuit and black leather pants with matching pumps. Leaning against the frame, she folds her arms and scowls once more.

"P, you haven't hooked up with anyone in the last six months. I bet your vagina is full of cobwebs at this point." *I don't hook up with anyone.*

Having sex has been exceedingly difficult for me to do since I ran away from home — from Mark. He shattered my ability to be intimate with anyone but my vibrator. Even then, that's difficult. The scars on my body may have faded, but the scars on my soul...they're permanent.

"Sarah, I am not interested in hooking up with a random guy at any bar or club we go to, you know that. You're lucky I'm even going out at all."

Her eyes sadden slightly but she recovers, "You'll regret your decision when you spot a guy who is sex on legs."

Doubtful.

I've had very few instances of consensual sex since I ran away, all of which were not with random men. They also weren't as intense as Sarah makes sex out to be. There wasn't much of a connection outside of physical attraction. I don't think I'll ever find someone I can connect with on a deeper level than sex.

I roll my eyes before replying, "Sure, Sarah, because we will *definitely* be running into someone like that, and I will *definitely* be hooking up with him."

"Don't say I didn't warn you," she says, shrugging.

Without another word, I walk past her and head toward our shared bathroom to shower.

Two hours later, Sarah and I exit our Uber and walk down the sidewalk toward *Skyline*. It's a new club that opened last month and from what Sarah says, it's the place to be if you're looking to have a night full of shit-faced fun.

Which is definitely not anything I'm looking for.

My idea of fun is sitting in my hammock chair reading a good romance novel. Losing myself in a world where women are strong and fierce and bring men to their knees. Now that is what I enjoy. But alas, I had to make friends with an extroverted party animal.

"Sarah, the line is huge. Let's just go somewhere else," I grumble.

The line travels down the long sidewalk before veering around the corner and out of sight. *I'm not about to freeze my ass off in this outfit to go inside a club I don't even want to be in.*

"Don't worry about it, Paige, I got us on the VIP list. We don't need to wait in line."

How the fuck did she manage that?

Shooting me a mischievous smirk, Sarah drags me by the wrist to the front door and we're met by a behemoth of a man who looks like he could stop a moving truck with his bare hands.

Jesus H. Christ.

"Name," he grunts in a voice that is as deep as Vin Diesel's but scary as fuck.

"Sarah Wilkson and Paige Henley," Sarah responds while batting her lashes.

After confirming our names on the list, the bouncer steps aside and opens the door to allow us through.

"Thank you," Sarah sets her hand on his forearm before winking and walking past. *Shameless flirt.*

He doesn't acknowledge her advances but does check her ass out as she strides through the doorway. *Barf.*

"Thank you," I say, also receiving no response. Which is a-okay with me.

At least you don't feel his eyes on your ass.

Once inside, I can feel the bass of the music reverberating in my chest as we walk down the narrow hallway lit by low red lighting. It's seductive and alluring.

"Let's go to the bar for drinks before we head to VIP for our table," Sarah shouts over the music, which gets louder the further inside we get.

I nod in response.

The hallway opens into a vast space of different colored lights and dark walls. There are multiple levels for people to socialize, dance, and drink. The DJ platform is in the center of the far wall and looks as though it can fill my entire living room and kitchen space. On the left is a massive oval-shaped bar with six bartenders serving patrons. On the right is the staircase leading up to the second level, where the VIP lounge is.

From this angle, I can't make out what it looks like up there, but I can see people standing by the railing looking down at the dance floor.

The place is packed full of people dancing — more like dry humping, to the music. Around the outer parameter of the entire space, tables, and booths are arranged comfortably.

We order our drinks – a Sex on the Beach for Sarah and a White Russian for me – before making our way up the stairs.

Men and women pretty much break their damn necks watching Sarah strut the entire way.

It's not surprising. Sarah basically looks like Rosie Huntington-Whitley. Legs for days, long blonde hair that cascades down her back, a beautiful trim figure, light blue eyes that you can get lost in, and plump lips that people pay money for but end up looking like fish. She draws attention every time she steps into a room, and she carries herself with such confidence.

That confidence is what I envy most about her. It's something I deeply wish I could have. My abuse started at such an important age in my life, I never had the chance to build it.

At the end of the VIP staircase, we are stopped by another bouncer. This one is just as bulky, but not King Kong-sized like the first bouncer we met. No less intimidating though.

Confirming our names, he lets us pass, and we make our way up the stairs.

The seating up here is much more intimate. The room is rectangular and dimly lit. The booths are black leather and placed along the back wall, hidden in the darker lighting for privacy. There are glass tables in front of them that help make the space feel more open. A door sits at the end of the walkway to what I'm assuming is a private restroom.

As we make our way to our table, the hairs on the back of my neck stand and my steps falter.

What the hell?

Goosebumps rise all over my entire body. Oddly, it's not an uncomfortable feeling. Which *is* unnerving.

"Are you okay?" furrowing her brows, Sarah lightly touches my arm to get my attention.

Shaking the feeling away, I meet her eyes and give her a small nod and smile before continuing my way toward our table.

Chapter 2

Declan

Sipping my whiskey and sitting with my best friend, Rhys, I watch as the bouncer lets two women through.

"God damn," Rhys mutters next to me and nudges my arm with his elbow.

God damn, indeed.

"I call dibs on the blonde," he says as he watches them walk past the front of our table.

"I wasn't even looking at her; have at it." I watch as one of the most beautiful women I've ever laid eyes on walks with a tall blonde.

She's without a doubt a tiny person. Her damn heels bring her to about five-foot-five. She's wearing figure-hugging jeans that accentuate her soft curves and a corset top that makes her breasts look fantastic. Her long, wavy brown hair stops just above the top of her waist.

I bet it would feel like silk in my grasp as I pound into her from behind.

She has a heart-shaped face, a small slender nose, and lips that have just the right amount of fullness. Even in this low lighting, I can tell her olive-colored skin is as soft as velvet. I can't confirm the color of her eyes, but they are a lighter shade, hazel or green maybe.

My mouth waters at the thought of having her body above me, beneath me, in front of me. I adjust my growing erection and watch the sway of her beautiful body as she walks.

This woman is mine.

She must sense my stare because she stumbles a bit and her brows furrow. She frowns at the ground and then she shakes off whatever feeling she just experienced, she gives her friend a small smile and a nod, then continues on her way.

With a smirk, I raise my glass to finish off my whiskey.

"Declan,"

Fuck.

Jackie's voice reaches my ears like nails on a chalkboard and my erection immediately deflates. Jackie and I fucked a few times in the past, but now I can't get rid of her. *No matter how hard I fucking try.*

I turn my head and watch as she walks towards me with a pout on her lips.

"You haven't been answering any of my texts or calls, baby. I've missed you," She whines, before perching herself on the arm of the seat closest to me. I scrunch my nose at my personal space being invaded.

With straight black hair that reaches just below the shoulders, tan skin with scattered freckles, deep blue eyes, and a body that makes porn stars jealous, Jackie is without a doubt a beautiful woman.

Unfortunately, her beauty is only on the surface.

She's a spoiled princess – thanks to her daddy never telling her the word "no". She's conniving and vindictive when she doesn't get what she wants, and I have no patience for her constant whining.

"Maybe because I don't want to talk to you, Jackie," if she notices the bite in my voice, she doesn't show it.

She takes my acknowledgment of her presence as an invitation to touch me and she leans forward, pressing her fake tits against my shoulder. I take in an annoyed breath.

"I just really miss you, Dec. Especially at night, all alone in my bed. I've really needed you to help this never-ending ache," she purrs, nipping at my earlobe. She continues pressing herself against me, which pisses me off.

I pull away with a growl.

"Get lost. I have a business meeting starting soon, and I don't need your dirty cunt around to spoil it."

Her body tenses and she jerks back as if I've slapped her before her face transforms into a rage-filled scowl.

"You know, you're such a fucking asshole. I miss you and you treat me like shit. I don't deserve this. I can find someone better than you, you know?!" Her high-pitched shriek rings in my ears.

I fight the urge to roll my eyes.

"I told you, Jackie, we were fucking and that was it. The last time was just that. *The last time*. Go find someone else's dick to sit on." I gesture toward the stairs.

With a growl, she curses "*Bastardo!*" and stands from where she was seated before stomping off toward the stairs.

Rhys chuckles next to me. "You're such an ass. I love it."

My mouth tips upward. "Yeah, well, she wouldn't be so bad if her voice didn't bother the fuck out of me and she wasn't a spoiled and whiny bitch."

Movement at the top of the stairs catches my attention and I see the bouncer letting my guest through. Rhys and I stand and button our suit jackets before striding toward him.

"Declan. Rhys. Always a pleasure." Antonio Romano – The Don of the Italian mafia and Jackie's older brother – greets us. He is accompanied by two men who look like they've spent too much time getting the shit kicked out of them.

"Antonio," I state with a nod.

Rhys stands next to me in a relaxed, yet protective, stance. The two men watch him warily. They're both very aware that Rhys could gut them in seconds if he wanted to.

Turning around, we stride to the opposite side of the room where the doorway to the next level is located.

I can feel her eyes on me when I pass her table. Knowing she's watching me as I watched her causes my blood to heat and travel south.

Fuck, I need to find out who this woman is.

Ignoring the temptation to meet her gaze, I continue toward the door.

Entering the security code in the hidden keypad, I make my way up the stairs once the door is unlocked.

After entering my office, I head behind my desk and face Antonio. His face is blank, and I motion for him to take a seat before taking my own. Rhys stands at my back and Antonio's men stand behind him.

"From what I see, business is good," he says nonchalantly as he looks around the room.

Here we go.

“You sound surprised.” Boredom laces my tone.

With a condescending chuckle, Antonio meets me with an amused gaze. “You only recently took over for your father, Declan. Forgive me for having my doubts that a twenty-five-year-old can handle a billion-dollar organization.”

I meet his stare with my own amused look. “You seem to forget that this twenty-five-year-old provides you with weapons for you to continue your drug trafficking.”

Antonio’s gaze becomes hard, but he keeps his mouth shut. *Bitch.*

Changing the subject, I say, “Let's discuss what you came for this time, yes?”

Chapter 3

Paige

"Did you see the asses on those men?" Sarah's excited voice cuts through my thoughts as I continue to stare in the direction the group of men went.

I guess it wasn't a restroom.

I turn my green eyes toward Sarah's blue ones. "Um... Yeah. That was weird though, right?"

"What?" her blonde brow raises.

"The way those guys were standing, like they were facing off or something, before heading through that door. I mean, they had bodyguards." My brows scrunch and I shake my head.

I know celebrities have bodyguards, but the vibe they all had was undeniably hostile.

"I honestly didn't notice anything past the fact that the second guy looks like he could pound your pussy into a wall if he wanted to." Her comment causes me to burst out in laughter.

"Sarah, your libido is ridiculous."

Unashamedly, she says with a shrug of her shoulder, “Yeah, well, I can’t help it if the male species can produce such a fine specimen.”

Rolling my eyes, I lift my drink and take a sip.

“Come on, let’s go shake our asses.”

I barely get a chance to set my drink down before Sarah grabs my arm and pulls me toward the stairs.

Six songs later, my feet have blisters, and those blisters have blisters.

You just had to pick your most uncomfortable shoes, didn’t you?

“I need to go to the restroom,” I shout to Sarah over the loud music. My chest pounds with each bump of the bass.

“Okay!” She starts pulling away from the guy she is dancing with, but I shake my head and put a hand up.

“Stay here, I’ll just be second. You can see the door from here.” I point out where the restroom is located just behind me.

Sarah looks unsure about letting me go alone. “I’ll be fine. Just dance.” I send her a reassuring smile before turning toward the restroom without giving her time to reply.

After relieving my near-exploding bladder, washing my hands, and double-checking my hair and makeup, I make my way back to Sarah.

I only make it five feet from the door when I’m frozen in place.

“Mark,” I squeak.

"Hello, Paige," the voice that has haunted my mind for so many years and thought I'd never hear again, burns through my eardrums like a hot knife.

Nonononono.

My breathing becomes shallow and erratic, and I start to sweat.

Mark's eyes slither down my body like a snake ready to strike and I instantly feel nauseous.

This cannot be happening.

"Did you miss me? You thought you could just dip out on me when you were eighteen and think I wouldn't find you?" His voice is tense, and he takes a step toward me. I take one back.

Don't throw up.

"I... I..." My tongue feels heavy in my mouth. My vision begins to tunnel as the heaviness in my chest becomes overwhelming.

DO NOT PANIC, PAIGE. You're in a club full of people. You're not alone with him.

My body is refusing to accept the truth of my situation.

"I knew you were dumb, but I didn't peg you to be stupid enough to think you could get away from me." He growls as he continues his stalk toward me.

Run. You need to run.

My head spins and I can feel the alcohol I drank climbing up my throat.

DO NOT THROW UP.

"Is there a problem here?" A deep voice sounds to my left, interrupting our exchange.

Thank God.

Mark and I both whip our heads and I meet the eyes of the man I saw in the VIP lounge. I'm instantly thrown into a blissful daze.

Holy. He's even more gorgeous up close.

When Mark speaks up, the man releases me from whatever the fuck kind of trance he placed and focuses on him.

The way he assesses Mark is as though he's nothing more than shit on the bottom of his expensive leather shoes.

Trust me, buddy, he's worse.

"Nah man, just catching up with my girl's daughter. Ain't that right, Paige?" Mark is so full of hot air that he genuinely believes he sounds tough.

The man meets my gaze once again.

God, those eyes are so blue, almost turquoise. Like the Caribbean Ocean in the summer. I could swim in them forever.

Whatever he must see written on my face, he doesn't like because his brows furrow and his eyes fill with questions, and... is that rage?

No, Paige. That's stupid.

"Um. Actually, I was just heading out." I try to slip past Mark, but he steps into my path. I tense and my throat tightens.

Shit. Fuck.

He dips his head to my ear and drawls, "This isn't over. I know where you live now Paigy, and I look forward to our visits again." He pulls away and the lump in my throat grows to ungodly proportions as I watch Mark disappear into the crowd. I can't pull my eyes away despite not being able to see him anymore.

I feel his presence behind me. My skin feels hot and sweaty. Nothing like that clamminess I felt around Mark. The air feels electrically charged – it takes my breath away. I don't turn around to meet his eyes.

"Are you alright?"

Damn. The voice of this man is husky and seductive without him even trying. My knees threaten to buckle.

What the fuck, Paige? Get it together. You can't go around getting seduced by a man's voice after just seeing Mark.

"Uh, yeah. I'm fine," my voice is so low, I doubt he even heard my response.

When he places a hand on my arm, my body stiffens almost painfully. It's quickly removed, and he doesn't attempt to touch me again. Instead, he comes around and stands in front of me.

I have to crane my neck to meet his eyes. Even in four-inch heels, I barely meet his shoulder. He has to be at least six-foot-three.

He has chestnut brown hair that is short on the sides and the top is just long enough to run your fingers through. The way it's tousled, I can't tell if it's intentional or if he's run his fingers through it too many times. His dark brows and lashes frame those gorgeous blue eyes. There is a barely noticeable crook in the middle of his nose as if it didn't heal properly from a break. His strong jaw is lined with enough scruff to rub your skin raw.

Stop. You don't need to sleep with some random man.

And his lips... Oh, those lips are perfectly plump. The bottom is slightly larger than the top, giving him a slight pout. His throat is covered in a big tattoo of an owl with wings that wrap around his neck.

His blazing stare makes me feel as though he is trying to reach my soul.

Why doesn't that bother me?

Nothing about this man makes me uncomfortable. In fact, I feel drawn to him in some way. *That* is what makes me uncomfortable.

"Thank you for helping me. I better go look for my friend now." I'm buzzing with the need to leave his proximity. It's so intense. Suffocating almost. But also… euphoric.

What the actual fuck?

The corner of his mouth lifts into a smirk.

Fuck, he has a dimple. Of course, he has a dimple.

He dips his chin in a small nod and then steps aside, allowing me to pass by him.

"Have a good night, *ghrá*." His voice makes shivers travel down my spine and into my toes. And my panties instantly soak.

I don't reply to him. I can't. I don't know what to say to the most beautiful man to ever speak to me.

You also have no idea what the fuck he just called you, Paige.

I find Sarah sitting at the bar with the same guy she was dancing with earlier. She catches me approaching and beams with her pearly-white teeth on full display. I send her a small uncomfortable smile which causes hers to falter, and she tilts her head in question with her brows lowering slightly.

I mouth to her, 'I'm heading out.'

Mark just said he knows where you live, dumbass. Do you really want to go there?

Nope, but knowing he's somewhere in the area is fucking with my head.

She gets up from her seat and walks over to me. "Is everything okay?"

"Yeah, don't worry about me. I just want to go home." *Liar.*

"Paige, come on, it's your birthday. You should enjoy it." She rests a hand on my arm and gently rubs it.

Something behind me catches her attention. Her eyes widen slightly and then she puts on her best flirty smile to whomever she is looking at.

Please don't be that guy. Please don't be that guy.

"Did I hear correctly? It's your birthday?" The voice has a sexy timber to it, but it's not *him.*

Thank the lord.

I turn and meet the eyes of the second man we saw in the VIP lounge. He's just as tall and sexy but with green eyes lined with dark lashes. The reddish-brown hair on his head is short on the sides and long on the top —styled to perfection— the crook on his nose is more pronounced than the guy who helped me. He has freckles scattered on his face which give him a slightly boyish look and his plump lips are symmetrical.

Where the fuck did these guys come from?

He places his hands into his suit pockets waiting for me to reply.

"Sure is. My little Paige here turns twenty-one today." Sarah wraps her arm around my shoulders in a sideways hug.

I stand there awkwardly as Sarah and this guy eye-fuck each other.

His smile reveals straight white teeth. "Well, I was coming over here to see if you lovely ladies wanted to accompany me and my friend. We were going out for a late dinner."

Before I can reject, Sarah answers with an enthusiastic "Sure!"

I shoot her a *what the hell?* look that she pointedly ignores.

His smile grows and his eyes light up.

Seriously, do they put something in the water here? This guy is too pretty.

With a glint in his eyes, he reaches his hand out. "Great, we're leaving now. My name is Rhys."

"Sarah."

Placing one hand in his, she wraps the other in mine, and we follow whomever this Rhys is toward the exit.

I guess this is better than going home and being ambushed by Mark.

Chapter 4

Declan

I knew it was a smart idea to send Rhys to invite those women with us. The brunette was timid toward me when I interrupted that dickwad who cornered her.

Something about him didn't sit right with me. His demeanor toward her was aggressive and possessive. Like she was his property. An object. Not someone to be worshiped. And she is someone you worship with your entire being.

The deer-in-the-headlights look she had on top of the blood draining from her face confirmed that he was not someone she wanted to be around.

Now, I'm no Saint. Shit, I love torturing people for fun. But there was no way in hell I was going to head out and leave her here.

Especially since my men couldn't find where the bastard went. Which is not something that happens.

I'm waiting outside my blacked-out Escalade - scrolling through my phone - when the door opens and Rhys steps out with the blonde and brunette behind him.

Sliding my phone into my pocket, I watch as they – correction, *she* makes her way over.

Fuck, she is beautiful.

The sway in her hips goes straight to my cock. I'm fucking grateful it's dark out, or she will see just how much I want her.

"Sarah, Paige, let me introduce you to my friend Declan," Paige's cheeks flush pink and she tries to avoid eye contact with me.

The blonde – Sarah, steps up to me and reaches out her hand. I take it and give it a small shake.

"Pleasure to meet you, Sarah. It's good to see you again, Paige," I don't miss the shiver her body makes when I say her name. I give her a smirk which causes her flush to deepen.

Her friend side-eyes me and then looks at Paige with a brow raised. Paige avoids looking at her.

"Alright, let's head out. I'm starving." Rhys claps his hands once and he opens the passenger door for Sarah to slide in.

He winks at me when he shuts the door then walks around the front of the car to the driver's side.

Opening the back door, I ask, "Anything in particular you want to eat, Paige?" *I know what I want.*

She slides into the backseat "I'm not really that hungry, so you guys can choose."

Her voice has a rasp to it that I didn't notice inside from how quietly she spoke. Fuck, it's sexy.

The scent of her perfume fills my nose when I slide in after her. It's light and airy. Like a rainy day in the summer.

"I honestly could go for a fat cheeseburger," Her friend chimes in from the front seat.

You'd think she hung the damn moon from the look Rhys is giving her. Not-so-subtly, he adjusts himself before starting the SUV and pulling out of the parking lot.

"I know a great diner about 10 minutes from here," his voice is eager. I roll my eyes at how he's salivating for this woman.

You're no different.

Sitting in *Shauna's Diner with* Sarah and Rhys on one side and Paige and me on the other, I try not to crowd her too much, but I want to be close to her. This booth feels too big, even though we barely fit as it is.

What is it about her that is doing this to me?

Everything about this woman is consuming me and I'm a willing victim.

Sarah and Rhys are scarfing down their cheeseburgers like it is their last meal before execution. I ordered myself a turkey melt with seasoned French fries that I essentially inhaled. Paige on the other hand, has barely nibbled at her chicken Caesar salad.

"So, I assume you own the club since you guys were able to get through that door in the VIP lounge that was obviously locked?" Sarah gulps her Coca-Cola.

"Declan owns the club. I'm just the muscle, sweetheart," Rhys sends with a wink.

"Paige, what do you do for work?" asking in as soft of a voice as I can manage.

She startles as if she was just lost in thought. "Huh?"

Chuckling lightly, I ask again, "I was just curious about what you do for work."

The flush returns to her cheeks, and God it is the most adorable thing I've ever seen.

"I work at an elementary school right now as an aid in the front office." A small smile forms on her lips.

"Sounds like an interesting job. I haven't been around kids in a long time, but I know they're wild and unpredictable," I tease.

She begins telling me about how much she enjoys her job and the kids she encounters. She tells me about a little girl named Sage, with whom she has a very deep bond. Her face is animated, and her voice is filled with so much love and admiration. She's mesmerizing this way.

I offer her a wider smile which she returns, and I'm struck right in the chest by her beauty. Her teeth are straight and white with pointed canines that I want sinking into my skin as I fuck her.

Where has this woman been?

Sarah and Rhys clear their throats from across the table, pulling me and Paige from our bubble.

"We just called an Uber. We're going to head out," Rhys says before he and Sarah slide out of their seats.

"Will you be okay, P? Do you want to come with us, and we can drop you off at home?" By the look in her eyes, I can tell she is hoping Paige says no so she can leave with Rhys alone.

I look over at Paige and she quickly averts her eyes.

"I can take you home." The need to be with her is overwhelming. I feel almost panicked at the possibility of leaving her side.

She will be mine if it's the last thing I do.

"Okay," she whispers, looking down at her hands. She tries hiding the small smile forming but I catch it and it warms something deep within me.

"Alright, it's settled. I'll see you later, Declan. Bye, Paige," Rhys says.

Sarah watches Paige momentarily before flicking her gaze to me. Her eyes narrow and her lips purse as she stares me down. "I know your face Declan. I *will* hurt you if something happens to Paige".

I'd rather slice off my hand than hurt her.

"I got her, Sarah. Rhys has my number. I can text him once I drop her off and he can let you know."

Satisfied, she nods her head. Blowing a quick kiss to Paige, Sarah spins around to Rhys before the pair walk hand in hand to the door.

"Since it seems you have no interest in your food, do you want to head home?" Her eyes flick over my face as she studies me.

"Whose home?" Her eyes bulge and I know she didn't mean to say that out loud.

I can't help but let out a laugh. "I didn't mean it that way, but I won't deny you if that is what you want."

"I am so sorry. I don't know why I said that. I... I'm not that type of person." The flush reaches up to her ears and it's cute as fuck.

Not bothering to hide my amusement, I chuckle "Not a problem, *ghrá*."

Her shoulders relax slightly with my response.

"I'm not usually this awkward, I promise. It's just been a rough night for me." She chews on the side of her cheek but holds my gaze.

Her light sea-green eyes captivate me. I would gladly lose myself in them.

Fuck, she's stunning.

"Do you want to tell me about who that guy was at the club?" I prop my elbow up on the back of the booth and face her fully.

"I'd rather not talk about it," she mutters. Once again, she lowers her head to look at her hands.

The need I feel to touch her skin is unbearable. Reaching out my hand slowly, I use my forefinger to lift her chin, so her eyes meet mine. Her breath hitches and her pupils dilate.

"If you're threatened by him, tell me. I'll take care of it." I don't remove my hand, but instead, move to cup her cheek and stroke her soft skin.

Velvet. I knew it.

She leans into my touch and offers me a small but sad smile.

Can't say I'm a fan of this look on her face.

"I appreciate your help earlier. He's just someone I knew and hoped I'd never see again." She moves her gaze away from me.

She doesn't elaborate further, and I don't push. There is something about Paige that speaks to my soul. I feel it deep within myself that she is meant to be with me. That our paths were meant to meet and continue side by side.

I'd be a damn fool to let this woman go.

"I'll still take care of it if he becomes a problem." I bring her eyes back to mine.

"But you don't know me," she whispers.

The corner of my lip tips up in a smirk.

"I will."

Chapter 5

Paige

Declan and I walk out of the diner into the night air that has enough of a bite, I shiver involuntarily.

"Here," slipping his suit jacket off his shoulders, Declan drapes it over me. It's gigantic and drowns my frame like a dress.

Jesus, he's bigger than I thought.

"Thank you. I wasn't planning on being outside any longer than to wait for an Uber at the club. I didn't think to bring a jacket." I pull the fabric closer to my body and I'm enveloped in his delicious scent of sandalwood and amber. I take a quiet deep breath to fill myself with more of his scent.

"No need to thank me, *ghrá*."

We slowly make our way toward his SUV. My body thrums with something I can't describe from being alone with him. Everything about this man makes me feel at odds with what I've always known. Despite his dangerous demeanor and authoritative presence, I feel this foreign need to be with him.

"Do you want me to take you home or would you be willing to walk with me for a little while?" Declan studies my face when I stare up into his eyes.

He brings me an odd sense of peace that I've never felt before. Being around him feels *right.*

"We can go for a walk," I say nodding.

His dimples are on full display when he smiles at me and my chest warms. He holds out his hand. Looking down, I take it. Electricity bursts through my body from the feel of his skin. His calloused hands rub against my soft ones, and I love the feeling. When I look back up at him, he winks, then spins around and leads me down the sidewalk.

We walk hand-in-hand, talking about everything and yet nothing at all. We joke and laugh about the oddest things. He makes me feel *seen.* Like a normal girl who isn't broken beyond repair.

Despite the strong presence Declan has, I feel so comfortable around him. It's difficult to navigate because I've never felt this before.

I feel him watching my profile from my peripheral. My blood starts to heat up and I try to avoid blushing.

"Why do you keep staring at me?" I ask quietly.

"You're unbelievably beautiful."

I bite down lightly on my bottom lip. Butterflies swarm my stomach.

Stopping, Declan turns to me and cups my face with one hand. He uses his thumb to gently pull it from my teeth. The corner of his mouth tips up in a small smile as he stares at my lips with such intensity that I can feel it in my bones.

We stand in our little bubble in the middle of the sidewalk, just watching each other. As the sounds of the city fade into the background and my heartbeat drums in my ears. I want so badly for him to kiss me. My thoughts are overtaken by the need for more of his touch.

I don't know what to make of this connection I seem to have with him.

Taking a deep breath, Declan clears his throat and releases my face. I instantly feel the loss of his warmth.

"Are you ready for me to take you home?" he asks as he runs his fingers through his hair.

My peaceful bubble pops and I remember my confrontation with Mark. I can't go home. I'll be completely alone.

"Not really," I whisper.

"Where would you like to go?" he asks in a low voice.

"Can we go to your house?"

Something that looks like understanding flashes across his face and he nods.

We pull into an underground parking garage and Declan swipes a badge before the security gate rises. We drive through into a near-empty lot with a few other expensive-looking cars and SUVs.

Definitely unlike the uncovered parking at my apartment.

Pulling into a spot close to the elevators, Declan switches the vehicle off and takes the key from the ignition. He doesn't make a move to exit the car but instead, shifts his body to face me.

"Are you sure you want to go up?" His eyes search mine.

Not really, but I'm scared to go home.

"Can I be honest for a second?"

He gives me a pointed look but doesn't say anything, so I continue.

"I'm scared to go home. That... that guy from the club was my mom's drug dealer when I was younger. I ran from home at eighteen because of him. I'm not sure how he found me here, but I don't feel comfortable going home knowing I'll be there alone." *But I feel comfortable with you.*

We're not going to touch that subject just yet.

He studies me with an expressionless face. *This guy must be amazing at poker because I cannot read him.*

"I will take care of him. In the meantime, let's go up to my penthouse. You can stay as long as you need to." He opens the door and exits the vehicle. A few seconds later, my door is opened, and Declan extends his hand out to me.

I slide my palm into his and that same electric current flows from his body into mine. He must feel it too because he inhales a sharp breath and his fingers flex. Our eyes meet and the atmosphere becomes thick.

Relaxing as much as I can, I wrap my fingers around his and climb out of my seat.

We ride the elevator in silence.

Why did I think this was a good idea?

With a *ping*, the doors slide open, and we step into a wide-open space.

Directly in front of me are wall-to-wall windows overlooking New York City. The lights of the buildings and cars below are breathtaking from here. To the right is a massive charcoal sectional with a white coffee table. On the wall hangs a huge flat-screen TV and a soundbar. On the left is an open-concept kitchen with white granite countertops, and charcoal-colored cabinets as well as matching stainless-steel appliances. Four black leather bar stools sit lined up against the large island. There is a rectangle-shaped dining table that seats twelve people. At the back left side of the room, I can see a doorway leading to what must be a hallway to the bedrooms.

Declan doesn't say anything as he watches me admire the space.

"This is amazing," I whisper under my breath. I'm in complete awe of how beautiful his home is.

"Thank you. My sister Emily said if I did the *typical male decor*, she'd castrate me." His tone is filled with love.

That comment makes me chuckle. "Well, I'm happy you took her threat seriously." I push my hair behind my ear.

He strides toward the kitchen and opens the refrigerator. Pulling out two water bottles, he hands me one before opening his and drinking down almost the entire bottle in two pulls.

Opting not to open mine yet, I walk to the windows and look out. We're so high up. I didn't pay attention to what floor we had stopped on.

I wonder how long it would take to reach the ground from this high up.

Cutting my intrusive thought, I feel Declan watching my back and my skin breaks out in goosebumps. I can feel the blood rushing to my cheeks, so I don't turn around. *Pull yourself together, Paige.*

I spin slowly, admiring the space. I stop when I see a photo on the wall of a woman who looks to be about my age. She has bright blue eyes, so similar to Declan's. Her red hair is draped over her shoulder and a beautiful smile is spread across her face.

"She's beautiful. Is this Emily?"

The sound of his shoes on the hardwood floors let me know he is making his way toward me. My stomach flips and my heart begins to race at the thrill of him being next to me. When he stops, he's so close to my back that his breath moves my hair.

"Yeah."

After a moment, Declan clears his throat lightly before the heat of his body moves away.

"I have a guest bedroom here that you can stay in for the night. It has its own ensuite, so you don't have to worry about privacy." His voice sounds strained.

He turns and makes his way down the hallway – I follow close behind.

He stops at the fifth door and opens it. "My bedroom is down the hall and to the left if you need anything." He points in the direction of his room.

I nod my thank you and step into the guest bedroom.

The space can fit both mine and Sarah's and *still* have empty space. Unlike the parts of the penthouse I've already seen, this room has plush white carpet throughout. On the left and centered against the wall is a beautiful white oak queen-size bed frame with a white comforter draped over the mattress and about a hundred pillows.

Not really, but still more than I use.

There is a matching dresser directly across from it with a large flat-screen TV mounted on the wall. Next to the dresser is the door to the ensuite. The window directly in front of me is huge and covers most of the wall. The view is just as beautiful as the one in the living room.

Do club owners really make this much money to afford places like this?

Entering the ensuite, there is a double vanity, also with white granite countertops. A large walk-in shower to the right and a jetted tub next to that. On the left, is the entryway of the walk-in closet.

There is a light knock at the door before it's opened and Declan peers in.

"I brought you a T-shirt to sleep in. I figured it was more comfortable than what you currently have on."

I offer a smile. "Thank you. I appreciate it. You can just set it on the bed.

He enters the room, sets down the black shirt, and then walks back to the door. Before he closes it, he turns to me and says, "I'll see you in the morning." And then he's gone. *Why does that bother me? You don't even know this guy.*

Yeah, but he makes you feel safe.

I walk toward the bed and begin undressing. Placing my head and arms through the proper holes, the shirt falls down my body and engulfs me just as the suit jacket did. The smell of sandalwood and amber mixed with laundry detergent fills my nose and I smile.

Ridding the bed of the multitude of pillows, I pull back the blankets, slide into bed, and burrow myself into a cocoon. The silk sheets slide against my skin and warmth envelopes me.

The weight of my eyelids becomes impossible to ignore, and I'm forced to drift to sleep.

Chapter 6

Paige

(Age 17)

There is so much blood. Too much blood.

Sitting on the cold bathroom tile, I try to calm my uncontrolled breathing but it's becoming overwhelming. I feel like I'm trying to breathe through a bendy straw. The smell of copper is so strong, it burns my eyes.

Mark bangs on the door again. Please go away.

"Open the fucking door, Paige!" His anger radiates through the wood with each pound of his fist.

When I told my mom I was pregnant and Mark was the father, she simply stared at me and said, "It better not mess with my drug supply." Before leaving me to go out on a drugged-up binge for three weeks. Her lack of reaction shouldn't have surprised me, but it was still painful to see how little she truly cared for me.

I tried going to a free clinic for an abortion but when Mark found out, he beat me until I could barely function. It took me just as long to heal from my wounds.

He wants me pregnant so he can use this baby to continue his "drug legacy". Whatever the fuck that means.

Well now, here I am, four months pregnant and miscarrying. I don't know how long the blood is supposed to continue but I feel I've passed the point of no return. The surface of the counter is covered in my bloody handprints. The blood has pooled beneath me and is now sliding through the grout of the tiled floor. But I don't want to do anything about it right now, I just want to bleed out and die.

Why can't he just kill me? I don't want to be here anymore.

I hear shuffling and then a loud bang before the door bursts open and Mark fills the doorway.

"What the fuck do you think you're doing?!" He roars in anger and disgust when he sees all the blood and me lying on the ground.

I don't reply. I can't. I feel so light-headed now, and very sleepy. Lowering myself further onto the floor, I lay my cheek against the tile. The stickiness of the blood coats the side of my face and hair.

Maybe if I just closed my eyes and relaxed enough, my body would let go.

"Fuck." I hear Mark mutter, then my body is lifted from where I lay, and I'm carried out of the house to his car.

Mark throws me in the backseat before slamming the door. The world around me spins and my vision loses focus. When Mark climbs into the driver's seat, he turns around and growls, "That baby better be alive when we make it to the hospital."

I better be dead by the time we make it.

I hear the steady beeping of a machine.

Well, I guess I'm alive. Oh, goody.

I open my eyes to see that I'm in a hospital room alone. I try to sit up but my stomach hurts like a motherfucker, so I have no choice but to fall back onto my pillow with a huff.

I wonder if I can "accidentally" overdose here? Not likely but a girl can hope.

With a soft knock, the door opens to reveal a tall slender old man with white thinning hair and a pair of circle-shaped glasses. He gives me a gentle smile.

"Hello, Miss Henley, my name is Dr. Grant. I am happy to see you are awake. How are you feeling?" Like I missed my one chance to rid myself of existence.

"My stomach hurts," I grimace.

"Ah yes, that is to be expected. What do you remember about coming here?"

"I honestly don't remember much. What happened?"

"Well, it appears, you had an incomplete miscarriage. Meaning, your body couldn't successfully remove all the tissue from the pregnancy. Your body hemorrhaged, which resulted in the extensive blood loss you experienced. We had to perform what is called a D&C, or, dilation and curettage, to remove the remaining tissue. The procedure was successful, and you should heal just fine. You may experience some cramping over the next several days as well as some spotting – all of which is normal. Do you have any questions?" he stands with his hands folded in front of him.

Can you perform an assisted suicide?

"Will that affect me being able to have any more kids?" I ask instead.

Maybe if I can't get pregnant again, Mark will get rid of me.

"That is difficult to say since we do not know the cause of this miscarriage. You're young and appear healthy, so I don't believe that you will have any problems in the future."

I can only nod in response.

"The man who brought you in, your stepfather – "

"He is not my stepfather," I growl.

"I apologize. The man who brought you in did not state whether he would return today but we will keep you overnight for observation since you lost a significant amount of blood. You should be able to go home in the morning. We have you on a steady regimen of painkillers to help with any discomfort you may have. Do you need anything before I leave you in the care of the nurses?"

A scalpel to slit my throat or wrists would be nice.

"No, thank you," I say with a tight smile that probably looks more like I'm in pain.

The smile he offers is warm and just pisses me off. "You're welcome. If you need anything, the nurses are available and can page me if needed."

He leaves the room, and I'm left alone.

The next morning, I'm wheeled out to Mark's beat-up Honda at the front of the hospital.

"Paige, baby, I've been so worried about you." With the fakest concern I've ever seen, he walks over to me and pulls me from the

wheelchair. He tells the nurse who helped me that he can take it from here.

I don't respond. I'm not sure what to say to him.

Mark opens the car door and I slide into the passenger seat. The smell of beer and cigarettes invades my senses and I grimace.

The car ride home is tense. Mark hasn't said a word since we left the hospital. From the way he is gripping the steering wheel, I know what's coming.

Maybe he won't stop, and you'll end up dead. *I think hopefully.*

Pulling up to my mom's house, Mark slams on the brakes and puts the car in park. Before I have time to register what's happening, Mark is in my face with my throat clutched in his tight grasp.

"You stupid fucking bitch! What did you do?! Did you purposely cause that baby to die?!"

The only response I can muster is a whimper from the tightness of his hold.

He shoves my head against the car window and stars dance around in my vision. Pain erupts in my skull. He suddenly releases my throat and exits the car.

I suck in deep breaths and fill my lungs before I step out of the vehicle and head inside.

Barely making it through the threshold, Mark throws my body to the ground and starts undressing me. I try to fight him, but he has at least eighty pounds on me, and I'm still weak from the drugs they gave me in the hospital.

He covers my mouth with his sweaty hand when I attempt to scream.

"Lie still!" He spits and droplets land on the side of my face.

I continue to fight as best as I can, which angers him more. In a swift motion, Mark punches my cheek and blood fills my nose and mouth.

You're weak. Pitiful. If you can't fight him off, then you deserve this.

The tears begin falling down my face and into my hair when I feel him line himself up with my entrance. The oppressive weight of my life is suffocating. Each day brings me new utter desperation for my life to end.

Following my routine for times like these, I find a corner to focus on and will my mind to go blank. I don't have a happy place to go to. My entire existence has been pathetic. I'm a waste of space unless I'm being used for the pleasure of others. But still, I try. I try my damn hardest to block out the sickening acts being done to me against my will.

His hot breath travels up my neck and he breathes me in. Tears spill from my eyes and I breathe in a ragged breath. His tongue drags up my cheek as he licks my tears and hums... and then he thrusts.

Chapter 7

Declan

Something's wrong. I don't know what, but I can feel it. The atmosphere has darkened and the weight of it is ominous. Straining my ears, I listen for any noise in the penthouse. For the longest time, I can only hear the sound of the central air working. And then, I hear soft whimpering.

Fuck.

Reaching over, I open my bedside drawer and grab my pistol. Shooting off the bed, I leave my room and go into the darkened hallway.

I need to get to Paige.

With my gun clutched in my hands, I stealthily make it to the end of the hallway and peek around the corner. When I see no one is there, I continue toward the room Paige is in.

Each step feels heavy. This feeling of panic in my system is foreign and I feel smothered.

Holding my breath, I place my ear lightly against the bedroom door and listen carefully. The muffled sounds of rustling and heavy breathing come from the other side.

Did someone make it past my security?

Reaching for the door, I hear "STOP! PLEASE!" My heart hammers into my ribcage and my protective instincts take control.

Fuck this.

I burst in with my gun pointed in the room. I whip it left and right quickly only to find that it's empty, except for Paige.

What the hell?

Paige is writhing under her blankets with a sheen of sweat on her forehead. Her face is twisted in agony.

Flicking the safety on, I tuck the gun in the waistband of my sweats before slowly approaching the bed.

She's having a nightmare.

"Paige," I whisper cautiously to avoid scaring her.

She continues whimpering like a dog in pain, thrashing around violently.

"*Mo ghrá*, wake up." I prompt louder.

Nothing.

Shit, I don't want to scare her.

When I reach the side of the bed, I bend forward and lightly touch a hand to her arm.

She jolts up with a shriek.

"Paige! It's me, Declan!"

She turns her panicked eyes toward my voice. Seeing that it is me, she relaxes.

"Hey, you're okay," I whisper. *What the fuck could she be dreaming of to cause this reaction?*

Her throat bobs as she swallows. "I'm sorry. I guess I had a bad dream. I'm sorry if I woke you." Her voice is hoarse.

"You didn't. I don't sleep much."

Releasing a deep breath, Paige pushes the blankets away from her body and climbs out of bed.

God, she's tiny.

The fabric of my shirt drowns her body and a strong sense of possessiveness and satisfaction travels through me at the sight.

She wraps her arms around her body tightly and hunches her shoulders. Shielding herself.

"Can I ask you a weird question?" she asks quietly.

"Ha, sure."

"Do you mind if I sleep with you in your bed? Or even just sleep next to you on the couch? When I have these nightmares, Sarah usually comes in and sleeps with me. But seeing as she isn't here, she can't do that."

Well okay then.

"Um, yeah. If you're comfortable with that, we can go to my room."

She nods and starts toward the door.

Once inside my room, I take out my gun and place it in the bedside drawer. Turning around, I notice Paige watching me nervously.

"It's just for protection," I reassure her.

She doesn't say anything when she turns and faces the bed. She stares down at it but her vision glazes over and I know she's not actually *seeing* the bed.

"I sleep on the side closest to the door. You can have the other side." I gesture to the opposite side of the bed.

Her trance breaks and she nods. Padding to the opposite side, she pulls back the covers, slides in, and tucks them up to her chin.

Shutting off the bedside lamp, I slide into bed next to her.

It's a good thing you bought a king-sized bed Declan, or this would be more awkward than it already is.

Her breathing doesn't slow, and I know she's still awake.

"Declan?" Her voice is so small, I want to pull her close to me and protect her from whatever is haunting her dreams.

"Yeah?"

"Thank you for letting me stay here. I know we don't know each other, but I'm happy I don't have to be alone."

I can't help the smile that forms on my face at her words.

"You're welcome, Paige. I'm glad you're not alone, too."

I feel her body shift a little closer and I will my dick not to rise.

Now is not the time.

"Paige?"

"Hmm?"

"What are you doing?"

She doesn't respond as she lays closer to me and tucks herself against my body. Her touch burns my skin in the most delicious way possible. There is no stopping my blood from traveling downward.

"Just wanted to get a little closer. Is this okay?" *Fuck yes, it is.*

Wrapping my arm around her body, I pull her close, silently answering her question. I catch a whiff of her perfume which causes my cock to press against the fabric of my boxer briefs and I groan inwardly. *Fuck. Bringing her in here was a bad idea.*

Hoping she didn't see my growing arousal; I twist my lower half slightly away from her. She notices and lifts her eyes to mine. Her expression is unreadable as she studies my face.

I lick my lips and her eyes track the motion.

"Declan," she breathes, eyes hooding.

My ma would whip me if she knew the thoughts that formed in my head from hearing Paige say my name that way.

She places her small hand on my chest, and I suppress a shudder.

"Will you kiss me?" she asks so quietly, I almost don't hear it.

"If I kiss you, I won't stop." The weakness in my warning is clear.

The color of her eyes darkens when her pupils grow. "Please… I want to forget." The natural rasp in her voice deepens.

I reach out and slide my hand down her silky hair and caress her cheek. Her eyes flutter closed, and she lets out a breathy moan. *Goddamn, I'm hard.*

Pulling her head close, I trail my nose against the underside of her jaw and breathe her in. *Summer rain.* She shudders and my mouth tips upward.

I twist my head to the other side of hers and trace my lips along her neck. Tipping her head back, her mouth falls open eliciting another erotic sound that goes straight to my cock.

"Are you sure this is what you want?" whispering, I make my way toward her mouth.

"Yes. Yes, please," she begs.

"I like the way you beg, *mo ghrà*," my lips hover just above hers. The rise and fall of her chest increases the longer I deny her request. The shirt she's wearing does nothing to hide her hard nipples. We maintain eye contact. Her eyes are filled with so much lust.

Our lips are so close, I can smell the mint of her toothpaste.

Losing her restraint, she smashes her lips against mine.

Chapter 8

Paige

Declan's urgency matches my own. Our tongues fight for dominance as we grapple for control. He pulls my body flush against him, pressing his erection into my hip. I don't feel any lingering effects of my nightmare, just him. Just this feeling of an all-consuming lust that might kill me if I don't tame it.

My panties are flooding with my arousal for this man. His allure is dangerous. His persona screams to stay away but it's like I have tunnel vision and all I see is Declan.

How can I stay away when he makes me feel safe?

He makes my body feel things I didn't even know were possible. I don't feel the suffocating self-loathing at the want in his eyes or touch. I feel sexy— desirable.

My hand travels up his broad and tattooed chest, up his neck, and drifts into his soft hair. When I give it a slight tug, an animalistic sound travels from deep in his chest. And he bites down on my lip.

I moan into his mouth as he moves his hand from my hair to cup my ass. He gives it a tight squeeze and then his touch travels up my hip and into my shirt. With every caress of his hand, my skin ignites with a flame so blindingly hot that it's hard to breathe. *But fuck does it feel good.*

Pulling away from our kiss, he pushes my shoulders backward, pushing me into the bed as he shifts so my legs fall open and he places himself between them. My pussy throbs with each beat of my heart. He nudges my head to the side and sucks on my neck. *That is definitely going to leave a mark.* His fingers grab hold of the fabric of the shirt, and he slowly pulls it up my body.

When he shifts his weight onto his heels to look down at me, the heat in his eyes is undeniable. It flows deep within me, and I soak up the burn I feel.

"You're beautiful," he rasps and then dips his head to take my hardened nipple into his mouth. I arch my back into his touch as he sucks and nips over and over. He repeats the motion with my other breast before moving away to look at me again. My nipples are so sensitive, I swear I could come from the sensation alone.

Holding eye contact, his thumbs curve around the band of my panties. Pulling them down, he tosses them across the room. His caress travels down from my hips. He grasps my knees in his large hands and pushes them down toward the bed, so I'm now fully exposed to him.

"Fuck, *mo ghrá*. You're exquisite." he moans, and my pussy grows wetter.

I bite my lip and watch him take in my bare skin. *Thank fuck I ended up listening to Sarah.*

His head lowers and I feel his hot breath on the inside of my thigh. I tremble. I'm completely wanton. My head dips back into the mattress. I've never been this wet before. I didn't even realize my body could get this wet.

He takes a deep breath in and groans deeply in satisfaction. "You smell so fucking good."

Using his thumbs, Declan opens my lips. The first swipe of his tongue is long and slow like he's savoring the taste. My hips buck from the sensation, and he wraps his arms around them to prevent me from moving.

Reaching my clit, he wraps his lips around it and sucks it into his mouth. I try to suppress the loud moan threatening to escape. *Fuck this feels so good.*

His assault on my pussy can only be described as a man starved. Each swipe of his tongue is long and delectable. The sounds of my moans fill the room. My clit is so sensitive and engorged – I can't last much longer. Declan's finger probes my entrance, then a second, and then he pushes them in.

FUCK.

"Oh my God, yes. Don't stop. *Please,* don't stop," My voice doesn't sound like my own, I'm so close to exploding. My stomach tightens and I can't help but ride his face with complete and utter abandonment. He pumps his fingers in and out of me and curves his fingers — rubbing that perfect sweet spot.

My orgasm builds and builds.

"Fuck, baby, your cunt is soaking my hand and the bed. Can you hear how she weeps for my touch?"

Holy shit.

With one final suck of my clit, I detonate. My entire body shakes, tears threaten to spill from my eyes, and I'm breathing heavily. *This feels like an out-of-body experience.*

He continues lapping at my pussy like it'll be his last meal. Like I'm a delicacy. The sensitivity becomes too much, and I need to push him away before I pass out.

He pulls his fingers out and brings them up. They're so soaked — glistening with my cum that starts sliding down toward his palm. He pushes his fingers to my mouth and rubs my arousal on my lips.

"Open," he says huskily. I obey his command and he slides his fingers in, forcing me to taste myself.

This is the hottest fucking thing to ever happen to me.

He stands at the end of the bed and drops his boxer briefs to the floor, freeing himself. I've never been one to say a penis is sexy or nice to look at. But Declan's dick is *mouth-watering.* It's large enough and thick enough that I know I will feel him for days.

Pumping himself in long leisurely strokes, he watches me admire his form. The head of his cock weeps with pre-cum that I want to taste.

That's never happened before.

"Can I take you bare?"

That question gives me pause. *Is he actually asking? No one has ever asked me.*

That's really fucking sad.

Raising my eyes to his, "Since this is our first time, I'd like to use protection."

He doesn't push or question as he leans over and takes out a condom from the bedside table.

Watching me, he places the edge of the wrapper in his mouth and rips it open. *Okay, that was hot.*

Don't ask me why because I don't know.

After he's sheathed, he grabs me from behind my knees and jerks me toward the end of the bed. I yelp in surprise at the manhandling. He rubs the head of his cock up and down my pussy – which is still sensitive – and then he lines himself to my entrance. He slowly pushes in. My head falls back, and I let out a low moan.

The stretch is phenomenal. Even through the condom, I can feel every divot and vein of his cock as he pushes further into me inch by glorious inch.

"Fuck me, Paige, you feel so fucking good. You're so fucking tight," He grits his teeth. Once he's fully seated, his hands push my knees into the mattress before he slowly slides out to the tip and rams himself into me with one hard thrust.

"Oh my God, Declan, yes!" I shout as he fucks me savagely. Each thrust makes my breasts bounce. He brings his mouth to mine and kisses me deeply while he continues his hard thrusts.

"That's it, *mo ghrá*, say my name as I take ownership of this delicious cunt."

He bows his head to watch where we are connected. The sounds of our bodies slapping together fill the room. The sounds of my *drenched pussy* fill the room.

He quickly pulls out, captures my waist, and spins me around onto my stomach. He slaps my ass causing me to yelp before he pulls my hips back, so I'm lifted onto all-fours.

He squeezes my ass cheeks in his fists and then spreads them. I feel a sudden hot wetness fall down my ass and to my pussy.

Did he just fucking spit on me?

He lines himself up with my pussy and then thrusts again, obliterating that train of thought. I feel his thumb press against my asshole, and I clench.

"Relax, *mo ghrá*. My cock won't be going there tonight." He circles the rim and presses his thumb further into me as he continues to fuck my pussy.

I've never had both filled at the same time, but my God, does it feel good.

I'm in sensory overload at the feel of his cock fucking my pussy, his thumb in my ass, his filthy words in my ears, and his lips all over me. My body begins to tingle, and I know I'm going to come again soon.

"Shit, you're gripping my cock so well. You're a greedy little bitch, aren't you?" he growls.

My muscles contract and I scream as I come so hard, my vision turns white. Declan's thrusts increase in speed, and he soon follows with a loud moan of his own.

I'm so sated that I barely feel him remove himself, clean us both up, and wrap me in an embrace before I drift off to sleep.

Chapter 9

Paige

I wake up with my head under the pillow, but I *know* this isn't my bed. The blankets feel too expensive. And the room doesn't smell like mine. It smells masculine. Like sandalwood and amber mixed. *Declan.*

I quickly lift my head and turn toward his side of the bed. He's not lying next to me, but I can hear noises from down the hall. *Did last night actually happen?*

The soreness between my legs tells me, "Yes, bitch, it happened." *Sarah will never let me live this down.*

Pushing myself to a seated position and wrapping the sheet over my breasts, I take in his room.

It's similar to the guest room but darker in tone and on a larger scale. It's very organized. Almost as if he doesn't even live here.

Hmm. That's weird.

I pull myself out from under the covers, take the sheet with me, and make my way to his bathroom. *It's huge.* The shower can fit about ten fucking people. The tub is jetted – like the guest bath – but this is even larger. I face the mirror and instantly hate what I see.

I look like an electrocuted lion with raccoon eyes. *Jesus.* I hurry and wash my face with the face wash Declan has on the vanity and try taming my mane as best as I can. The brush he has will disappear forever if I even attempt to use it.

Fuck my genes for not giving me straight hair.

After I've deemed myself presentable enough, I dress in the T-shirt he gave me last night, and a pair of his boxers, then leave the room and head toward the kitchen. The smell of French toast, coffee, and bacon hits my nose and my stomach grumbles excessively.

You burned a lot of calories, Paige. Better go replenish.

God, I can't believe I did that.

Declan is standing in front of the stove wearing only a pair of gray sweatpants, *of course*. I bite my lip as I watch him work like he's done this a thousand times. His back is covered in different gray and black tattoos. His muscles ripple with each motion he makes, and the heat builds between my thighs. *I guess Mark didn't completely break me after all.*

Or it's just this man that looks like a God.

Sensing my presence, Declan turns around and smiles at me, his dimple on full display. I return his smile and walk closer to the kitchen island. *Okay, Paige, don't be awkward. You're an adult. This is fine.*

"Coffee?"

"That sounds amazing, thank you."

He turns around to the coffee maker and returns with a small black mug.

"There's creamer in the refrigerator if you want some. My sister has a bunch of different flavors in there."

"Does she live with you?"

"Yes. She is currently in Ireland visiting my ma."

"Is that where you're from?"

I open the refrigerator and choose a cinnamon roll-flavored coffee creamer.

Declan is setting the table with our plates of food when I finish pouring the creamer and put it away.

"I was born there, but moved to the US when I was very young, so my accent is gone at this point."

We sit across from each other at the dining table.

He points to my plate with his fork, "French toast, eggs, and bacon. I didn't know what you'd like but I figured most people like this combo." *Do. Not. Blush. He's just being nice.*

"Looks delicious. Do you always cook?"

"Yeah, Emily can't cook to save her life, and I don't want to pay someone else to do it here."

So, he's not an arrogant rich boy. Shit. I need to find something wrong with him. He's too perfect already.

"I don't mean to sound rude, but why not pay someone to cook for you? It seems to me that you make enough money."

His eyes fill with amusement. "I have a cook. Just not here."

I open my mouth to ask what he means, but he changes the subject.

"Are you feeling any better after last night?"

My chewing stills and I look up to see him already watching me. I finish chewing and then set my fork down before replying.

"Uh. Ha. Yes, I do. Thank you. I'm sorry for keeping you up." *You know because you were fucking me into a coma.*

He sets his utensils down and drinks from his coffee mug.

His smirk is too fucking sexy "Paige, I haven't slept that deep in at least three years."

When my cheeks flush, he winks and then resumes eating.

After breakfast, Declan leaves for his room. Twenty minutes later, he returns wearing a white button-up shirt with the sleeves rolled up to the elbow showing off his tattooed skin and dark blue dress pants that emphasize his thick thighs.

As Sarah would say, this man is sex on legs.

I can't quite wrap my head around the fact that *this man* had sex with me last night.

Mind-blowing, out-of-this-world, delicious sex.

He spots me standing in front of the windows overlooking the city and smiles. Placing his hands in his pockets, he leans against the doorway of the hall and watches me. His eyes roam over my features like a warm caress.

Normally, being watched so intently would make me uncomfortable, but the way my blood is pumping is definitely not from being uncomfortable.

"I kind of like seeing you in my shirt, *mo ghrá*." *There's that word again.*

"What does that mean?"

"I'll tell you another time."

I narrow my eyes at that. I guess I could always Google it, but I'd rather hear it from him.

He lets out a chuckle and walks over to me, crowding my space. His cologne fills my nose. *God, he smells good.*

"I do like what is under the shirt more, though." The look he gives me is heated and makes me melt like butter on a hot pan.

I don't have a chance to reply when the elevator doors slide open, and Sarah and Rhys walk in.

"I brought you a bag with some clothes, shoes, and makeup. Go get ready!" Sarah throws the bag at me and then pushes me toward the hallway.

I dig my heels into the hardwood. "What the hell, Sarah, why do you need me to get ready so fast? You literally just walked through the door."

Declan answers for her, "Sarah and Rhys let me know it was your birthday yesterday. Since the night ended young, I bought a trip for you and Sarah to a spa this morning." *What?*

My jaw drops and I stare at Declan like he's grown a second head. "Why would you do that?"

He just shrugs in response. *Who fucking does that?*

"Don't question a man when he buys you a day at the spa, P." Sarah scolds, and continues to push me toward the guest room. "Now go get yourself ready so we can go." She quickly swats my ass.

An hour later, I am showered and ready to head out.

Sarah is sitting on the couch when I return to the living room.

"Where are Declan and Rhys?"

She spins around to peer over the top of the couch, "Oh, they said they would meet us for lunch later today. I guess they had some work to get done. But Declan sent a car to take us to the spa."

"Why?"

Sarah lets out an annoyed sigh and rolls her eyes. Standing, she makes her way over and stops in front of me.

"Because, Paige, he wants to do something nice for you since you didn't really have a good night last night." We've literally known these men for a night.

That didn't stop you from letting him fuck you.

Ignoring my internal monologue, "How do you know that?"

Her eyes soften and she reaches her hand out to push my hair behind my ear. "Declan told me about Mark."

I rub my front teeth with my tongue. "He doesn't know anything other than Mark was my mom's drug dealer and the reason I left home. He doesn't even know his name."

"What did he say to you?"

I contemplate lying, but considering he said he knows where I live, that puts Sarah at risk.

"He knows where I live. And he said he's looking forward to our visits again." My skin breaks out in a sweat just thinking about it.

Sarah's hands ball into fists and she growls. "That motherfucker! When I get my hands on him, he's going to wish he never met you."

"Sarah, he's dangerous. You know what he's done. I just need to find a way to keep him out of my life and away from me. Maybe we should find another place to stay."

She mulls over my suggestion. "I don't know, Paige. The building might be shit, but the apartment itself is perfect for us."

It is and I love it but what other option do I have aside from fleeing the state again?

"Just... just think about it, please. I don't want anything bad to happen to you because of my past catching up to me." *My stomach falls into my ass thinking about something happening to Sarah because of me and my fucked-up past.*

She wraps her arms around me in a tight hug. "Don't worry, babe. Mark might be in the city, but he's never met me before. I grew up with four older brothers and I know how to hide a body." She winks deviously.

I keep forgetting she is batshit crazy.

"You really need to lay off the crime shows, Sarah," I tease, returning her hug.

"The dopamine they give me is just what my brain needs," she purrs.

Our hug ends but we continue to hold hands as we head to the elevator.

An indoor waterfall sits in the center of the spa's foyer and calm music plays in the background. The smells of eucalyptus, jasmine, and lavender flow through the air and I already feel more relaxed.

We walk to the check-in counter, where a petite blonde with big brown eyes stands, smiling. "Welcome, Ladies. Do we have an appointment today?" she asks.

"Yes, it should be under Mr. Moore," Sarah answers.

The girl scans the computer in front of her and then nods. "Perfect, I have you both down for full body massages and manicures and pedicures."

"Thank you so much." She gestures for us to sit and wait for someone to take us back for our appointment.

A waiter walks over holding a tray. "Can I interest either of you ladies in a mimosa?"

Sarah and I share a sly smile and then reach for a glass.

"Cheers!" We laugh.

Our names are called and when we stand and turn around, two massive men stand in front of us. My wide eyes meet Sarah's, and she mouths *holy shit.*

"Hello, ladies. I am Scott and this is Dan. We will be your masseurs for today. If you'd follow us, we have a room with two beds ready for you."

When we step into the room, it's dimly lit with two massage tables in the center. There are large oil diffusers in the corner. Gentle trickling water sounds play through hidden speakers.

"Please undress from the neck down. If you wish, you can stay in your underwear. We just need to be able to access the glute muscles without any restrictions." Dan says.

"We'll give you ladies some privacy. When you are undressed, please lie face down on the table with the sheet on the bed draped over you from the waist down."

Scott and Dan exit the room and gently close the door behind them.

Once we're undressed and lying under the sheets, a light knock comes from the other side of the door.

"Ready?"

"Yes, we're ready."

"Are there any areas you want us to focus on?" They ask as they set up different oils on the bedside tables.

We both shake our heads no and they begin working on our muscles.

"*Oh my God*. Yes. Right there."

"Sarah! Will you quit moaning like that? You're making this weird!" I whisper-shout from my massage table.

Without lifting her head, she replies, "Rhys twisted me up like a pretzel last night. I need my muscles worked."

Lord, if you can hear me, why did you make her this way?

"Well, I don't want to hear you moaning like you're about to orgasm."

She chuckles under her breath but doesn't say anything else.

Chapter 10

Declan

Fucking Paige was a feeling I never thought I'd experience. The way her pussy molded to me. The sounds she made. Fuck, just everything about her was perfect.

I'm not an addict but I already need her again.

"Dec?" Rhys' voice cuts through my thoughts and I'm brought back to our meeting.

I meet his eyes. "What?"

"Cillian was saying that one of our warehouses was ransacked over the weekend. They burned the fucking place down."

What the fuck?

I flick my icy glare to Cillian, who nearly pisses himself.

"Why in the fuck are we just now being informed of this?" I bark, causing everyone in the room – aside from Rhys – to jump.

"W... Well, Boss. We... We... Well..." Sick of the stuttering, I pull out my pistol and shoot him between the eyes.

He falls to the ground with a loud *thud*.

The color drains from the other men's faces as they watch the blood flow from the bullet hole.

"Does anyone else care to explain – without stuttering – why my warehouse was fucking hit?!" I shout.

"Boss, we had a very small group of men guarding the warehouse at the time. They caught us during position changes. Cillian — there, was the only survivor." Finn, one of my father's original men, answers.

I set the gun on the table and cross my arms over my chest.

"Who did it?" My anger begins reaching boiling levels.

No one answers.

My rage erupts and I flip the table.

"WHO THE FUCK DID IT?!"

"We have our suspicions, Dec. But so far, nothing concrete for us to be able to make a move without starting an outright war." Rhys sets a hand on my shoulder. "Don't worry brother, we'll take care of this."

"We just lost $100,000 in weapons. This better be fucking taken care of soon or I will shoot every one of you cock-suckers between the eyes, chop you into pieces, and send you to your fucking families. Now get the fuck out."

The men quickly leave the room without uttering a word.

"Sarah and Paige should be done at the spa in about thirty minutes, so we should start heading out if we're going to meet them for lunch."

Right.

Pulling up to *Duke's*, I spot the car I had pick up Sarah and Paige parked by the curb. Tom, the driver, steps out and opens the door for the girls.

Rhys and I are met with warm smiles from both of them when we step out of Rhys's Audi.

Without missing a beat, Rhys strides over to Sarah and pulls her into his arms.

Paige slowly walks up to me. "Hi."

I pull her into my arms and breathe her addictive scent in. "Hi, baby. How was the spa?"

"It was great. Thank you for doing that."

"Anything for my girl."

Her cheeks are flushed when I release her. Chuckling lightly, I place my hand on her lower back and lead her inside.

Now seated at our table, Paige is much less tense than when we arrived.

"Can I take you out to dinner tonight?" I ask abruptly.

"Becoming a little obsessed, Declan?" she teases, amusement filling her phenomenal green eyes.

"What can I say? I like being around you." *More than I can understand at this point.*

She bites down on her bottom lip, and I watch the move intently.

We're interrupted by the sound of glass shattering and people gasping. When we turn around, Antonio is forcefully pushing a man into a table as he stalks toward us. Rhys and I stand as he gets closer.

Stealing glances at each other, we shift so we're blocking the girls from view. Rhys adjusts himself enough to be able to pull out his gun if necessary.

"You cock-sucking motherfucker!" Antonio spits.

When he goes to strike me, Rhys spins him around by his arm, twisting it behind his back, and slams his face against the table across from us. The sounds of glass and silverware echo in the now-quiet restaurant.

"To what do I owe this unwanted visit, Antonio?" I push my hands into my pockets and tilt my head to the side.

His goons try to intervene, but the glare Rhys shoots their way makes them stop short.

"Jackie came home last night completely plastered and high off her ass because of you!" Antonio's yell is slightly muffled from his face pressing into the table.

Jesus fuck, this woman is going to continue to be a problem, isn't she?

"What Jackie did last night had nothing to do with me. I spoke to her for all of three seconds before she left."

I nod to Rhys to release him. Antonio rises and rubs his wrist while glaring at Rhys.

"Bullshit. She came home and said you were all over each other, but you threw her out like trash when she mentioned wanting to get back together."

"First, we were fucking. Not dating. Second, what Jackie does on her own time is none of my fucking business. She's not my responsibility."

Jackie has struggled with drug addiction for two years now. She's been in rehab multiple times and her family even set her up with a personal "sobriety coach" to tag along whenever she was going to social events. What is ironic is that her family traffics drugs, but she doesn't get her poison from them. She buys off the street.

I've never really cared about her addiction, that's the fault of her family. But our arrangement ended the moment she wanted more. Jackie is a woman you fuck, not keep.

"What did you say to her?" He demands.

"I didn't say shit other than for her to leave me the fuck alone and I had a meeting — with you, I might add." The boredom of this conversation is beginning to irritate me.

The look he sends me says he doesn't believe a word coming out of my mouth. *Too fucking bad, it's the truth.*

"If she goes down this hole again, Declan, this is on you."

"Leave me out of it," I snap. "She and I have no personal relationship. You and I barely have a fucking work relationship. Once this deal we have is done, we're cutting ties. Now, fuck off so I can enjoy the rest of my lunch."

Antonio peers behind me and sees Paige.

A deep growl leaves my chest at the obvious interest in his eye. Antonio lifts his hands in surrender before backing away and heading to the exit. *Good choice, motherfucker.*

Spinning around, Rhys and I are met with an amused look from Sarah and an intrigued look from Paige.

"That was badass!" Sarah exclaims as she reaches for Rhys and pulls him down to his seat. "I need you to teach me that move."

Blocking out their conversation, I sit down next to Paige.

"I'm sorry about that. Are you okay?"

The corner of her mouth tips up and I can see the lust filling her eyes.

"What's that look for?" I ask with a smirk, scooting closer so our knees are touching. I place my hand on her thigh and trace circles with my thumb.

She shrugs her shoulder, feigning indifference. "Oh nothing, just that what just happened was probably one of the hottest things I've ever witnessed." She sends me a sly smile. The blood rushes to my cock at that comment and my brain fills with thoughts of repeating what we did last night.

Chuckling, I reply, "I'm happy you saw it that way." I tuck a strand of hair behind her ear as I study the perfect features of her face. She blushes and dips her head shyly.

Then an idea strikes me. "How do you feel about going away with me this weekend?"

Placing her elbow on the table, Paige rests her chin on her palm. "Where to?"

"I'll make it a surprise," I wink.

She purses her lips to hide the smile trying to spread on her face. "Okay."

"Give me your phone so I can put my number in it." I hold my hand out.

She sits up straight, grabs her phone from her purse, and hands it out to me.

Taking it, I put my number in and hand it back.

"Perfect."

Chapter 11

Paige

The doorbell rings and I hear Sarah's bare feet padding lightly on the laminate flooring.

"Declan is here!"

I ferociously throw my shoes, one by one, from my closet.

"Don't let him in! I can't find my other sandal!"

"Too late," whipping around from my crouched position, Declan stands in my doorway wearing a pair of black jeans, a white V-neck that molds to his chest and arms like a second skin, and white trainers.

How is this man even real?

"Give me like five minutes. I can't find the other shoe I was going to wear."

"We have time." Waltzing into my room, he sits at the end of my bed.

He looks so out of place here. Even in casual clothes, Declan's aura is too dominant, too powerful for my small bedroom.

"You didn't really tell me what we would be doing this weekend other than to pack clothes for the beach... Declan, we live in New York and it's November. The beaches are going to be too cold."

He must find my question amusing because his eyes light up playfully and a smirk plays on his lips.

"We won't be going to a New York beach, Paige."

Huh?

Pausing my search, I turn to face Declan.

"What do you mean we're not going to a beach here? Where else would we be going on such short notice?"

"You'll see." *That's not helpful at all.*

After spending another fifteen minutes digging through my apartment for the damn shoe and confirming that Sarah will be staying with Rhys while we're away, we are finally ready to leave.

"You packed for the whole weekend, right?" Declan confirms as we stride to his SUV. His hand is placed at the small of my back and the warmth of it is distracting.

"Yeah. I wasn't sure what else to bring, so I kind of brought everything."

God, Paige, you're so fucking awkward.

One of Declan's men – Liam – steps out of the car and greets me with a dip of his chin. I offer him a smile and he reaches a hand out to help me with my bag. After I've handed it to him and he's loaded it into the trunk, he slides back into the passenger seat and shuts the door. There are two additional SUVs – one in the front and one in the back. I meet Declan's eyes and raise my brows in question.

"Planning on having a police escort too?" I tease, though I begin feeling uneasy about the clear protection detail.

Declan caresses my arm and then takes my hand in his, "My job requires... a certain level of protection. We will be having some of the men I employ accompanying us on this trip, but they will be very discreet. You won't even notice they're there.

His reassurance does nothing but make me more nervous about this trip.

What does he even do for work?

What kind of person needs round-the-clock protection?

Seeing my indecision, Declan closes the gap between us and clutches my chin with his forefinger and thumb. He lifts my head as he brings his down. His lips brush over mine in a feather-like touch. Our kiss ends far too soon, and I find myself mourning the loss.

"I promise this trip will be enjoyable. You will be safe, and you won't have anything to worry about. I got you, *mo ghrá.*"

He peers at me through soft, ocean-blue eyes, and my heart flutters. Those eyes can make me do just about anything. There is something about Declan that speaks to a part of my soul, letting me know that I can trust him. I find myself involuntarily gravitating toward him all the fucking time.

The side of my lip tips in a small smile. "Okay, let's go."

His eyes light up and a smile spreads across his gorgeous face. My soul soars with pride that I'm the reason for it.

Laying my head against the back seat window, I watch the city pass by as we drive toward the airport. The sounds of cars honking and people shouting and cursing at each other bring a smile to my lips.

"What's that smile for?" Declan asks in a playful voice.

I turn to face him and shake my head. "I just never really realized how much I enjoy the city."

His head tilts and his brow arches, "What makes you say that?"

I gesture a hand toward the passing buildings. "I grew up in a rundown part of a small town; it was very quiet." My eyes dim slightly. "I was constantly trapped inside my own head. The sounds of the city help drown out the thoughts that exist."

Declan studies me through intrigued eyes.

"I'm glad you ended up in this specific city. It would have been a shame to have to travel all over the globe in search of you."

My face grows warm as a blush spreads over my cheeks.

He sends me a wink that immediately makes my heart race before turning to face his own window.

As we get closer to the airport, I think about how much I hate flying.

The confinement of the cab, the smell of other people, and the uncertainty if you're going to even land safely make my anxiety skyrocket.

If you'd asked me about it when I was sixteen, I would have begged you to crash the plane into the closest mountain regardless of how I felt about being inside. I had spent years wishing and praying for an early death. My life was a bottomless abyss of pain and suffering at the hands of people who should not have been a part of my life in the first place.

A mother is supposed to nurture and protect you. I picked the short straw with mine because there has not been a time in my life when my mom actually took care of me. The earliest memories I have include being home for days at a time – alone.

I learned to rely solely on myself. Found myself being a real-life Matilda. Cooking, cleaning, and being my own teacher.

My suicidal thoughts and self-harm started shortly after Mark started coming around. I had already had a level of self-loathing – who wouldn't with a mother like mine? But after I was persistently raped, I needed something to numb the pain. I learned very quickly how to be discreet with my self-inflicted wounds so I would not end up being pounded into by my mom or Mark for 'ruining the merchandise'.

The one and only time they saw my cuts, they locked me in a room for five days with no food or water. But you bet your ass they beat me before then. After that, I made sure to cut myself along the back of my hairline, behind my ears, or under my nails.

Since meeting Sarah, I no longer self-harm, but my intrusive thoughts make appearances more often than I would like to admit. I've tried different anti-depressants but none of them made me feel like *me.* I became a zombie – slowly walking through life in search of sustenance. Therapy was useless. They all scrutinized me like I was in search of sympathy or controlled substances.

So yeah, fuck them.

With the threat of Mark being in the air, I really hope I don't fall back down into that pit I found myself in before I met Sarah.

Paige

(Age 18)

I've never been afraid of death.

In fact, I've craved it for the last five years.

I've spun around different ideas of how I would kill myself. Fire. Drowning. Overdosing. Slicing my wrists. Jumping off a building. Getting hit by a truck. I mean, the possibilities are endless.

Every option gave me so much hope that my pain would finally end.

Running hasn't been an option for me because I have nowhere else to go. I have no family, no money, no place to stay.

Nothing.

Death is my only way out of this hellhole.

The wind whips my hair around violently as I peer over the edge of the bridge. The sound of the rushing water below only barely drowns out the sound of my blood pumping in my ears.

It's such a far drop.

Would it hurt?

Would I be dead before I reached the bottom?

Since I couldn't decide what option would be best, I picked two different ones. First, I'd slice my wrists. Then, I'd jump to the ravine at the bottom of this bridge.

I figured if I didn't die from the impact, the water would help me bleed out.

I know *it's a painful and stupid way to die. But honestly, nothing could hurt more than my entire existence.*

I've been beaten, raped, drugged, forcefully impregnated, and humiliated over the last five years of my life. On top of being abused by my mother my entire childhood, I doubt there is any death that would hurt more than that.

I step closer to the edge with my pocketknife in my hand. The metal thrums with anticipation of what's to come.

Flipping it open, I twist the handle around to watch the sun reflect off the blade.

I smile as I drop my arm to my side and stare up at the sky.

Maybe my soul will be lost to a never-ending void because it's not worthy of heaven.

What soul is if they've been tainted the way I have?

I'm too dirty, too sickening for even Hell to accept.

"What are you doing?"

I spin around and meet the blue eyes of a beautiful girl – she can't be much older than I am – whose eyes flick from me to the knife and the edge. They narrow when they return to me.

"You're not going to jump, are you?" She takes a step toward me.

I stick my hand out, halting her. "Don't come closer. What do you want?"

She stops and tips her head to the side. "I asked first. What are you doing?"

Someone must truly hate me because apparently, I can't even get killing myself right.

"Go away." I dismiss her with a turn and face the edge again. There is no way I'm letting this girl mess up my chance at escaping this shithole.

I lift the knife to my wrist, press down, and begin slicing vertically. Wincing from the pain, I watch as the blood pools and then begins sliding down my hand.

The hood of my jacket is grabbed, and I'm thrown backward onto the ground. I hit the gravel hard from the force.

"What the fuck?!" I yell, stumbling to my feet.

The girl puts her hands on her hips and scowls like I'm a kid caught stealing from the cookie jar.

I return her scowl. "Fuck off," I growl through clenched teeth.

I stumble when she pushes me back as I try to move around her.

The blood from my cut falls down my wrist and onto the ground in a steady drip. Her eyes quickly fall to my arm and then back to me.

"Whatever you have going on, that isn't going to fix it," she says pointing to my wound.

My nostrils flare as my irritation grows.

"I didn't ask for your fucking opinion. You know nothing about me or why I want this. So again, Fuck. Off."

I spin around and start walking away. I'll find somewhere else to do this.

"I can get you out," she says quickly.

My steps stop and I turn my head to the side, peering at her over my shoulder.

"What do you mean?" My eyes narrow.

"Whatever you're going through, whatever situation you're in. I can get you out. I'm heading to New York today. Come with me."

I turn fully toward her. "Why would you offer me that?"

Her face remains blank but her eyes... they're like mine. Sad. Pained.

"Because I'm running too."

When I don't say anything, she offers her hand and smiles softly. "I'm Sarah."

Chapter 13

Declan

By the time we make it to the privately owned airstrip, Paige has fallen asleep with her head against the window. She looks so peaceful. Her youth shows now that her face isn't tense with panic.

I'm not sure what her sleeping habits are, but from what happened that night at my penthouse, I think it's safe to assume she gets about as much sleep as I do.

I'm taking her to Florida for a short weekend trip while also still being in the U.S. I need to be close in case my men get any leads on who was dumb enough to steal from me. There is not a chance in Hell they get to torture the fucks before I do.

As we round toward the private jet, I lightly pat Paige's leg.

She jolts but luckily doesn't scream. She blinks her fatigue away and looks around.

When she sees me, she relaxes further and gives me a warm, tired smile.

I know there is a fierce woman inside that timid exterior. I just need to find a way for her to let her out.

Mhamó would think she's some kind of witch from how quickly I've come to care for her.

Her eyes widen when she takes in the jet. "Declan, is that yours?"

"Mmhm," I nod.

Tom stops the car next to the jet steps. Liam climbs out and begins working with the crew to get the luggage from the trunk.

"We're going on a trip to Florida. Nothing fancy this time around. I promise the next time I take you on a trip, we'll go somewhere you'll love."

She gapes at me, and her mouth falls open "We're flying to *Florida* on a weekend trip? That'll cost a lot of money just for two days, Declan. How can you even afford a private jet? I thought you just owned a club."

"I never said I *only* owned a club," I say smugly.

She eyes me suspiciously. "You don't traffic drugs, do you?"

The laugh that spills out of me is so sudden, that it catches me off guard "No *ghrá*, I don't traffic drugs. That's for the Italians."

She narrows her eyes as she assesses me.

"Come, let's get you comfortable aboard." I exit the vehicle and offer my hand to her. She's slower to take it than I would have liked, but at least she takes it.

Placing my hand on the small of her back, we walk toward the jet.

Once aboard, we are greeted by the pilot and flight attendant. "Good morning, Mr. Moore. We are all set for takeoff as soon as you're ready."

"Perfect. Allow me to get Paige comfortable and then we can go."

They both bow their head in a quick nod before stepping away to continue their tasks.

Paige looks around the space. Her face is blank and I can tell she's inside her head. It's your standard private jet, white and tan colors with a couch in the back next to a table as well as a private bedroom for sleeping.

"Would you like something to drink?" I ask as she continues to look around from the seat she chose.

"What do you do for work?" She watches me warily.

"Let's get up in the air and then I will answer all the questions you want to ask." *I can't let you take off on me if you don't like what you hear.*

Liam boards the jet and takes in mine and Paige's proximity. Choosing the seat furthest away, he sits and tells the pilot we are ready for take-off.

Once in the air, I move closer to Paige. Leaning to rest my elbows on my knees, I face her. "I am the head of the Irish mafia in New York."

She purses her lips "You're awfully young to be a mafia boss, Declan." Her brow raises, but I can see the amusement dancing in her green eyes.

She thinks I'm kidding.

The corner of my lip lifts. "I recently took over for my father, Conor. He was killed by one of our rivals."

Her face becomes expressionless as she stares into my eyes. I shift so my thigh touches hers. She's so damn addicting.

"So, when you said you'd take care of Mark, you meant you'd kill him?" She asks and raises her brow.

I slowly lift my hand toward her face, allowing her time to reject me. When she doesn't, I cup her cheek and stroke her bottom lip with my thumb.

"Whatever you want me to do with him... I'll do it," I whisper.

She studies my face intently. This time, her eyes show an emotion I can't quite place.

My heart speeds up the longer she continues to stare at me without speaking a word. I try removing myself from her proximity, but she rests her hand on my thigh, stopping me.

"And you really don't traffic drugs?"

"I promise you, Paige, we don't deal with drug trafficking. The only business we have is weapons."

"Drugs are where I draw the line. I spent my entire life around them and saw what they do to people. I refuse to be around that again."

"You don't have to worry about drugs, mo ghrá."

She nods and purses her lips as she studies my face, deep in thought.

"What are you thinking?" I ask.

"I must really be fucked up in the head because I'm completely okay with what you do. You make me feel safe, and I don't understand it."

I chuckle and lean in to kiss her lips lightly. "Well good. I want you to understand that I will do everything in my power to keep you safe."

She smiles softly at me and then grows serious.

"I want to know more," she says.

"About what?"

"Everything. What you do. Why you do it. And how you became a part of it."

I lean back slightly and narrow my eyes. "Paige, there is no way in fuck you will be a part of anything other than being *with* me. You won't be participating in any of the activities Rhys and I are involved in. It's dangerous."

Her nostrils flare as her face reflects her growing irritation.

"Declan, my life has been full of danger since I was thirteen years old. Maybe even before then, but I didn't know about what my mom was fully involved in until that time." She turns her head toward the window, and I'm forced to drop my hand from her face.

"I told you I'd take care of it. You don't need to worry about anything." I try reasoning with her, but she isn't having it.

"I can't live my life scared of the next time Mark, or someone else my mom gets herself wrapped in, comes around. You're my chance to learn to defend myself. To have people willing to protect me."

"Paige, I understand. I do. But this life, what Rhys and I do… We have enemies who will not hesitate to kill you just for the fact that you know how the organization works. If they find out you're associated with *me*, they'll hurt you just for the fun of it."

She doesn't move her eyes from the window. Her face remains expressionless but by the rapid movement of her eyes, I can tell she is thinking over my response.

"Ghrá?"

Rather than responding, she gets up and heads to the bedroom.

Chapter 14

Paige

I'm not stupid. I know there are consequences when it comes to knowing about the *mafia*.

I know there is danger involved in knowing things that only certain people in the world do. I don't want to know this shit so I can use it against people who actually want this life. I want to know so I can use it to keep Mark away from me.

This is so fucking ridiculous.

With a huff, I fall face-first onto the bed of the private bedroom. Ironically, it feels like I'm lying on a cloud.

Declan makes it seem that anyone hurting me would affect him in any way. That doesn't even make sense. I don't *know* him. We've slept together, and I feel safe with him, but that doesn't mean he feels the same way I do.

After what feels like hours of laying in the room alone, I eventually fall asleep.

The trip from the airstrip to the beach house is quiet. Declan either doesn't want to talk to me or doesn't know what to say. I don't know what to say to him either. I don't think my request is unreasonable, but I could be wrong.

I've spotted Liam watching from the rearview mirror multiple times but just like Declan, the man is a master at hiding his emotions and thoughts.

This was supposed to be a fun weekend. Maybe you're overreacting.

I roll my eyes and then peer over to Declan, who is typing furiously on his phone with his brows drawn in.

"How old are you?" I ask as I continue to watch him.

He answers without lifting his gaze. *Okay, so I guess he doesn't want to talk.*

I turn away from him and face the window as the ocean comes into view. The waves crash into the shore in a clash of white and blue. The beautiful sandy beach calls for me to lay there and soak up the sun's warmth and breathe in the ocean-scented air. To listen to the waves crashing and the birds calling to each other.

"He's got a lot of shit going on right now, Paige," Liam says from the front seat, watching me once again from the rearview.

"Shut the fuck up, Liam," Declan grumbles before shoving his phone into his pocket. He slides his hands through his hair and lets out a big, annoyed sigh.

Not annoyed... Stressed.

When I ask him if everything is okay, he waves it off before looking out his own window. I purse my lips and narrow my eyes as I assess his profile. *He really is a beautiful man, isn't he?*

Right now, an annoying beautiful man.

My mind drifts to our first night at his penthouse and the heat begins to form between my legs. I lightly squeeze my thighs together to relieve the pressure that starts to build.

I see Liam watching me again through the rearview. He winks and chuckles under his breath before returning his eyes to the road.

One of these men needs to teach me how to improve my poker face.

The beach house we're staying in is beautiful.

Where I was expecting a massive mansion on the beach, this is small. Almost like a bungalow. The exterior walls are glass. You can see inside the entire house. It gives the place a luxurious feel. The floors, countertops, and cabinets are all different shades of white that complement each other effortlessly. The furniture is a light brown to complement the sandy beach. The paintings on the wall do not look to be mass-produced, and they're of different ocean life.

"In case you couldn't guess, Emily also gave her two cents about the decor for this place too."

"Oh, so *now* you're talking to me?" I ask, full of sarcasm.

Declan stands just inside the front doorway watching me take in everything. His eyes fill with amusement as he walks toward me. Once he stands inches away, he tips my chin up with his forefinger and thumb.

"Keep giving me lip and see where that gets you." Then his mouth crashes against mine.

I instantly melt into his touch. His words and this kiss cause my pussy to weep. He groans into my mouth when I start exploring his chest with my hands. The muscles feel carved of granite.

His heart beats rapidly against my palm, showing just how much I affect him. It's absolutely amazing.

Cupping the back of my head, Declan deepens our kiss and pulls our bodies closer together. His erection presses against my stomach due to our height difference. I moan softly into his mouth when he grinds himself against me. I need him inside me right now.

Someone clears their throat from behind Declan and I pull away from him so fast, I nearly fall on my ass. Declan doesn't turn to meet whoever wants our attention, so I peer around him to see a gentleman who looks to be in his mid-forties. I offer him an awkward close-lipped smile and then look up to meet Declan's amused eyes. *Motherfucker.*

"Sorry to bother you, boss, but I just wanted to check in and make sure you didn't need anything before the team and I head out for our posts."

"No, Finn, we're all good here. Fuck off."

Finn's eyes flick to me for a moment before he chuckles darkly. With a shake of his head, he leaves the room.

Declan's stalks toward me like a predator after his prey and shivers travel down my spine.

My panties are soaked, and I can feel my heartbeat in my clit from how fucking turned on I am.

Jesus Christ.

"Now, where were we?" He gives me no time to respond before bending and swiftly lifting me by the back of my thighs. My legs wrap around his waist, and he bites down on my neck, making me groan, while making his way down the hallway.

Once inside the bedroom, Declan throws me onto the bed and I land on my back. My hair falls over my face as I bounce on the mattress.

Propping myself on my elbows, I see him reach behind his neck and start to pull his shirt off.

His entire body is a walking art gallery of tattoos. He has very little skin untouched. His muscles flex when he pulls the shirt completely over his head.

God, if you can hear me, thank you for creating this man's body because damn.

Tossing it to the floor, he works on lowering his shorts and boxer briefs. I bite my lower lip when he fists himself and pumps slowly.

"Crawl to me," he says in a low husky voice.

Crawl? Oh, my fuck. Okay, okay. Be seductive. Think sexy panther.

I turn from my back onto my hands and knees. Maintaining eye contact, I slowly crawl across the mattress to him, swaying my hips and rolling my shoulders as I go. He watches my every move with hooded eyes, and it feels amazing to see how much he wants me. He bites down on his lip as I get closer.

Sitting on my heels, I stare up into his eyes. His pupils are blown, making his eyes appear like the deep ocean. *I want to drown myself in them.*

"You're so damn stunning," he reaches a hand out to thumb my lower lip.

I suck his thumb into my mouth and roll my tongue over it while hollowing out my cheeks. A deep, animalistic rumble escapes from deep in his chest and it goes straight to my core.

"Undress." The dominance in his voice turns my pussy into the Nile River.

I remove my clothes as quickly as possible before returning to my kneeled position.

Without needing any prompting, I wrap my hand around his cock and bend forward. Flattening my tongue, I lick him from base to tip. I lick the pre-cum from the head and roll my tongue slowly around.

Opening my mouth wide, I relax my throat as best as I can and swallow him down as far as I can manage without gagging.

His eyes burn into mine as bright and as hot as a blue flame. They are filled with an untamed lust that rivals my own. His head falls back, and a low breathy *"fuck"* leaves his lips when I hollow my cheeks and suck.

I continue working his cock with my throat and tongue. Using my hand to cup his balls, I squeeze them lightly. Declan grabs a fist full of my hair and pulls my head away, making me release him with a *pop*. I let out a whimper.

"I'm not about to come in your mouth when I already know what your delicious cunt feels like. Now, lie back and spread your legs," he growls before pushing me back.

When my back meets the mattress, I spread my legs as wide as I can. His eyes travel down my body and stop on my pussy that is now throbbing with need. Feeling bold, I use my fingers to spread my lips so he can see how drenched I am.

"Fuck, *ghrá*. You're remarkable. Why don't you show me how you finger yourself?" He strokes his cock as he continues to watch my arousal slide down my pussy and land on the bed.

I unhurriedly slide my finger up and down my center before circling my clit. I'm already so sensitive from his stare.

"Oh my God," I moan as my head tips back. I alternate my movements between rubbing my clit and fingering myself, building my orgasm.

Delcan's name falls from my lips like a prayer. Hearing his ragged breaths from the foot of the bed arouses me to no end and I pick up the pace.

I'm so close to coming that my body feels on fire. I'm riding my hand like a woman possessed and my moans become screams.

"That's it, baby. Make yourself come."

My eyes roll to the back of my head as my body seizes with the intensity of my orgasm. My thighs shake as my pussy clenches around my fingers. My forehead is covered in a thin line of sweat and my breathing barely begins to slow when Declan grabs onto my ankles and pulls me to the end of the bed. He presses my knees down, keeping me exposed.

He bends down to lift his jeans and digs into the pockets. Pulling out a condom, he rips open the wrapper and quickly sheaths himself.

In one swift thrust, he bottoms out inside me, and my scream echoes off the walls.

"Fuck!" Declan shouts before grabbing onto my hips and fucking me vigorously. Our bodies slap against one another and the sound of my wetness fills the room. With each of his thrusts, my clit rubs on his pelvic bone, making it sensitive and swollen.

Grabbing my hair tightly, Declan pulls me forward. "Look how gorgeous you look taking my cock," he rasps through gritted teeth. "Hear how your cunt weeps from how good I make her feel. She's a slut for me and soon I plan to feed her my cum."

"Please don't stop, fuck, Declan. *Please* don't stop." My voice is now becoming hoarse from my screaming. *But damn am I in ecstasy.*

With each roll of his hips, my orgasm builds, and my body starts to shake. "Shit baby, you're squeezing me so fucking tight. Be a good girl and come on my cock."

"Yes! Yes! Oh, fuck yes!" My orgasm hits me like a freight train, and I burst.

A gush of fluid escapes me and covers Declan's lower stomach and the bed sheets. *Holy shit, no one has made that happen before.*

"Oh, fuck yes. You're such a good fucking girl, baby, squirting all over me. Painting me. Fuck." He doesn't slow his tempo as he fucks me through my orgasm. The intensity is too much.

"Declan. It's too much," I rasp.

Moving his hand between us, he circles his fingers on my clit and my body feels like it's going to explode.

"Give me another one, baby. Come on. You can do it. Come all over me again." His encouragement is all I need for another orgasm to barrel through me. My back arches and I tighten my legs around his waist. My mouth falls open in a silent scream as I come all over him.

His thrusts begin to lose control, and Declan's orgasm crashes into him. He bites down on my shoulder and groans as he presses himself so deep into me our bodies almost fuse.

Catching our breaths, we remove ourselves from each other and make our way to the bathroom.

Lifting me by my hips and placing me onto the countertop, Declan runs a washcloth under some warm water and cleans my thighs and swollen lips. The level at which he cares for me even after having his way with my body makes my heart flutter.

Once he's finished, he cups the back of my head and kisses me gently before helping me down from the counter and walking with me to the shower.

There is something so intimate about showering with another person and not having sex. It's hard to explain. We're both on full display and touching each other, but not *touching* each other.

He already makes me feel the safety I've never had the pleasure of knowing. I need to be careful before I let my foolish heart latch onto him.

Once showered, we walk back into the room and Declan slides into bed completely naked. He pulls the blankets back and beckons me to join him.

The butterflies in my stomach flutter insanely about him wanting to be skin-to-skin with me while we sleep. When I climb into bed, he pulls me into his chest, and I nestle in as if we've done this a million times. His heart beats against my ear and I feel blissfully content.

Just as I'm drifting off to sleep, a thought pops into my head.

You're already getting attached... you stupid, stupid *girl.*

Chapter 15

Declan

Sitting on the beach with a beautiful woman is always nice. Sitting with *Paige* on a beach is heaven.

The Florida sun reflects on her suntan lotion-covered skin and my cock stands to attention. Her gorgeous dark hair falls down her shoulders in beautiful natural waves and moves softly in the ocean breeze. She has sunglasses perched on the bridge of her nose and she lays on a lounge chair with her head tipped up.

If Paige is the only thing I see for the rest of my life, I'll die a happy man.

Today is our last day here and we haven't spent more than an hour without falling into each other. I've fucked her against every surface in the house. Her pussy was made to be filled with me and only me. We barely know anything about each other, but it feels like I've known her my whole life. She's my other half. I have no doubts about it. And soon, she will feel the same.

"Boss."

I turn my head at the sound of Finn calling out to me.

He jerks his head for me to follow.

"I'll be right back, baby," I whisper to Paige, placing a kiss on her forehead. She hums in contentment, and I smile.

"Another one of our warehouses was hit."

A deep growl leaves my throat, "But we were able to capture one of the men behind it. He's not someone I'm familiar with." A quick shake of his head displays his irritation. "I told our men to leave him in the cellar for you."

My eyes narrow as I stare at a spot on my desk in the beach house office. I have many enemies—it comes with the territory—but not being able to narrow down who is responsible is pissing me the fuck off.

"Are you ready to send a message?" The bloodthirst in my voice matches the look in Finn's eyes.

The tightness of my fists as we land in New York does little to lessen my anger. I've hidden my vile thoughts from Paige as best as I could, the closer our plane has gotten, but she's too observant. She knows something is wrong.

"Tom will take you home from here. I have something that requires my attention," I say, helping her into one of my SUVs.

"Take me with you."

"I've already told you, you will not be participating in any part of this," I snap.

She jerks back at my tone.

Firing back, she bares her teeth, "I don't know what your issue is, but you've been an ass since the beach this morning."

My hand shoots out and I grip her jaw tightly. I bring her inches from my face. "I will not be repeating myself, Paige. My world is dangerous, but I'm deadly. I own half this city and I will not be disobeyed. Now get your sexy ass in the car and go home." I release her and watch as a defiant smile plays on her face.

I knew she was in there somewhere.

"Goodbye, Declan." Paige slides into her seat and slams the door in my face. Fuck, now my cock is hard.

Thirty minutes later, I arrive at my estate. The Irish-style mansion towers over the twenty acres of land it sits on. I have a hundred men who scour the grounds on rotations. With a forest of trees surrounding the road and perimeter of the property, as well as the iron gates, and concrete wall, it's an impenetrable fortress.

Making my way inside, I'm greeted by Ingrid, my lead housekeeper in the foyer.

"Welcome home, *leanbh"*

She hasn't stopped calling me *child*, even though I haven't been one since my father had me kill my first man at twelve years of age.

My father wasn't a *cruel* man, per se, but he wasn't a nurturer in the sense that I had someone to lean on. *That was reserved solely for Emily.* He wanted a legacy to continue what he built. Someone who can meet his opponents head-on and *win.* After leaving Ireland, my father molded me into that legacy.

Little did he know, his son would grow up to enjoy skinning and gutting people for sport.

"Hello, Ingrid. You are free to retreat to your room. I have some things I need to attend to in the cellar."

"I am not a fool to what you do down there, *leanbh.* I have been privy to the ins and outs of this organization since before you were born. You will do well to remember that." She pivots toward the kitchen and leaves me in the foyer. Her amusement should irritate me, but it helps reduce my rage minutely.

I open the door leading to the cellar and begin my descent. With concrete stairs and walls, the air is much colder down here. My builders were told not to place any windows in the room and to ensure the door was fully soundproof. It's the perfect place for me to play whenever the need calls for it.

Once I reach the bottom, I push open the large steel door. Rhys and Liam stand next to a man hanging from the ceiling by his wrists. He is as naked as the day he was born.

"Get me my tools," I demand and circle the man.

He's unconscious. *Now that won't do.*

I land a swift and forceful punch to his ribcage. The crack is instant, and he wakes with an agonizing shout. *Music to my ears.*

"Now that you're awake. Let's skip the formalities, shall we?" He levels me with a glare and spits at my feet.

An amused chuckle leaves Rhys as he returns and sets my tool bag on the metal table at the back of the room.

"I do love it when they start this game with a fight. It makes it much more enjoyable when I break them."

"Aye, Sir," Liam agrees.

Making my way to my bag, I flip it open and lay out the tools neatly on the table.

"Stupida feccia irlandese," Stupid Irish scum. Ah, so he's Italian.

Rhys and Liam exchange a glance before exiting the room.

I truly enjoy torturing the life out of people. It's remarkable to see how much pain the human body can withstand.

Settling on the largest hook I have; I stalk toward him and jab the hook into his shoulder. It cuts through skin, muscle, and bone effortlessly. His scream echoes throughout the entire space, and blood spills from the wound and slides down his body.

"Now that I have your undivided attention, why did the Romanos think they could steal from me?" I question calmly despite the rage I feel inside. *Motherfucker thought he could do this, and I wouldn't find out? Foolish.*

"Non ti sto dicendo un cazzo." I'm not telling you shit. Another spit to my feet.

I grip the hook tightly and yank it, so he is inches from me, eliciting a whimper from his lips and more blood to ooze out. *"Oh, ma lo farai." Oh, but you will.*

Returning to the table, I choose my carving knife. When he spots it, the color drains from his face, and his eyes widen. He begins jerking on the chains holding his body up. Just as I reach him, the door opens, and Rhys returns. He regards our *guest* curiously.

Returning to my task, I grab hold of his ear and slice it off. He shrieks in pain and thrashes around. Blood gushes from the wound, splattering onto my face, neck, and shirt.

I toss the ear onto the ground, and it lands with a wet *plop*. I continue to carve into different areas of his body, removing skin and meat as I go. Asking him question after question.

Snot and tears stream from the man's face. His eyes are rimmed red, but he continues to deny me information. *Fuck, this guy is tough.* The stench of shit and piss has permeated the air.

I've ripped out all his fingernails and toenails, taken off his bottom lip, and carved into him like a damn turkey on Thanksgiving. The only reason he is alive right now is because we've given him adrenaline to keep his heart pumping. But he still hasn't given me any answers.

I stand next to the table, content with the work of his body. He's still alive, barely. If it weren't for the fact that I needed him to send a message, I would have chopped him up already and fed him to my pigs. *Thanks, Criminal Minds, for that little idea.*

"What do we do now that the fucker won't give us information?" Rhys asks as I wash my hands in the utility sink we have down here.

I purse my lips in thought. "We know it's the Italians, that much is obvious. What I can't figure out is why. Antonio just struck a deal with us so there shouldn't be any motive for this."

"What about the issue with Jackie?"

Shaking my head, "Nah, she's a pain in the ass, but her brother wouldn't fuck with me over her."

Rhys stands next to me as we continue to watch our unconscious prisoner.

"What if she's behind this?"

I snort at that thought. *Ridiculous.*

"She'd better hope she's not behind this. I'd make what we just did here, look like child's play if that were the case." I nod to the now-dead hanging man "Have Finn and Liam drop his body off at the Romano's estate."

I need a night out. Pulling out my phone, I send a message to Paige.

Me: Be ready in 1 hour.

Paige: No thanks.

Me: It wasn't a suggestion.

Paige: And what, *Mr. Mob Boss,* makes you think I want to see you?

Me: Don't care if you want to or not. I'll be there in 1 hour and you better be ready.

Chapter 16

Paige

I'm sitting on my hammock chair reading a dark romance novel. Reading these types of books makes me realize that I'm not surprised by my desire for Declan. Morally gray is the only way. And Declan no doubt fits in that category.

What *does* surprise me, is the way I responded to him squeezing my throat when we got back from Florida. My panties were so soaked that I had to masturbate in the shower as soon as I got home to relieve the ache.

Mark used to hold me down every time he violated my body and I've hated being restrained since. But with Declan... I *want* him to hold me down. Dominate me. Take what he wants from me.

I'm not exactly sure what to do with that revelation.

"Paige, Declan is here!" Sarah shouts from the living room. *Ugh, stupid men.*

I roll my eyes and climb out of my chair with an annoyed huff.

I'm likely being childish, but he was being an ass for no reason.

Declan stands in the entryway looking like a dream in black slacks. The white button-up he's wearing has the first three buttons undone, revealing his beautiful, tattooed skin. His eyes assess my disheveled appearance with disapproval which I meet with an innocent "oops" look.

The muscle in his jaw ticks but he doesn't say anything.

Crossing my arms, we maintain eye contact. Neither of us willing to let the other win.

What in the fuck, Paige? When did you get your balls back?

"Paige, I told you to be ready." His voice laced with annoyance.

I can't help the smirk that appears on my face. "And I told you no thanks, *Declan*," I add emphasis to his name just to piss him off.

Declan takes in a deep breath and rubs the bridge of his nose with his thumb and forefinger.

"I want to take you out. Go get ready," he grunts.

I straighten my spine and lift my chin defiantly. "I'm not going out. I'm perfectly content reading in my bedroom. You're welcome to leave now." I spin on my heels and walk down the hall.

Sarah meets my eyes from the doorway of her bedroom and shoots me a look of approval with a thumbs up.

When I told her about everything Declan shared with me, she was just as pissed that he outright refuses to teach me anything that could benefit me with Mark's situation. It doesn't make sense that he wouldn't want me to at least learn to defend myself.

Just as I reach my bedroom doorknob, Declan grabs the back of my neck and spins me around. "Your defiance turns me on just as much as it pisses me off, Paige. So, unless you want your ass to be spanked raw and your pussy dripping with my cum, I suggest you get ready so we can go."

My body is instantly on fire, and I couldn't hold back the moan even if I wanted to. "That doesn't sound as much of a threat as you think." My voice dips low just as my pussy starts to throb.

Declan's pupils dilate and then he presses his body against mine. "Maybe if you behave like a good girl for me tonight, I'll eat your sweet cunt until you're screaming and squirting all over my face."

Don't listen to your pussy, Paige. He's corrupted her.

Although I don't answer, Declan can clearly see that I'm turned on by his statement. He leans down into the crook of my neck and breathes me in. "Tell me, *ghrá*, if I slide my fingers into your tight little cunt, will she be weeping for me? Will she be begging for me to stuff her with my cock?"

My eyes flutter closed, and a whimper escapes me.

Sarah clears her throat from behind us, "As riveting as it is to watch you guys get each other all hot and bothered, I don't have Rhys here to help me get off. So quit it and leave."

I glare at her over Declan's shoulder, and she playfully rolls her eyes.

Declan chuckles under his breath. "Go get ready, *ghrá*. We're going to my club."

Sarah gleefully claps her hands and then darts back into her room.

"I guess she's coming with," I say with a smile and a shrug.

He huffs out a small laugh, "Alright, I guess I'll have to wait for *both* of you to get ready."

Placing a gentle kiss on my lips, he pulls away and opens the door for me. When I turn around, he smacks my ass and follows me inside.

An hour later, we are walking into Declan's club. Rhys stands at the entrance, waiting for us. I'm wearing a short wine-colored silk dress paired with matching pumps. My makeup is smoky and makes my green eyes stand out. I've styled my hair in a messy bun to accentuate my slender neck and I have small strands of my wavy hair left out to frame my face.

Sarah is wearing a gorgeous gray sequin dress that emphasizes her blue eyes beautifully. She has nude pumps, and her blonde hair is curled and cascades down her back like a waterfall of gold. She's decided to go with a more natural makeup look and it's perfect for her.

"What would you like to drink?" Declan asks as he gestures for a waitress to come to us in the VIP lounge.

"You choose for me."

The smirk on his beautiful face makes my body and heart swoon.

"We'll take four glasses of the Teeling Vintage Reserve." The waitress nods her head and leaves to fulfill the request.

Standing at the railing, drinking the Irish whiskey, I watch as people dance to the music playing. They're all blissfully unaware of the travesty that goes on around the world. The disgusting humans that walk among us.

I feel Declan's gaze burning my back every so often and I smile to myself at how that makes me feel.

"Pezzo di merda!" someone shouts at the end of the stairs. We all turn our heads to see the same man from the club and lunch being manhandled by the bouncers below.

"Let him pass," Declan says with a lazy wave of his hand.

The man storms toward the table shaking in anger. Rhys stands at the ready once he is within striking distance.

"What the fuck were you thinking in sending a man to my home, beaten to death, *stronzo?!*"

Beaten to death? What the fuck? I meet Sarah's eyes, but of course, she's eating this up.

To some, Declan appears calm and collected.

To me, I can see the menacing hatred behind his blue eyes. Okay, *he looks like he would beat someone to death.*

"Antonio, how about we head up to my office, huh? Then we can sort out this little *tantrum* you're throwing." The contempt in his voice is unmistakable. And just like the restaurant, the change in Declan is so sexy.

"Move," Rhys barks and pushes *Antonio* toward the door at the end of the walkway.

Declan glances at me and I watch as his eyes soften. *Don't swoon, don't swoon, don't swoon.*

Approaching me, he bends to whisper in my ear.

"I'll only be a few short minutes." He places a soft kiss on my lips, and then he leaves Sarah and me alone.

Sarah leaps over to me. "That was fucking hot!" she exclaims.

"I'll admit, that was pretty hot," I agree with a chuckle.

Turning around, I continue my people-watching.

It's been thirty minutes since Declan and Rhys left and I'm beginning to feel on edge. Maybe it's the alcohol talking but I can't get over the sensation that I'm being watched. My skin feels covered in tiny bugs. I'm fidgety and feel the need to leave.

That's ridiculous, you're in a club filled with hundreds of people.

I scan the club and spot Finn standing in the shadows, staring in my direction. When someone crosses in front of him, he's gone.

Did I imagine that?

"I need to go to the restroom, want to go with?" Sarah asks, straightening out her dress.

I set my glass down and we head toward the stairs.

"Son of a bitch!" Sarah's shout echoes in the empty restroom.

"You okay?"

"No, I'm not okay! I just started my fucking period, and I don't have shit with me. Do you have anything?"

I rummage through my clutch, but I already know I don't have a tampon. I don't even get periods anymore because of my birth control implant.

"Sorry, babe, I got nothing. Let me text Declan that we're heading out and we can go home."

Sarah is muttering angrily under her breath when she exits the stall to wash her hands. I roll my lips to avoid giggling but fail when I meet her glare through the mirror.

"It's not fucking funny, Paige. I just ruined a damn good pair of underwear *and* had to use like half of the toilet paper roll so I'm not bleeding down my leg."

I raise my hands in surrender. "You're right, I'm sorry. I shouldn't laugh, but you always start your period at the worst times, yet you still don't carry anything with you."

"Let's just go home," she grunts, swinging the door open.

I follow her as we make our way out of the club.

Chapter 17

Declan

"I didn't order anyone to steal from you. We struck a deal regarding those weapons. You know that I need them. I have done many awful things, but I won't betray the deals I've made."

His voice remains strong but his eyes and the trickle of sweat above his brow reveal just how nervous Antonio is to be in this room with me. *As he should. I've skinned people alive for less.*

The contents from the top of my desk crash to the floor when I violently sweep my arm across it. My computer is shattered, and important documents are now mixed. I can't concentrate on anything but the uncontrollable rage flowing through my body.

He's a damn fool if he truly thinks I'll believe his lies.

"Then explain to me how a group of Italian men were ransacking my warehouses? The man I tortured wasn't just some lowlife off the fucking streets. He was trained to withstand that level of pain without breaking."

He dips his chin, and his eyes bounce around in thought as he stares at the ground.

"All I can give you is my word that it was not me who ordered that hit. I'll look into my men and find out who sent them and why."

Walking into his space, I shove my finger into his chest powerful enough that he grunts and winces. "You're going to do more than that, Antonio."

I point to Rhys, "He's going to stay in your ranks — under my order — until this is sorted. If he finds anything that contradicts what you've said to me, I will burn everything you own, love, and cherish to the ground."

He's taken aback by this demand and begins to sputter, "You don't honestly believe I would allow that, do you? I've given my word, and I will help y—"

His blabbering is cut off by my hand grabbing his throat like a vice.

"I don't give a flying rat's ass about your *word,* Antonio. I have over $100,000 worth of weapons missing, two warehouses that have been burned down, and nothing to show but a dead Italian that I tortured until he shit and pissed on my floor."

Clawing at my hand and wrist, Antonio's face begins to change into a deep purple. When his eyes start to roll back into his head, I release his throat and he falls to his knees on the ground.

"If... you... send him to my home... he will return... in pieces," he says through each gasp.

Squatting down to his level, I say, "Don't make an enemy out of me, Antonio. You will lose." I give him a firm pat on the cheek before rising to my full height. "Now get the fuck out of my office. You're drooling on my floor."

Rising to his feet, Antonio straightens his suit and hair before glaring at me venomously. "I'll keep my word. It might not mean anything to *you, coglione,* but it does to me. When I prove to you that I had nothing to do with this, I expect double the weapons I requested."

He leaves my office with a slam of the door and the walls shake.

I fall back into my seat and rub my hand down my face.

Fuck!

"Hate to make this situation worse... But the girls left." Rhys' apologetic face pisses me off more than I already am. Picking up my whiskey glass, I throw it at him. He ducks and it shatters when it hits the wall.

"Why did they leave?" I mutter, rubbing my temples. *This was supposed to be a good fucking night.*

"Something about Sarah bleeding from her vagina and needing new underwear," he shrugs and watches me as though we didn't spend nearly an hour in a heated argument with Antonio.

A deep sigh leaves my chest and I run my hands through my hair. *I need an outlet for the homicidal thoughts running through my mind.*

Composing myself, I stand.

"Well then, let's go get shitfaced." *It's not what I want but it will have to do for now.*

Rhys's face beams like I just told him we were going to a fucking orgy.

"I have a better idea."

We pull up to one of my newest warehouses by the docks. It's empty, as our shipment from Ireland is not set to arrive until next week, and my men have been setting up the security system in the meantime.

Climbing out of the SUV, the air is cold with the approaching winter. Rhys and I stride side by side to the door, the metal groaning as we open it and step inside.

I'm greeted by the sounds of grunting and angry mutters. My eyes meet Rhys, and he wiggles his brows with a conniving smile on his lips.

In the center of the room is one of the lower gang members from around the city. He's not someone we usually waste time on but considering the night I've had, I intend to play.

"When did you do this?" I ask Rhys, gesturing to the kid in the seat.

He shrugs, "Found the kid hanging around one of our warehouses earlier today. He could have waited until tomorrow for your attention, but after what happened at the club with Antonio, I thought you'd enjoy having some fun."

Not far from him is a steel table with my tools spread out like a buffet. My mood begins to improve with the prospect of letting this rage out.

Torture and pussy are the greatest forms of pleasure. And fuck am I ready to indulge.

Hearing the sounds of our shoes as they meet the concrete floor, the kid stops his poor attempts at loosening his confines. His face drains of all color, and his eyes widen with fear when he sees me step closer to him.

"Whatever you think I did, sir, I didn't. Whatever you think I might know, I don't," stammering, he begins to shake as Rhys and I stop within inches of him and stare down into his eyes.

"Oh, we know you don't know shit. This is just for fun," Rhys mocks him with an evil smirk.

"F-fun? What the fuck is wrong with you?! You just take people off the streets and tie them to chairs for *fun?"* His eyes are wide with a mixture of panic and anger.

"Not *people,* lowlife wannabes who think they can snoop around our warehouses," Rhys replies. Shrugging off my suit jacket, I walk toward the table and inspect my instruments. "We're also not just tying you to a chair, you dumbass, you're going to die today."

The chair begins rocking back and forth as he tries to get some momentum to break the chair and escape.

Unfortunately for him, Rhys grips his hair as close to the scalp as possible. He stops moving and hisses in pain.

"P-p-please, sir. I will do whatever you need me to do. Need someone to play bitch and do shit for you? I'm your g-guy. Just don't kill me."

A small snort leaves me.

"I have hundreds of men at my disposal. What would I need you for?" I lift my butcher knife and slide my finger down the blade — testing its sharpness. Setting that down, I spot a car battery to the right with jumper cables. *Perfect.*

"Please! Please! Listen, I know you have some stuff going on with your warehouses; rumors have been going around. I don't know who's doing it, b-but I can help you! Like you said, I'm just a lowlife. No one will pay attention to a lowlife asking around. Right? *Right?!"* He shrieks as the anger disappears and the panic increases.

Rhys steps up to my side and whispers under his breath, "The kid has a point, Dec. We could use him to listen around the city. Someone will slip up at some point."

My thoughts run wild with this idea. It does make sense. But this kid isn't loyal to me. He's one of those people who would spill everything he knows or make a deal to save his ass, just like now.

"I'll have someone come in from Ireland. They won't know who it is. They've never been to the States."

Spinning around with the battery in hand, the thrill of torturing this guy is making my heart race rapidly. The high I get from causing excruciating pain to others has been unlike anything I've ever felt.

Until I met Paige.

With a thud, the battery hits the concrete at his feet. The crotch of his pants darkens as he soils himself.

"Declan." Resisting the urge to strangle him, I turn toward Rhys. He gestures for me to walk to him.

"What do you want?"

"Bringing someone from Ireland wouldn't do a damn good thing here, man. Think about it: this kid has already established relationships with the underworld *here*, not in Ireland. People on the streets will be more likely to talk when he's around."

I hate that he's making sense. I need someone's organs to spill at my feet to release this tension.

"I also don't think I need to go to Antonio's. Part of me doesn't really believe that he's behind this, despite the Italian we caught."

"So, what? We just let Antonio off the hook?" I growl.

"No. I think we send the kid to scope out the streets and confirm if any word about any more Italians doing shady shit comes up."

I sigh and run a hand down my face, "I trust you more than I trust anyone else, Rhys, so if you think this is a good idea, then fine. I'll trust your judgment."

He slaps a hand against my back and smiles, "We got this, brother. We'll catch whoever this fucker is."

"What's your name, kid?" I say when I turn and face him.

His spine straightens, and he wipes his face on his shoulder, "Tyler, but I go by Bean."

"Bean?" I deadpan. *Who the fuck wants to go by Bean?*

"Uh... yeah, it's technically short for string bean because of how tall and skinny I am."

Fucking stupid.

"Well, *Bean*, thank Rhys for saving your life. I'm taking you up on your offer."

His shoulders drop and he breathes out a sigh of relief. "Thank you, thank you so much. I will do whatever you need me to do."

I pick up the electric branding iron from the table. "First, we need to make sure that you understand what will happen if you fail to maintain your loyalty to me." *Now where to place this? I can't have people noticing my organization's symbol on his body while he's snooping around for me.*

"W-wait! Wait! You don't need to do anything! I'll be loyal, I swear it!"

Shaking my head in mock disappointment, "Well you see, *Tyler*, you belong to me now. I can't just take your word for it about your loyalty. You signed your life away to the devil when you offered yourself up. As your reward, I'll place my brand on your body. Just for fun, I'll take a finger or two. Maybe a piece of your tongue." I shrug. "Who knows? The night is still young, and we need to discuss what you will be doing for me."

I capture his jaw in my hand and force his head upward to meet my eyes.

"If you so much as *think* of betraying me, I will rip out your intestines and have you watch as my pigs feast on them. Got it?" I growl.

He blanches and whimpers when I squeeze his jaw tightly and then shove him back into the seat when I release him. Without a word, he nods repeatedly.

"Now, let's see where this brand will be placed."

Rhys takes one of the smaller knives from the table and cuts the front of the kid's shirt and the legs of his pants. I examine his body for the perfect location.

"What about his foot?" Rhys suggests. "It'll hurt like a bitch, and it'll be easy to hide from people if needed." Tyler releases a small whine at the suggestion.

"I actually like that idea. Take off his shoes and socks. We'll do both feet."

Flipping the switch, the branding iron begins to glow orange and red as it heats. The steam flows upward.

"Hold his feet still." I jut my chin outward, gesturing at his feet.

Rhys steps on his toes with his boots, pinning Tyler's feet down.

A smile forms on my lips and I watch as the kid slams his eyes shut tightly and he chokes out a sob.

When the brand meets his skin, it sizzles and the smell of burning flesh invades my nose. His screams are music to my ears as they echo off the concrete walls and tears slide down his face. I don't give him a chance to catch his breath before I press the brand to his other foot. His screams crack as his voice becomes hoarse.

I toss the brand to the side after I've finished and then stand to admire my work.

"Now that we finished that part, what part of your body do you want me to take?" I walk over to the table and scan its contents.

Through short gasps, he replies "I-I don't know. Is this necessary?"

I shrug, "Not really, but it'll be fun." I settle on some pliers and then walk back to him.

"I'll go easy on you this time around. I'll just take a fingernail. It'll grow back...eventually," I chuckle.

Walking around him, I grip one of his hands that is tied behind the chair and rip out one of his fingernails. He stifles a yelp.

Rhys steps up with some bandages and tends to the wound.

"Now, just like you offered, you'll be my hidden ears around the city. If you hear *anything* related to me or my warehouses, you will report it immediately."

He nods rapidly, "Yes. Yes. I can do that."

I pat his face, "Excellent. Make sure you don't disappoint me, *Bean.*"

"Never, sir." He shakes his head.

Rhys unties him and he stands, rubbing his wrists. "Give me your phone," I say.

He does as I say, and I enter my number and then hand it to him.

What he doesn't know is that I'll be placing a tracker on him to keep eyes on him as he does what he was ordered.

"Now leave." He bends down to grab his belongings and then limps out of the warehouse.

Chapter 18

Paige

(Age 14)

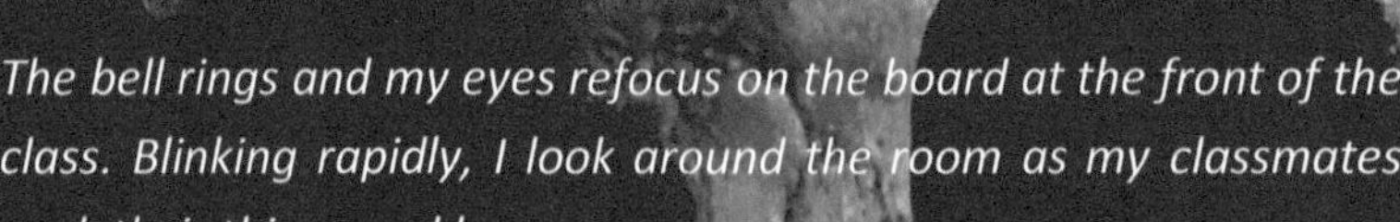

The bell rings and my eyes refocus on the board at the front of the class. Blinking rapidly, I look around the room as my classmates pack their things and leave.

I close my notebook and shove my belongings in my old and faded black backpack. Slinging it over my shoulder, I shuffle to the door. I'm swarmed by the sounds of lockers opening and closing, people laughing or shouting at each other, and feet stamping on the laminate flooring.

Not a single person in here knows the inferno-filled Hell that is my life.

Keeping as close to the wall as possible, I make my journey toward the exit.

My day at school ended far too quickly. I'm not ready to go home. I'm not ready to return to the continuous pain I feel there. Dread is a constant emotion. Hopelessness is right along with it.

"Paige, wait up!" someone yells from behind me.

I spin around and see Adam running in my direction. He stops just a few feet from me and bends at the waist to set his hands on his knees and catch his breath.

I don't say anything as I wait for him to stand upright and tell me what he wants.

"Sorry, you walk faster than I was expecting," he says sheepishly.

Because I'm in a constant state of fight or flight.

Studying my face, Adam gives me a soft smile and then dips his head down. "So, uh... The reason I followed you is because I wanted to see if you wanted to hang out sometime." I don't miss the hope in his eyes when he returns his gaze to me.

I know Adam has liked me since last year. But the girl I was at that time is not who I am now. He would be disgusted by me if he knew. Everyone would be disgusted.

I don't get a chance to reply when we're interrupted by my mom's shouts.

"Paige! Get in! We have shit to do." Her impatience fills her words.

Adam chews on the inside of his lip as he swings his eyes between me and my mom's car. He reaches into his pocket and slips out a folded piece of paper. "Here's my number. I'd really like to hang out if you're up for it."

I take the paper into my palm and offer him a sad smile. "Thank you."

Don't let yourself feel something. It won't happen.

VHe smiles at me and then leans in and places a small kiss on my cheek. I watch him jog back toward the buses. Once he's out of sight, I turn and walk toward my mom.

"Don't go around thinking you can go and get a boyfriend, Paige. I won't have you fucking up my deal with Mark." She snatches the paper from my hand when I climb into the passenger seat and rips it to shreds before throwing it out of her window.

The hollowness in my chest expands as I watch the pieces fly into the sky when we drive off.

We drive toward Mark's house in silence. I peek at my mom from the corner of my eye and watch a cloud of smoke leave her mouth from the cigarette she's smoking.

Mom used to love me. Or at least I think she did. In her own twisted way. She used to be beautiful too. Like me, her hair is brown. But, unlike mine, hers is constantly matted and lacks any resemblance to being healthy. Her eyes are also green, but more emerald in color. Where my skin is olive and tan, hers is grayish from her malnourishment. I struggle to remember the mom I had before the one that sits next to me. Even if the one I used to have would beat me, she was still better than the one I have now.

"Why the fuck do you keep staring at me? Got something to say?" She flings the cigarette butt out the window and rolls it back up.

"No, I'm sorry. I didn't mean to stare." I shift my body away from her, embarrassment filling me.

"Whatever. Listen, when we get to Mark's he's got some buddies there that you need to entertain."

My tears flood my eyes and my vision blurs. Entertaining *Mark's friends is a new thing that I have been forced into.*

I guess these guys have 'the good stuff', according to my mom, and she needs to use me to get it. She's always needing to use me to get things.

What did I do to deserve this? Why does she hate me so much that she lets these guys hurt me?

"Okay," I mumble under my breath and lean my head against the window.

"You also need to start actually fucking these guys, Paige. You can't just keep lying there until they're finished. My supply will be cut off if you don't start acting like you like what they're doing."

"I don't like it, mom! Would you like having gross grown men gang-rape you so your mom can get drugs?!" I hiss before I can even process my reaction.

My mom slams on the brakes, nearly causing the car behind us to rear end the car. It swerves around to avoid crashing into us and the driver flips us off while laying on the horn.

"What my mom did to me was worse than what I'm doing to you. Quit being a fucking baby. I need Mark around and he wants you. So here is what is going to happen: we are going to go to his house, you will *fuck as many of his friends that are there, and you* will *act like you're enjoying it." She reaches for her pack of cigarettes and places a new one in between her lips to light.*

She blows a cloud of smoke into my face, "If you fuck this up for me, it'll only be worse for you." The disdain in her eyes causes my chest to hurt.

I don't have time to stop her before she pushes the cigarette onto my neck and burns my skin.

No matter how many times she does this, I still can't hold my cry. It's not so much from the physical pain of the burns as it is from the excruciating emotional pain. My mom hates me, and I'll never understand why.

She holds the cigarette to my skin for what feels like hours. When she removes it, I slump down and curl into myself. The burn throbs but I resist the urge to touch it. Doing so will only make her do it again.

We don't exchange any more words when she shifts and starts driving down the road.

"There she is!" Mark's voice booms from the kitchen when I walk in.

He pulls me into his body and spins me around to face the group of six men sitting at the table. My stomach churns as they all watch me.

"She's too covered up. How are we supposed to decide if she's even worth the shit we're giving you?" One of them says. He's short and fat with a giant bald spot at the top of his head.

Mark pushes my body away from his and I stumble toward the men. "Take off your clothes," he grunts.

I have no other choice but to comply.

My body trembles as I remove my top and pants. Standing there in my underwear and bra, I try to cover my body with my hands.

"All of your clothes, Paige," Mark grunts.

Reaching around, I unclasp my bra and it falls off my shoulders. My stomach churns as I feel the intensity of their stares.

"That's better," one of the others hums.

I reach down and slide my underwear down my shaking legs. Standing upright, I cover myself as best as I can but Mark swats my hands away.

"Don't fucking cover yourself. Show them what they're getting," he says through clenched teeth.

I remove my hands but keep my eyes on the ground. I'm disgusted with them, with myself. Why can't I fucking fight?

"Look at us sweetheart," the gigantic bald one coaxes. Don't. Do not look at them.

A shove to my back throws my body into the lap of the one closest to me and he wraps his arms around my torso with his hands on my breasts.

I squirm to get away, but my legs are grabbed by another set of hands before they're spread apart.

"Oh, she has a very nice pussy, Mark. What do you think guys?"

The five other men shift to look at my exposed flesh and they all hum in approval. Their eyes sear into my skin and I feel like I'm burning alive.

"Please… Let me go." I beg in a broken voice.

The man holding me dips his head low, his lips rub against my ear, and I struggle to hold my cry as he mutters "Don't worry little one, we will make your tight little pussy feel good with all of our cocks." I feel his erection pressing into my back as he pushes upward.

My ears drum from the blood pumping. My throat feels like it's about to collapse from the tightness and I feel like I'm suffocating. The walls are coming in so tightly, I'll never escape.

The hands holding my legs open start sliding up my body toward the apex of my thighs. When I try to close them, the man holding my torso growls. His chest vibrates and it travels through my body. I tense as my fear intensifies.

The sounds of chairs shifting and bodies moving closer fill the room. My breath shallows with each noise. The room darkens when all of them hover around me. I'm a carcass being stared at by scavengers before they devour me.

Tears now run freely down my face. Each one taking a part of me with them.

"How about we take you to the room, huh sweetheart?" A man with greasy black hair asks. His voice wraps around me like a straitjacket. The smell of his breath travels into my nose and I gag.

"The room at the end of the hall is all set up for you." My mom's voice rings in my ears from somewhere in the room. Completely void of any concern for what her daughter will suffer. Her demeanor makes it appear that she set up a room for a family guest and not a bunch of rapists.

Mom... please...

It's no use. She doesn't care. As long as she gets what she wants, she'll never care what happens to me.

"Excellent, let's go then."

My body is shifted, and I'm now being carried bridal-style down the hallway. The fabric of the man's shirt rubs against me, scorching every layer of skin in its wake. The little bit of a soul I had left dies with each passing second. The emptiness in my chest deepens until I'm left feeling barren of any resemblance of humanity.

I'm set down on the bed once the door is closed and the lock clicks. The room smells of moldy wood, cigarettes, and torment. On the nightstand is a large bottle of lube, some rope, some tape, and a few other things I don't recognize.

A skinny man with scars all over his face puts my wrists together and wraps the rope around them. The frayed material rubs against my skin. The redness and irritation taking form.

"Lay down," he grunts, and reluctantly I comply. If I follow orders, maybe, just maybe this won't be worse than it will no doubt already be.

My arms are lifted above my head and the man straddles my hips as he secures me to the headboard. He pulls them taut, leaving no room for any sort of movement.

When he's finished, he dips his head into the crook of my neck and breathes in deeply. Shivers travel down my body and my heart hurts from the force of each beat.

"Please... please don't do this..." my pleas fall on deaf ears and they all completely ignore me and begin undressing.

The one straddling me slides down my body and the feel of his clothes on my skin feels like I'm being cut open. He forces my legs open, and he lowers his mouth. The unbearable burn of his tongue sliding up my slit is instant. I whimper in pain.

"Fuuuuck, she has a tasty fucking pussy," he moans and dips down to lick again.

It hurts.

"Move the fuck over, I need a taste." He's pushed off my body and the space is filled with the man with the bald spot. He's

completely naked and his body is covered in black hair. The touch of his fingers inside my labia scrapes my skin.

I cry out.

My head whips to the side as I'm slapped across the face. I can feel the sting of each finger's outline forming.

I bite down on my lip so hard the skin breaks and I taste blood.

"Shut the fuck up," someone hisses. My vision is completely blurred from my tears, I can't tell which one hit me.

Try as I may, I cannot hold back the sob from passing my lips as more hands touch my body.

"Hand me the lube," he nods toward the end table and one of them tosses the bottle to him.

He shoves a finger into my body, and I cry out in pain. He thrusts a few times before removing the finger and sucking it into his mouth.

His eyes roll to the back of his head and he moans. "You were right, her pussy is delicious."

The bed shifts as more bodies join us. I'm drowning in such desperation for escape. An escape that I know will never come.

I hear the cap of the bottle flip open and the lube is distributed around for them to coat their dicks. I try bucking his weight off me but he's too heavy. He doesn't move an inch.

Their laughs fill the room at my sad attempt and then one of them shoves their dick into my face.

"Open," he growls.

I roll my lips and try to move away from him, only to be met by another dick in my face. I start thrashing my head from side to side when they bring themselves closer. The acidic burn of bile touches the back of my throat.

I'm stopped by a large hand clasping down on my neck and squeezing. My body goes rigid when I meet the black eyes of a man with a large, raised scar that spans from his left eye to the bottom of his jaw.

"We said open," he growls.

Once I open my mouth, he lets go. A dick is shoved into my throat at the same time another is shoved inside me. My scream is muffled. Hands are all over my body, squeezing, pinching, and kneading. My body is in absolute agony as the thrusts to my throat and pussy become violent.

Grunts, moans, and watery gurgles of my choking drown out my cries for mercy.

The thrusts only stop for a second before new bodies replace them. My hair has been grabbed so hard, there must be patches missing.

I'm flipped onto my stomach and forced to my knees causing my wrists to scream out in pain as the rope squeezes them to the point of circulation loss. Someone aligns themselves with my back entrance. My screams of pain echo in the room when he thrusts.

I can feel my flesh ripping from the intrusion. I have no time to adjust to his size before he pulls back out and shoves forward once more.

Someone bites my neck and my shoulders so roughly that I have no doubts blood was drawn.

The torture goes on for several hours. Each time one would finish, a new one was ready for me. The cycle repeated until I was used multiple times by each of them.

I'm lying in bed with my hands still bound to the headboard. I'm alone.

Finally.

The final man left about an hour ago and I've been stuck here ever since. The sounds of my whimpers are all that fill the space.

No one comes in to check on me. No one ever comes to check on me.

My wrists are bloody from the rope rubbing incessantly on my skin. There is dried cum and blood all over my body. I'm itchy with no way to relieve it. My throat burns so horribly, I honestly believe there's permanent damage. My skin is littered with black and blue bruises from their hands... And the pain between my legs.... Excruciating.

Chapter 19

Paige

I wake to my screams bouncing off the walls. Covered in sweat, my heart is beating like I just ran a marathon, my skin feels hot, and I have tears streaming down my face.

Fuck, that one was bad.

My nightmares have plagued me for so many years, but they still bring such horrible reactions out of me. After being cornered by Mark, they've only worsened. Become more detailed – more *real.*

The progress I've made since leaving is starting to become a thing of the past. I'm back to being a terrified eighteen-year-old on the run from her monster. I've reverted back to the fight-or-flight mode I had as a kid. It's eating away at me. I can't sleep. I can't eat. My mind races non-stop creating horrific scenarios of what will happen when Mark finally visits me.

Sarah opens my door and immediately climbs into bed with me. She pulls me in close to her body. I lay my head on her chest, and she strokes my hair gently.

"You're okay. You're safe. I'm here. We're home." She repeats those same words every time she comes to console me. Her voice is soft and comforting.

I haven't seen Declan since the night at the club. He reaches out but unless I'm going to work, I don't leave the apartment. It's been ten days.

Every time I step out of that door, someone is watching me. I can feel it in my bones. The hair on my body sticks straight up the moment I leave the threshold of my home. I constantly look over my shoulder thinking someone is directly behind me.

Sometimes, I hope I actually spot someone so then this psychological shitshow will end.

A knock at the door causes my bones to nearly jump out of my body and I wrap my arms so tightly around Sarah, I doubt she can breathe.

"It's okay, it's Rhys. I forgot he was coming to take me out to breakfast. I'll tell him we'll hang out another time." She pries herself out of my grasp and leaves to open the front door.

A few minutes later, I expect to see Sarah in my doorway when it reopens, but it's Declan.

His eyes fill with alarm when he sees me in the fetal position on my bed. He's next to me within three strides.

"What happened? Are you hurt?" His hands hover above me as his panicked eyes scan my body for injuries. I shake my head softly and he relaxes his shoulders.

He climbs into bed and pulls me into his arms. My body instantly relaxes into him, and I burst into tears. The panic I've been holding so deeply inside explodes out of me in waves.

"Paige, what's wrong?" He strokes my hair as I continue to cry into his chest. "Baby, I can't help you if I don't know what's going on." The heartbreak I hear in his voice hurts. Sarah is the only person in my life who has ever worried about me.

"It was another nightmare. I'm sorry." I sniff and wipe the tears away from my eyes. When I look up at Declan he looks as though my pain hurts him. My cheeks flush with the embarrassment of him seeing me in such a vulnerable position again.

He pushes a strand of my hair behind my ears and his eyes travel over my face. "Don't apologize, *mo ghrá.* I simply want to know what's wrong so I can fix it," he whispers.

You can't fix me. I'm not repairable.

Sarah and Rhys walk into my room. They simply watch me and Declan being wrapped in each other. *Great, let's have a 'watch Paige have a meltdown' party.*

"Why are you here?" I croak, continuing to rub tears away from my swollen eyes. My skin around them burns as I rub layers away.

"I've missed you. You won't come see me or talk to me, so I came to you when Rhys said he was coming to see Sarah." His fingers thread through my tangled hair. He doesn't seem to mind needing to separate the knots with each pass.

"Declan, we need to talk about you and Rhys teaching me how to defend myself." I prop myself on his chest and meet his eyes.

His expression changes and his jaw ticks but I continue to push.

"My nightmares are about Mark. What he's done. How my life was before I came to New York. I can't live like this, Declan. *Please.*" A choked sob breaks through my mouth, but I keep my eyes on his.

"He's stayed under the radar for the last few weeks, but I'll catch him, baby. Nothing will happen to you as long as I'm around." His voice is full of promise, but I can't trust in that. I can't trust that someone who I barely know will remove a threat I've known for so long.

I push away from him to create space. His proximity is overwhelming.

I need to breathe.

"You don't understand, Declan. I can't leave my fucking apartment because someone is watching me!" I scream and his face jumps back in surprise.

"What the fuck do you mean someone is watching you? How do you know?" He whips his head to Rhys who takes his phone out of his pocket and leaves the room.

"I feel it every single time I walk outside. Someone is watching me leave here and go to work. When I come back home, someone is watching me. I feel so unsafe, petrified. I don't know what else to do. I'm always seconds away from a fucking panic attack."

Declan jumps off the bed and begins filling one of my bags with my belongings. He opens drawer after drawer, shoving whatever clothing he sees into the bag without seeing what they are.

"What are you doing?" My brows furrow as I watch his movements.

He doesn't spare me a glance, "You're not fucking staying here. You're coming to live with me."

"That's not happening." I climb off the bed and try to take the bag from his hand. His hand tightens on the strap, and he shrugs me off. He continues packing my things.

"Paige, if this is how you've been feeling, maybe it's a good idea that you stay with him for a little while," Sarah slowly walks toward me like I'm a cornered animal. I feel like a fucking cornered animal. The only difference is they bite when they're scared. I freeze. I'm fucking pathetic.

If I go with Declan, I'll be safe. What about Sarah? I can't leave her in this apartment knowing someone has been hanging around the place.

As if reading my mind, Rhys returns and stands next to Sarah. "I'll have Sarah stay with me until we catch this Mark guy, Paige. You don't need to worry about her. I got her."

He wraps his arm around her waist, and she melts into his embrace.

This is too much, too fast. I ran from Mark three years ago. Our lives were happy. I *was happy.*

But you'll be with Declan.

The smell of sandalwood and amber fills my nose. It's so comforting – but also scary – I'm falling too hard too fast. This will only end in disaster.

That hasn't stopped you up to this point.

Shut up! Shut up!

I press my hands against my ears and shut my eyes. The room is too fucking small. I'm drowning. I can't fucking breathe.

"Baby," the gentle tone in his voice cuts through the barrier I've created with my palms, I lift my head and meet his beautiful blue eyes. "I know it's not what you asked for, but staying with me will keep you safe. *I* will keep you safe."

His eyes soften. They're filled with such sincerity.

"This is too much," I say, shaking my head.

"So much is happening and it's happening too fast. I'm trying to navigate this... whatever this *thing* is between us," I point to him and then myself, "but I'm also trying to wrap my head around the fact that the man behind all my fucked-up trauma is in the same city as I am."

My heart beats rapidly and my panic grows again.

Declan cups my face with both of his hands. *"Mo ghrá*, you are mine. You always have been, and you always will be. I *swear* to you, I won't let anything happen to you."

My head and my heart fight between staying with him and that this is a serious mistake, and it would be better to run away again.

"I'll keep you safe," he says in a firm voice.

"This isn't a good idea." I shake my head again.

"Don't fight me on this, Paige. Stay with me."

"No, I'll find somewhere else for me to stay."

Declan's face grows with irritation. "Why? Why can't you let me take care of you?"

"I don't need you," I fire back.

He lets go of my face and takes a step back. "You're coming with me."

"I don't need you to be some hero, Declan. I've been taking care of myself long before you came around." I stand taller to emphasize my stance on the topic.

"You're mine and I take care of what's mine. You're coming with me whether you want to or not," he growls.

I bite down on my tongue to avoid yelling at this infuriating man.

When I glare at him, he lets out a sigh and runs a hand through his hair.

Dropping his arm to his side, Declan looks at me with pleading eyes. "Please, Paige," he whispers.

The wall I've built around myself cracks and I feel my reluctance falter. I close my eyes and sigh.

"Fine... I'll stay," I whisper.

A gorgeous smile spreads over his face, "But only until we can find Mark and get rid of him. After that, I'm moving to another apartment."

He smirks. "We'll see."

Placing a kiss on my forehead, Declan lifts my now-filled bag and grabs my hand. "Let's go home. I'll have some of my men come and pack up and move both of your things."

"This isn't the way to your penthouse." We're traveling down a winding road that is hidden by a forest of trees.

There is an obvious amusement in Declan's eyes that I don't understand. Then I remember what he had said the first morning we spent together, 'I have a cook, just not here'.

It shouldn't surprise me that he owns another home or apartment. I mean, he's a rich man. Most people with the amount of money he must have, own a ridiculous number of properties.

The trees open up and an enormous mansion is revealed. It looks like a castle that you'd see in Ireland and not a home you'd see in New York. It's absolutely breathtaking.

The outside is made of gorgeous stone with phenomenal arches. Multiple windows made of colorful stained glass depicting different Celtic gods face us. It's whimsical, foreboding, haunting, entirely unbelievable. I'm completely entranced by the beauty of this home.

The property goes on for what feels like forever. Horses are grazing in the pasture. Pigs, goats, sheep, and chickens fill their respective pens.

This fucking mob boss has a farm.

"You have a farm? What kind of mob boss are you?" My eyebrows rise to my hairline.

Declan's laugh fills the cab of the SUV, and it warms my soul. I love hearing him laugh. It's deep and flows over my body like a warm blanket.

"My dad wanted to make sure we kept some Irish traditions in our life. So, we grow a lot of our own produce and care for farm animals." He smiles over at me and winks.

"That's amazing. I couldn't — still can't —picture you having a fucking farm." I continue scanning the grounds in awe. This place is a completely different world than the one I've assumed Declan has lived.

Parking the SUV, we unbuckle our seatbelts, exit the car and make our way toward the steps. I crane my neck as we step closer to the mansion, not wanting to miss a single detail.

Inside opens to a grand foyer with vaulted ceilings. A crystal chandelier hangs from the center, the light reflecting off of it brightens the room. The decor consists of old Irish relics, likely authentic. The walls are white as well as the marble flooring. I'm blown away.

Mouth falling open, I spin slowly and admire the amazing craftsmanship of this place.

Wow. Just, wow.

"You look stunning in our home, Paige." Declan's eyes are heated as he watches me.

Blood rushes to my cheeks at the sound of him calling it 'our home'.

You're a fucking idiot. You're getting attached and you plan to leave.

"Hello, *leanbh.*" A cute, petite old woman with gray hair and green eyes walks down the stairs.

"Hello, Ingrid. This is Paige. She will be moving in with me today," he says calmly, as he steps closer and places his hand at the small of my back.

She studies me closely. While her eyes aren't cruel, she still gives off a *take-no-shit* vibe.

"And why is she doing that?" Her voice is filled with obvious suspicion.

"Just get her a room ready, Ingrid." Declan presses against the small of my back and leads me toward the kitchen.

The kitchen is filled with huge professional-grade appliances. It's open concept and the ceilings are also vaulted in here. The countertops are made of butcher board and the cabinets are charcoal. It's absolutely gorgeous.

A small older man with crazy hair is standing by the island working on some dough.

"Hello, Niall. This is Paige, she will be staying here with us."

The man lifts his gaze from the dough and smiles widely. He reminds me of Doc from *Back to The Future.*

"Welcome, Paige. I am Declan's chef. Is there something I can make for you to eat? I have yet to find something I can't make," the triumphant tone in his voice makes me smile.

"No, thank you. I appreciate the offer," I politely decline.

"Very well, if you change your mind, I will be here working on the dough for some scones." He resumes kneading and forming each scone with precision.

We continue through the mansion and Declan points out the unique features and rooms. The craftsmanship is remarkable, and I can tell a lot of work has been placed into the home.

We climb a long flight of stairs to the second floor and walk down a long hallway. Other hallways branch off in different directions. I will have to make sure I don't wander around because I know I'll get lost. The walls are covered with different art pieces from all sorts of painters and photographers.

Making a right, we continue down a smaller hallway before coming to a stop at the third door made of gorgeous cedar wood.

"I wanted to show you this room first before I take you to the one you'll be staying in."

Pushing open the door, a library comes into view. I'm rendered absolutely speechless. The sheer number of books in this place would take me three lifetimes to finish. My mouth falls open as I take in the space. It's unbelievable. I've never seen so many books outside of an actual library. Even then, I think this has more.

"Do you like it?"

"This is...wow, Declan, this is something else."

"When you had said you wanted to go back to reading, the night we went to my club, I wanted to make sure this was ready for you."

I turn to meet his eyes. They're filled with so much adoration. My heart doesn't quite know if it should be happy or scared.

Both. Definitely both.

"You got this ready for *me?* As in, it wasn't already here?" I circle my finger around motioning around the room.

He shakes his head and leads me further into the library.

"This was just a large empty room that we couldn't decide what to use for. After that day, I took one look at this and knew this room was yours."

Mine?

"Declan, why would you make this room for me? How did you know I'd ever even come here?"

"Because one day, you'll be my wife."

Someone get an AED. My heart just stopped.

"W-what?" I stutter like a fool.

Declan cups my face and caresses my cheeks with his thumbs. A soft smile remains on his lips as he stares into my eyes.

"You've been mine since the day I saw you walk up the stairs in my club. I intend to have you take my last name."

I gulp audibly which causes him to chuckle. He kisses my forehead lovingly and then steps away and faces the room.

My heart is racing with the new information. *Wife? His since day one?*

Who just decides that you belong to someone?

Mark decided that when you were thirteen.

And cue the panic.

Abort. Abort. I can't let another man own me.

After all this is done and over with, I'm leaving. I need to get away from Mark, New York... Declan.

As much as I know it'll hurt to leave, I'm not strong enough to withstand the crushing weight of being someone's property.

He's never made you feel like property.

Declan is a mob boss. I can never be an equal to that. He might be working to lure me in with his charm and pretty words. He'll change and be a monster of his own. I know it.

I've seen enough monsters in my life. I refuse to belong to another – no matter how good it feels.

I'm sorry, heart. I need to follow my brain right now.

"Declan, I can't thank you enough for this amazing gesture, but I'm not staying here once Mark is taken care of."

His shoulders tense, and he stands straighter but doesn't say anything.

We stand in the room in silence.

After several awkward moments, Declan spins on a heel. He grabs my hand and leads me out of the room.

Chapter 20

Declan

I need to figure out a way to find this *Mark* and remove him as a threat.

Him being in New York — being alive - is messing with my chances of keeping Paige. She wants to run because he's here.

I'll be damned if I let that happen.

She's mine.

I had thought showing her the library would have solidified her wanting to be here with me. Obviously, that was a dumb fucking assumption on my part.

A fucking library, Declan? Seriously. You're a fucking moron.

I'm good at fucking women and leaving them. They always come to me. I don't have to say a single word before they're bouncing on my cock. I have no idea what the fuck to do about wooing someone to want to stay with me.

With her hand wrapped in mine, Paige and I walk down toward the bedrooms in the West Wing of the mansion.

I thought briefly about not giving her an option but to stay in my room, but then I decided if I really wanted to keep her, I needed her to come to me.

Handcuffing her to my bed won't bode well for me in the end.

"This is your room" We stop in front of a set of large solid-wood double doors.

Swinging them open, Paige sucks in a breath.

The room would easily fit four of her apartments, and that's just in the main living area of the room.

With dark hardwood flooring and white walls, the room is well-lit with receding lighting, but the main source of light comes from the massive windows on the far end with French doors that lead to its private balcony. In the middle of the room and against the wall on the right is a king-sized bed with a charcoal gray duvet and an array of different throw blankets and pillows. Emily has a weird obsession with pillows and blankets. Every property I own has hundreds of both.

Along the wall, opposite the bed, a large flat-screen TV is mounted. There is no dresser in here due to the massive walk-in closet just off the ensuite.

"I should really stop being surprised by your things, Declan. Everything is so extravagant." Paige nudges my shoulder playfully with a smirk.

"This is all my mother's doing. When we first came to the States, she came to design the home to be similar to our home in Ireland."

"That's really beautiful. So, you've always been a part of the mafia, even there?"

"Yes. My family has led the mafia in Ireland for generations. My father was sent to the States to take over after a leader here was killed. So, my family runs both."

She walks further into the room and lays down on the bed.

I continue to watch her as she appears to melt into the mattress. The magnetic pull I feel toward Paige is so foreign. Her entire being is all-consuming. I need her like I need air.

She props herself onto her elbows and shoots me a beautiful smile. She pats the spot next to her and beckons for me.

Can't say no to that.

I stride into the room. Once I'm lying next to her, I pull her body into mine.

Being with Paige calms my mind, body, and soul.

I can feel it with every fiber of my being that she was destined to be mine. Figuring out a way for Paige to feel the same way is a challenge in and of itself.

"Thank you," she whispers and nestles into my chest.

I take in a deep breath and release it slowly. My fingers run through her silky strands. The action has started to become a comforting habit.

"Paige, I'd do anything for you," I whisper.

She doesn't reply, but instead burrows further into me. We lay there wrapped in each other and stare at the ceiling.

A soft knock on the doorframe interrupts our peaceful bubble.

Looking up from our position, Ingrid stands, studying us closely. I know she's apprehensive about Paige being here. She doesn't know her or where her loyalties lie.

It's not clear how her feelings about the situation will be once she sees that Paige isn't a part of this life. She'd probably deem me foolish and reckless for bringing her into this. But Paige is a once-in-a-lifetime woman. It'd be idiotic to let her go.

"Hello, Ingrid. What do you need?" I ask.

She studies Paige warily before meeting my eyes. "You're needed downstairs. Rhys is here and says it's important."

Her eyes flick to Paige once more and then she exits the room.

I place a kiss on Paige's temple, "I'll be back, mo ghrá."

Standing from the bed, I walk toward the door. Turning around in the doorway, I look longing at the magnificent woman lying in the bed. A soft smile forms on my lips before I leave the room.

"How can this lowlife cock sucking motherfucker outsmart our men? Where the fuck is he?" I growl.

This *Mark* is becoming more of a headache to track down than he's worth. Every time my men finally locate him, he slips through their fingers. There has to be someone with connections in the city helping him. It doesn't make sense.

And it's fucking pissing me off.

"I'm not sure, Dec. But with how evasive he is, we need to be careful with Paige. There is no doubt in my mind that he's the one whose been following her."

With my back to Rhys, I stare out my office window at the grassy acreage of land.

I can't understand who would help him, though. From what Rhys was able to uncover, Mark is nothing but a low-grade drug dealer.

"We need to make sure she has constant eyes on her. *Nothing* happens to Paige. Understood?"

"Of course, brother. I can see how much she means to you already. We'll make sure she's taken care of."

I spin and meet his eyes. His face is set in determination.

"He goes straight to the cellar the second he is caught. I want to drain the life from him."

He nods his head sternly.

"Do you know what he's done to her other than selling her mom drugs?"

I chew on the inside of my cheek. I have my suspicions but even those make me nauseous. My thoughts are far too dark, and I can't fathom my Paige going through any of the things I've thought about.

"A couple of things come to mind, but she's never told me. She has nightmares. Often. Sometimes, it's nearly impossible to wake her up from them."

Rhys's brows furrow.

"Maybe you can talk to Paige and find out if he knows people out here that would help hide him." His suggestion is a great one, but Paige is a vault whenever I try to ask about Mark.

"Maybe we can get Sarah to help. Paige all but refuses to talk to me about this fucker."

"I'll check with her about it."

"Great. Send Finn in when you head out, will you?"

Rhys nods and strides out of the room. A few minutes later, Finn steps in and stands with his arms behind his back in a practiced military stance. *Perfect little soldier.*

"I want you and whomever you deem good enough to be on Paige's watch. Until we figure out this Mark situation and the stolen merchandise on top of the destroyed warehouses. I want her under twenty-four-hour protection."

"Boss, are we sure the drug dealer is even worth our time? He —"

I pin him to the wall by his neck so forcefully, the drywall cracks.

"Let's get one thing straight. *I* am the boss. *You* take orders from *me.* Don't ever question what is worth our time or not. Paige is worth *everything* and this drug dealer is a threat to *her.*" The growl in my voice is feral.

He holds his arms up in surrender and nods.

I release his throat and walk to the wet bar on the right. Pouring myself a hefty amount of whiskey, I swallow the amber liquid in one shot. The burn helps little to ease my irritation regarding this whole situation. It's ridiculous that one man – one *insignificant drug dealer* – can evade us.

"I want to know every person she comes in contact with."

"You got it, boss."

"Good. Now, leave."

The door shuts with a click and I hurl the shot glass. It shatters against the wall. I slump in my seat behind my desk and rub a hand down my face. I'm beginning to feel like a failure. No one has been able to best me in years and it's pissing me off, especially since it involves Paige.

The chime of my phone interrupts my thoughts.

Jackie: When can I see you?

Why can't this woman take a hint?

Just before I'm going to tell her to fuck off, I get an idea. Rhys's comment the other day, about her being behind our issue, resonates in my mind.

Me: Meet me tonight at my club. I want to talk.

Jackie: Perfect! I'll see you then.

I quickly send a message off to Rhys about this impromptu meeting. He wasn't too happy when I told him not to tell Sarah about where we were going, but he can get over it. The last thing I need is for Paige to ask about Jackie and have to explain why I would meet her. I can't allow Jackie's ridiculous obsession with me to threaten the life I want to build with Paige.

When I hear a knock on my door, I set my phone down and invite them in. Ingrid enters the room and closes the door behind her.

Her hardened stare meets mine when she spins around.

"What are you doing with this woman? Why is she here?"

"Watch your tone, Ingrid. I'm still your boss and I lead this organization. Not you," I warn.

She straightens her shoulders and lifts her chin.

"Who is she?" she demands. Ingrid and Rhys are the only two people who can speak to me this way without getting a knife to the throat. She's been around long enough that I have established a close relationship with her.

"Someone important to me. She's not a part of any underground life, Ingrid."

"And you're certain? How long have you known this woman?"

I understand her concerns, but I don't have the patience to explain myself right now. I don't *need* to explain myself.

"Ingrid, she is *my woman*. You do not need to concern yourself about her. She is loyal to me, and I am loyal to her. As I've said, she knows nothing of the underground life. I want her here and you will be sure to treat her with the respect she deserves."

She rolls her eyes and waves a hand in annoyance. "I care about you more than I give a damn about this life, *leanbh*. I want to make sure this woman is not going to become a problem."

I let out an annoyed sigh, "Ingrid, Paige is not a problem."

"She's too quiet and unsure of herself, Declan. This life will eat her alive. You need a strong woman at your side."

"Enough, Ingrid!" I slam my hands down on my desk. She doesn't flinch or falter. "Paige is *it* for me. I will not have this discussion with you again. You know nothing about her. When you get to know her and her strength, then you can talk to me. Until then, I don't want to hear another negative thing come out of your mouth regarding Paige."

She doesn't say anything.

"Am I clear, Ingrid?" I growl.

"Crystal," and then she leaves the room with a slam of the door.

When I enter Paige's room, the restroom door is slightly ajar, and the shower is running.

I make my way over and lightly knock on the door, "Paige?"

"Uh, yeah? Come in."

I push the door open and walk inside. Paige is in the walk-in shower. The steam has fogged up the glass, but I can still make out her delectable brown nipples and beautiful curves as she rings out her hair. My cock hardens in my pants.

"Enjoying your shower?" I tease.

"I would enjoy it more if you weren't watching me," her tone suggests otherwise.

"Can I join you?" I ask as I begin unbuttoning my dress shirt.

"I mean, I guess you can." The playfulness in her voice excites me.

I'm ready to play baby.

Chapter 21

Paige

Declan is getting undressed far too slowly. It's agonizing waiting for him to expose that beautifully tattooed skin of his. My body tingles in anticipation.

I'm turning into Sarah - my libido is ridiculous because of this man.

"Don't worry, take your time. My skin isn't shriveling up in here or anything," I say sarcastically.

He chuckles "What have I said about giving me lip, baby?"

"Why don't you come in here and remind me?" I challenge.

He finally finishes undressing and enters the shower. My clit throbs in sync with my heart.

His eyes travel up my body hungrily. Chills travel through my bloodstream despite being in the hot water.

I arch a brow and then spin around to rinse my face under the spray.

He closes in on me. The warmth of his body overpowers the warmth of the water. He places his hands on my hips and pulls me back into his chest. His erection is pressed up against my back. It's so hard, I cannot wait to be filled with it.

He dips his head down and places a gentle kiss on my shoulder. The moment his lips touch my skin, I shiver. He chuckles and places a kiss on the opposite side. The reaction is the same.

"I thought you were coming in to teach me a lesson?" I mock and press my ass into him.

I feel a sharp bite to my shoulder and gasp. His fingers dig into my hips.

His hands move up my body from my hips leisurely, his calloused fingers heightening my arousal. Stopping just below my breasts, his thumbs lightly caresses the underside.

My head falls back against his chest and a soft moan escapes my lips.

"I can teach you lessons without dominating you, ghrá." The low seduction in his voice heats my body into an inferno.

My body becomes more aware of each and every brush of his fingers on my skin. It's blissful torture.

"Declan," I moan in disapproval.

His touch is too slow.

"Yes, baby?" he says in a husky voice.

"Please..." I beg.

He chuckles as his hand takes an excruciatingly slow pace toward my pussy. I'm soaked and aching. I need him to make it go away.

When his finger lightly brushes my clit, my knees buckle. His opposite hand holds me steady at the hip and he begins rubbing slow circles with just the right amount of pressure.

"Fuck," I whisper, and my hips start to roll of their own accord. *I need more.*

His hand pulls away and I whine in exacerbation.

"Declan... Please..."

"Tell me what you want, *ghrá.*" His lips brush up the column of my neck and I moan again.

"Fuck me. Please. *Fuck me.*"

I'm spun around and then hoisted up by my thighs. My legs are draped over his forearms and in one forceful thrust, I'm filled to the brim.

"Fuck! Yes!" My screams echo off the shower walls as we meet each other thrust for thrust. The stretch is euphoric. *Declan* is euphoric.

"Scream for me, baby. Let everyone on this property know this pussy is mine," he growls and bites down on my neck.

My nails dig into the skin of his shoulders as he fucks me against the shower tiles. The warmth of his body mixed with the coldness of the tiles is amazing.

"Your cunt is phenomenal, Paige. It was made for me," he grunts.

I can't form a coherent sentence. I'm floating in a cloud of ecstasy.

Declan sets me down on my feet then pushes my front up against the wall, so I bend at the waist. I barely have time to catch myself before I face-plant into it. Once I'm steady, he lifts one of my legs, splitting me, and then thrusts into me once more.

I let out a loud moan at the stretch he gives me.

He pounds into me with so much force, I will likely bruise between my thighs. *But these bruises will be welcomed.*

A hand wraps around my throat and I'm pulled back against his chest.

"Do you like feeling my cock deep inside your tight cunt, baby? Do you feel how greedy she is to be filled by me?" he rasps in my ear.

"Yes, God, yes I do. You feel so good Declan."

He smashes his lips to mine and kisses me like his life depends on my breath.

"Tell me you're mine, Paige."

I shouldn't. I know I shouldn't, but I can't help but let the words fall out of my mouth.

"I'm yours, Declan. I'll always be yours."

"You're never getting away from me," he growls.

Declan's hand that is wrapped around my neck drops down to my clit and he rubs circles while continuing the same pace of his thrusts.

"Come for me. Paint my cock with your cum, *ghrá.*"

My eyes roll to the back of my head and my entire body tightens before I'm thrown into the orgasms of all orgasms. A kaleidoscope of color bursts behind my eyelids and I can't contain the animalistic moan that falls from my lips.

My thighs shake and I stand onto my toes.

"Fuuuck, Paige. Your pussy is squeezing my cock so well. Look at you. You're gorgeous falling apart for me."

His thrusts increase before Declan pushes into me one final time. With a deep groan, he fills me with his cum.

I'm panting and completely spent when he pulls himself from me. I feel his cum slide out of me. A finger scoops up what is oozing out before it's pressed back into me.

"I can't wait to put a baby in you," he whispers.

I freeze. *A baby?*

Nonononono. I can't do that.

I quickly rinse off my body, grab the towel I have draped over the door, and exit the shower without a word.

"Paige?" Declan calls but I can't turn to face him. I need to get away from him.

I can't get pregnant again. I *won't* get pregnant again.

I scramble to the closet and throw open a drawer to find a pair of panties and some clothes to sleep in.

"What was that?" Declan's soft voice comes from the entryway of the restroom.

I can't control my tears from flooding my eyes. I can't face him. He'll see the fear and the pain there and I'm not ready to open that door to my past. I don't know if I ever will be.

Ignoring his presence, I continue to dress in silence.

I feel him come up behind me and my eyes flutter closed. My hands tremble and my lip quivers. Taking a deep breath in, I spin to face him. My head remains down although my eyes are closed.

"Baby?" The concern in his question is obvious. But I *can't* open that door. It needs to stay closed.

He'll become repulsed by me if he learns about what has been done to me. It'll crush me to have Declan look at me with disgust.

"Paige, talk to me. Please." His pleas hurt my heart. I swallow the lump that is stuck in my throat and raise my head.

His blue eyes are filled with so much concern for me. The tears I was holding back begin to slide down my cheeks.

He cups my face with both of his hands and wipes away my tears as they fall.

My lip trembles at the tender gesture and I begin to sob. My face crushes against his bare chest and he wraps his arms around me.

"I-I…. I can't talk about it, Declan. It hurts. I can't take you looking at me differently once you know the truth." Each word comes out in gasps, and I sob uncontrollably.

"Shh, Paige. I would never see you any differently than the woman who I want to be mine." His sweet words are supposed to make me feel better, but they are suffocating.

"I can't be yours! Don't you get it?" The sudden anger in my voice surprises both of us. I can't contain my rage about the thought of being owned by someone. Used for someone else's pleasure.

"What are you talking about?" He shakes his head in confusion and steps back.

"I refuse to be owned again, Declan. So, if your idea of me being yours is ownership, you're in for a shit ton of disappointment. I'm out of here the second we find Mark and he's gone."

I storm out of the closet before he can convince me to change my mind.

You're running because you're scared of wanting to be owned by him.

Yeah, well fuck you, heart.

Declan leaves me alone for the remainder of the day.

My heart had hoped he would have come for me but obviously, that was fucking stupid and childish. I can't want someone to come to me after I just ripped them apart and stormed out.

I'm walking down the hallway when I hear a hushed voice. I slow my steps when I reach the corner. Leaning against the wall, I peek around to see Finn on the phone, speaking in a low voice. I can't make out what he is saying but he's tense and he sounds angry.

"Just make sure you get it done," he barks, shoving his phone in his pocket. He huffs out an annoyed breath and then marches in the opposite direction from where I'm hiding.

That was very odd.

I stand quietly for a few more minutes to make sure he doesn't come back before I continue on my path toward the front door.

When I make it outside, I scan the property and see a lone horse in a round pen.

"Hi, beautiful girl," I whisper lovingly as I approach her slowly.

She watches my every move in a tense stance. I don't crowd her but simply wait at the gate for her to come to me.

After several minutes she takes a step forward. When I make an excited movement, she pauses and stares at me again.

This goes on for a while before she's finally pushing her nose against my hand.

"That wasn't so bad, now, was it?" I keep my voice as calm and quiet as possible as I stroke her velvet hair. I feel a peace in her presence I've never felt. Silent tears fall down my face as I continue to stroke her.

I move to her blonde mane, and she bristles. I pause my hand to make sure she's okay with my touch there. She relaxes her muscles and I begin stroking her again.

This is what I need.

This serenity is what my heart needs. What my mind needs.

Life has become a shitshow of panic and anxiety. I don't know how long I will be able to hold out this time before the need to escape becomes my only option.

Chapter 22

Declan

I watch Paige with one of the newest horses. She hasn't been given a name quite yet. The horse has refused any human contact since she arrived yesterday and refuses to leave the pen.

Paige's outburst today pained me as much as it enraged me. Mark has done a number on her, and I can't even find the man to make him pay for it. My failure to eliminate this threat is weighing on me.

I can give Paige the life she deserves. I only need to remove anything that could threaten to take her from me.

The chime from my phone catches my attention and I spot a message from *Bean.*

Tyler (Bean): I found out some information about your warehouses. Someone heard there is supposed to be another hit on one of them tonight. No one would say which one.

Me: Who did you hear that from?

Tyler (Bean): A dude named Bones. He's a bouncer at a bar down in Brooklyn.

Me: Meet me at Skyline.

I pocket my phone after sending Rhys a message to meet me at the club and stride for the door.

"Ingrid, I'm heading out for some important business. I need you to keep an eye on Paige while I'm out. She's standing out by the new horse."

She glowers at me but agrees.

Once I step outside, I make my way over to Paige.

"I'll be back later tonight."

She doesn't face me when she responds. "I'll see you later then."

"Whatever is going on in that beautiful head of yours, you can tell me."

Her shoulders tense but she doesn't reply. She continues stroking the palomino's mane.

"We haven't decided on a name for her if you want to give her one. She also hasn't allowed anyone close to her since we got her yesterday."

She continues to ignore me, so I turn and leave without another word.

I will end your suffering, Paige.

Me and a couple of my men pull up to *Skyline* where we see Tyler and Rhys standing outside. They both make their way over to the car when we park.

Climbing in, Rhys nods a greeting to me, and Tyler gives me an awkward smile.

"Where is this club?" I demand the moment the door shuts

We pull up to a rundown building in downtown Brooklyn. There is graffiti littered across the entire building and people hanging around outside. When we step out of the SUV, everyone scatters like cockroaches.

My reputation of taking random people off the streets to torture precedes me, so people steering clear of my vicinity is nothing new.

"That's him." Tyler points at a man at the front door. He looks like your stereotypical club bouncer with a black tee that covers his large muscles and a bald head.

"Evening," I drawl as we get closer to him.

His eyes flick to me and narrow.

He doesn't recognize me. This is going to be fun.

"What do you want, pretty boy?" he grunts and puffs out his chest.

"Just came to ask a few questions. Hoped you could answer them for me," I say in a relaxed tone.

He looks between my men, Rhys, and me several times before returning his eyes to mine.

"I don't know shit." His stance becomes defensive.

My eyes flare as my blood pumps in excitement. Cutting into this man will be just what I need to help keep my anger under some semblance of control.

"Ah, well you see, that's not what my buddy Bean has told me. Now, I'm sure you're a busy man, but I'm afraid you will be coming with us tonight to answer my questions."

When I signal my man to grab him, he pulls out his gun and aims it at me.

I let out a sigh in feigned disappointment.

"That's not necessary. You'll be coming with us, *calmly,* or I'll blow your kneecaps and then drag you. Take your pick." I arch a brow.

He doesn't lower his gun, but it begins to shake as he flicks his gaze around the area, looking for an escape.

Running out of the little patience I have, I draw my pistol. My movements are quick, and he doesn't have time to react when I blow the first knee out. His screams echo into the night as he crashes to the ground, and I blow out the other.

"Load him into the trunk," I order the two men who accompanied me and Rhys, then spin around and saunter back to the car.

We pull up to my estate and the men use the outdoor entrance to get the bouncer into the cellar.

"Are we still meeting Jackie tonight?" Rhys asks as we watch the men carry Bones to the door.

"Yes, let's go."

I don't go inside to speak with Paige. I want to push for answers but right now, I have business to handle.

Rhys and I walk up into the VIP lounge and spot Jackie sitting in a short red dress and 'fuck me' red heels. Her hair is down and styled straight. Her makeup is heavier than usual.

"Delcan, I'm so happy to see you." She saunters over to me, and I further assess her appearance. She's thinner, and her complexion despite the makeup is sickly.

She's fucking using again. That might actually help with finding this drug dealer.

"Jackie," I grunt as she leans in to kiss me. I turn my head in time for her red lips to press against my neck.

"Mmm, you smell absolutely amazing." Her face brightens when she sees Rhys standing next to me. "Will he be joining us this time?" she purrs.

"I'll pass," Rhys says, and he leaves to take a seat.

"I came here to talk, Jackie." Placing my hand on the small of her back, I sweep my arm out and gesture for her to take a seat.

"I don't want to talk. Why don't we go to your office? I know how much you love to fuck me on your desk." She goes to stand but I wrap my hand around her wrist.

"Sit down," I growl.

Her face morphs into surprise and then confusion, but she sits.

"I need to ask you a few questions about a new drug dealer in the area. From what I can see, you're using again."

Her face flushes red. "I've been *doing a little dabbling,*" she mumbles with a shrug.

"Well, I just need to know who you're buying from. There's a new drug dealer running around, his name is Mark."

She sucks in her already thin cheeks and steels her face.

She knows him.

"I go through a guy who goes through another guy. I don't know his name."

Rhys snorts from behind me but I ignore him.

"Now, now, Jackie. You know how much I hate when you lie." I mock scolding with a smirk.

"I've heard you've been fucking a new girl, heard she's a pretty little thing." She quickly changes the subject and I instantly feel rage.

"Choose your next words very carefully, Jackie," my voice deepens, and my glare becomes murderous.

She shrugs a shoulder and pushes her hair behind it. "What was her name? Paige?"

I ball my fist to avoid choking the life out of her. I need to remember I'm in a crowded club, even if it's mine and we're in VIP. I don't have the entire police force on my payroll.

"What do you know?" I question through clenched teeth.

"Oh, not much. Don't worry, Declan. I won't tell her about us fucking tonight." She shoots a wink at me.

"We will not be fucking tonight or any other night, Jackie. Now tell me what you know about Paige."

Her smile is conniving, and her eyes fill with hatred.

"Just that you might want to keep an eye on her."

Fuck this.

I whip my hand out and fist her hair tightly, no doubt ripping a few strands out at the root.

"You are going to tell me everything you know." I bare my teeth at her, and she slightly shrinks away from me.

"Let me go," she hisses and tries pulling away.

Jerking her by her hair, I pull her in close. "Tell. Me." My jaw is clenched so tight, it might break.

"Take me back. *Be with me* and I will."

I let out a loud laugh that causes a few other patrons to whip their eyes to us.

"I won't be doing shit, other than skinning you alive, if you don't tell me what you know about Paige."

"She's damaged goods, Declan. I know what you want. What you *need*. We've always been good together."

"Get this through your thick fucking skull, Jackie. We are *nothing. You* mean *nothing* to me. If something happens to Paige, I will come after you. I will nail you to the wall and pour acid on your body and watch as your face melts. Then I'll fuck Paige next to your corpse."

Her face blanches and her fight increases as she tries to get away.

"Where is Mark?" I bark.

"I-I don't know! Last I heard, some guy named Bones knew where he was at! Now let me go!" she shrieks.

I let her go and she scrambles to her feet before running away without a second look.

Turning to Rhys, we share a look filled with malicious promise.

"Let's go see our friend, Bones, shall we?"

With blood splattered over my face and clothes, I look down at the dismembered body of Bones. The name seems fitting now that he's just a pile of them.

My breaths are ragged at the exertion I placed on myself to cut off his limbs. He was a big guy so cutting him required more of a workout.

He was able to give us a general location of where Mark would be as well as a little tidbit that he recently came into some money and set up some kind of deal with the Russians.

Bad fucking idea.

Vladimir Solkolov — the Pakhan of the Russian mafia — and I have had bad blood ever since I refused his merger request. I don't trade flesh and made that very clear to him. Since then, we've had shootouts, sabotaged deals, and deaths across both of our territories.

"Get his body parts to the pigs," Rhys orders two of our newest members. They gag as they load the pieces of flesh, bones, and organs into the wheel barrel before leaving for the pig pens. They've turned green multiple times and completely lost their stomachs once I started cutting off limbs.

"How do you want to play this? If he's involved with the Russians that explains how easily he's been slipping through our fingers."

Rhys undresses and dumps his blood-coated clothes into the burn bin. I follow suit. We both dress in some jeans and black tees that we stored down here for this reason.

"We need to meet up with Ivan to find out about this deal. If someone has been watching Paige, that could only mean one thing."

"Do you think he sold her to them?"

I don't think. I know.

"That's the only thing that the Russians would be willing to take from a small drug dealer."

The Russian Bratva runs the biggest sex trafficking ring in the world. If a woman is sold to them, she's as good as dead. Once sold, it's nearly impossible to find them until they are killed and dumped once they've reached their usefulness.

He growls under his breath as we both exit the cellar.

After we've checked every warehouse for any potential threats, we come up clean and head back home.

I walk up the steps and down the hallway. My steps slow as I reach Paige's room. The need to see her is too much for me to ignore. I knock lightly and open the door.

Paige is lying in bed reading a book when the door fully opens. She peers up at me, closes the book, and sets it aside.

"Uh, hi," she smiles tentatively.

"Hi, how are you?" I take a few steps closer.

She lets out a small sigh before motioning for me to sit on the bed next to her.

I sit and lay a hand on her thigh.

"I'm sorry about how I reacted earlier. You didn't deserve that, and I know you don't understand why I did it. But I need you to understand that I can't tell you everything about my past. It's filled with awful things, and I can't have you look at me differently."

My eyes bounce between hers and I can see the pain behind each word. Destroying Mark and showing her my love will be the only way I can help remove the pain she carries.

"Nothing in your past will ever change the way I see you. I'm the leader of the Irish mafia, Paige. I don't give a shit if you tell me that you've killed hundreds of people. My feelings for you were solidified the moment I met you."

A small laugh leaves her lips, and it fills my heart with warmth.

"Will you stay with me tonight?" The question leaves her lips as if she's scared I'm going to say no.

"I'll always stay with you, mo ghrá."

I stand and remove my clothes. After I'm down to my boxer briefs, Paige scoots over to allow space for me to lie with her.

Once I slide under the blankets, I pull her close to me.

Paige traces the lines of my tattoos on my chest and then my neck.

"Why an owl?" she asks as her finger moves over the owl tattooed across my throat.

"In the Celtic culture, the owl is a guide to and through the underworld. The reason I tattooed it on myself is so my enemies can see I will be what takes them there."

"Do you have many enemies?" she asks quietly.

"I'll have enemies even among those I call friends, Paige."

Chapter 23

Paige

I just reach the front door when Ingrid stops me.

"Where do you think you're going this early in the morning?" Her voice echoes through the large foyer.

I turn around to see her walking down the steps. Her eyes bore into me with each step she takes.

"I wanted to go out and spend more time with the palomino outside before I have to work today."

She studies me with pursed lips. I'm unsure of exactly what she is looking for, but she's watching me like a parent watches their teenager, expecting them to try and sneak out to a party.

"Don't leave the grounds." Spinning around, she walks down the hallway leading to the kitchen and leaves me alone in the foyer.

Okay then...

"Hi girl," I whisper once I'm outside by the pens. The brisk morning air covers the grass in a frosty dew.

The palomino's ears perk up and she lifts her head in my direction. She comes to me and nudges my hand with her nose. A smile spreads across my face and I stroke her gently.

The time I spent with her yesterday was exactly what I needed. It also seems to have been what she needed too. Her entire aura is calming. She feels like a kindred spirit. We spent hours together.

"Thank you for letting me spend time with you yesterday," I whisper as I continue to stroke her soft hair.

She snorts as though she understands what I'm saying, and I chuckle.

"I need to think of a name for you. Can't keep calling you 'girl', now, can I?" I tease and she bobs her head up and down.

The horse just agreed with me.

I tap my finger against my chin and purse my lips in thought.

"What about Lily?"

She nudges me once more. *I'll take that as a yes.*

"Yeah... I like Lily too."

I pat her cheek softly.

It's probably a stupid fucking idea but she seems to like being around me.

I approach the gate and swing it open. Lily regards me warily. Once I'm inside and the gate is locked, she ambles toward me at a slow pace. I don't move, allowing her to approach on her own.

Sticking my hand out with my head bowed, I wait. It feels like forever before I finally feel her nose press lightly against my hand. My body tingles with excitement that is difficult to contain but I don't want to frighten her, so I force my body to remain calm despite my desire to jump up and down in excitement.

Raising my head, I look and see Lily has her eyes closed. Closing my eyes, I lean forward and press my head against hers. I breathe in a deep sigh and relax into her.

"You're good with her."

Lily and I startle at the sound of Declan's voice. He's standing just outside the gate with a tender smile.

"She relaxes me." I turn away shyly.

"I'm glad. I wanted to come out and let you know that we found some information about Mark, and I think we have a pretty good idea of where he is." He places his arms on the railing.

Lily recognizes my change in demeanor and shifts slightly.

"That's good. Maybe then I can move out sooner than we thought."

I need to set a clear boundary, so it won't hurt as much when I leave.

Stop sleeping with him then.

That is the logical move to make but the thought of not sleeping wrapped in his arms or the feel of his body pressed against mine when we're connected makes me feel sick.

You're going to make everything harder if you don't push him away.

"You're not leaving any time soon," his voice hardens, and his jaw tightens.

"What do you mean? You just said —"

"I know what I said. But it's more complicated than you think. Until any threat to your life is completely taken care of, you will be staying here."

With one final stroke of her hair, I leave Lily in the pen. I stand in front of Declan with my arms crossed. My blood simmers just below the surface but lashing out won't get me the answers I want.

"Define 'complicated'," my voice is cautious.

He avoids my gaze and rubs his teeth with his tongue.

"Declan."

"There's nothing to worry about; nothing is going to happen to you. I promise." He kisses me on the forehead and walks toward the front door.

My thoughts begin to spiral with what could possibly complicate my situation more.

I pull my phone from my back pocket and text Sarah.

Me: Has Rhys talked about anything weird?

Sarah: You're going to need to be a little more specific. We have weird conversations all the time.

I smirk at her reply. She's always been an interesting person, so her answer doesn't surprise me.

Me: Just about the situation with Mark. Declan mentioned it being more complicated than just Mark. So, I'm kinda freaking out a little.

Sarah: He hasn't really said anything other than he made some kind of deal with some dangerous people. He probably won't tell me anything more since he knows I'll tell you.

Me: Ugh. Okay. Thanks.

Sarah: I'll try and get him to tell me more. Don't worry. Rhys and Declan will make sure we're safe.

Me: Yeah... I'll talk to you later. Let me know if he says anything.

Sarah: Love you!

I don't answer her message.

Placing my phone back into my pocket, I head inside to get ready for work.

My anxiety is through the roof. Not knowing what the fuck is going on is driving me insane. Declan seems to think that keeping me in the dark is the best thing for me but that's absolute fucking bullshit.

I only arrived fifteen minutes ago, and I can't focus on anything but the awful prickling sensation of being watched. Every time I turn around, I expect to see someone. There is nothing that can tell me I'm not going completely insane with paranoia.

"Miss Henley?" a small voice sounds from the other side of the desk, and I nearly jump out of my skin.

Peaking over, I spot Sage. She's a first grader here and comes to the office every morning so I can braid her hair.

She's neglected like I was as a child. I don't know the extent of her home life, but she comes to school in the same clothes for days at a time and her hair is never brushed unless I do it. Her family has been reported multiple times, but the system continues to fail her. If I can give her a support system and any sort of comfort, I will.

My smile is instant. "Hi, honey. Are you ready?"

She nods and rounds the desk to sit at her designated 'braiding chair'.

"What kind of braid would you like today?" I pull out my comb, detangling spray, and elastics and lay them on the desk.

"You pick." Sage plops herself in the chair and rocks her feet back and forth with her hands crossed on her lap.

After spraying the detangler, I rake the comb down her long blonde hair.

"Alright, let's see. How about two Dutch braids?"

"Yes, please." Though she's facing away from me, I can tell she's smiling.

She tells me about her weekend as I work through her knots and twist her hair into two neat Dutch braids.

Sage's posture becomes rigid and my brows furrow at the sudden change.

"Um, Miss Henley." The nervousness in her voice increases my anxiety.

"What's going on?" I peek around her shoulder and follow her line of sight.

A large baldheaded man in a black suit leans against a blacked-out car with a lit cigarette. The rain plummets down on his daunting form as smoke bellows out of his mouth. I feel his penetrating stare down to my very core. It's ominous and dangerous.

I squeeze Sage's shoulders gently, attempting to offer her reassurance that I barely feel myself.

"Go on and get to class," I whisper and then calmly push back from my seat and put my supplies away in the drawer.

Sage leaves quietly, but not before she studies the man outside. She furrows her brows and leaves with a disturbed look on her face.

Pulling my phone out, I send a message to Declan.

Me: There's a strange man outside of the school. He's staring at the building.

Declan: I'm on my way.

By the time Declan arrives, the man is long gone. But the effects of his presence linger. The sour taste in my mouth hasn't dwindled in the slightest.

"What did he look like?" Declan asks, running his fingers through his hair.

"I only saw him from afar, but he was really... *big*, like might as well have been a bear, big. He was bald with a clean-shaved face but that was all I could make out. Oh! He was in a black suit and had a blacked-out car. He was also smoking a cigarette."

To say that I feel like a disappointment at not being able to give him more information is an understatement. Declan crosses his hands behind his head and looks up.

School is still in progress, but Declan, Rhys, and I stand huddled outside while Declan has a few men checking out the nearby area.

I don't understand why that man would be here. Mark didn't know people like that when I was younger.

Declan drops his arms and then marches toward the doors of the building with determination.

"What are you doing?" I run to catch up to him right as he flings the door open and strides toward the office.

"I just want to talk with the principal here about setting up some security," he says under his breath.

I grab onto his arm, and he stops to face me.

"That's absolutely ridiculous and unnecessary. I don't need a freaking bodyguard on school grounds, Declan." I roll my eyes at the preposterous idea of having armed guards in an elementary school.

He growls in irritation. "Do you intend to fight me at every turn when it comes to your safety?"

I ball my hands into fists and take a deep breath to calm myself.

My retort is interrupted by Principal Nolan exiting his office. When he sees Declan, his brows furrow then he flicks his gaze to me.

"Can I help you?" he deepens his voice to seem more intimidating. Unfortunately for him, Declan would probably shoot him between the eyes if he wanted to.

"Are you the principal here?" Declan looks down at the stout man.

"I am. And you are?"

"My name is Declan Moore. I've come to discuss security for Miss Henley."

Principal Nolan is taken aback, rightfully so. He meets my eyes and arches a brow before turning back to Declan.

"Let's head into my office." He motions for us to pass, and Declan wastes no time heading into the room.

The three of us are sitting in his small office. I'm mortified at Declan's behavior. I didn't mention the man so he can come barging in and establish some sort of ivory tower to put me in.

"Why would Miss Henley need to have security on school grounds?" Principal Nolan asks with a tilt of his head.

"That is none of your concern. I just need to ensure that she has them." Declan's tone leaves little room for negotiation.

"Mr. Moore, was it? This is an elementary school. We have procedures that we follow that ensure the students and staff here are safe. I'm afraid I cannot allow armed men to walk the grounds. It would be stressful for everyone here."

"I think you misunderstood me. I wasn't asking for permission. I was informing you that Miss Henley will be having security," Declan growls.

"Declan." He whips his glare in my direction, and I snap my mouth shut.

Principal Nolan shifts uncomfortably in his seat before clearing his throat.

"Your demands will need to be cleared with the board and superintendent. We will also need to communicate with the staff and parents of each of the students here."

Declan growls and then storms out of the room. I offer an apologetic smile to Principal Nolan before following him.

"Are you out of your mind?!" I yell once we are outside. "You can't just expect to be able to have *armed* men on school grounds, you maniac!" my arms flail around me.

Declan halts and I nearly crash into him. He spins on his heel and is inches from my face in seconds. He looks ready to murder someone. His eyes are wide and his hackles are raised.

Not saying anything, he spins back around and jumps into his car. The tires screech as he barrels out of the parking lot.

"Well, that went well," Rhys says from behind me. I completely forgot he was even here.

"Shut up, Rhys," I say under my breath as I watch Declan's car disappear down the road.

I let out a defeated breath and head back inside.

Chapter 24

Declan

It's late into the night by the time I make it back home. I drove aimlessly for several hours, attempting to calm down before coming home. I was so angry at Paige, the principal, and myself.

I took Finn and Liam with me to meet with Ivan when they should have been watching Paige. I blindly believed that she would have been okay at the school. Maybe teaching her how to shoot a gun and self-defense is a good idea.

You should be able to protect her. You're failing.

I don't make stupid decisions. Everything I do is calculated. But when it comes to Paige, everything is unpredictable. My emotions get the best of me despite my best intentions to keep her safe.

I don't know what the fuck I'm even doing at this point. Everything is a jumbled mess of chaos. I've always thrived on chaos and have never struggled with maintaining my control. This situation is turning whatever discipline I've had into dust.

Paige is in my head and I've become distracted. The empire I've built is falling as I turn all my focus to protecting her and finding any threats to her life.

Which you're failing at finding.

I also can't protect her if she fights me any chance she gets. It's as though she doesn't want me to keep her safe. She questions everything and doesn't trust in my feelings for her.

If she'd let me, I'd worship the earth on which she stands. She just has to fucking let me.

She's *mine.*

My mind is in turmoil that I can't reach into the part of her heart that wants to be with me. She built such a fortress around herself as a child, and it's only been reinforced with the reappearance of her past.

I'm on my fifth glass of whiskey when Paige opens the door to my office. The numbness in my body is beginning to set in. I need an escape from this fucking *pain* in my chest.

I raise my eyes from the spot on the ground I've been staring blankly at from my seat.

She hesitantly enters the space before closing the door behind her.

"Are you okay?" she asks quietly.

I only grunt in response. Draining the rest of my whiskey in one gulp, I stand to fill the glass once more. I know that alcohol is a depressant but right now I don't give a shit. The ache in my chest can only be numbed by the burn whiskey provides.

Regret for whatever comes out of my mouth tonight will likely take over once I'm sober.

I stumble on my way to the wet bar and Paige hurriedly attempts to catch me. Her hand touches the skin of my arm and I find comfort as well as absolute torture in her touch.

She's fucked with my head to the point that I don't know how much more I can give without just forcing her to accept my love.

Shrugging her off, I grab the bottle and chug directly from the spout. The liquid flows down my throat in a now muted burn.

"Declan, you're drunk. Why don't you go to bed?" She tries to take the bottle from my hand, but I tighten my grip.

"What do you want, Paige?" I say in a low growl.

She pauses to look at me with her brows furrowed. "I'm checking on you. You left and I haven't seen or heard from you in hours."

Snorting, I take another swig of the whiskey. She can pretend to care all she wants. I fell in love immediately and she won't even try to see the life I can give her. She has one foot out the door at all times.

I get it. I do. She's been a victim in her past. But now, she's a survivor. A warrior. She just needs to let it out. Let that Goddess take control and obliterate her monsters.

"Go to bed, Paige. I'm fine." I stumble back to my seat. Flopping onto the cushion, I drape one leg over the arm, leaving the other on the ground.

Paige walks toward me and kneels at my side. The skin between her brows creases as her face morphs into worry.

"What's going on with you? Is this because I don't want a bodyguard at the school?"

If only it was just that. I'm failing at my promise to keep her safe. She doesn't want me like I want her. I can't fucking eliminate the demon that haunts her dreams. I can't find the culprit behind the burning of my warehouses. The emotions I've always been able to control are raging a war inside my mind.

Nothing is going right.

"Don't worry about it," I whisper, my head lulls back and hangs from the opposite arm. I stare at the ceiling and let out a frustrated sigh.

"Declan... I know you want to keep me safe but having those men there doesn't just affect me. There are children there who would be in danger if we have the place swarming with mafia men. I'm going to be putting too many people in danger."

I understand her worries. But I can't muster up a fuck to give right now.

Completely ignoring her, I take another swig and then drop my arm. The bottle slips from my hand and rolls onto the ground. The whiskey spills onto the floor and travels toward the rug in the center of the room.

Paige leans down and picks up the bottle. Placing it gently on the coffee table, she turns to look at me again with those eyes that I love so much.

She's so fucking gorgeous. Angelic.

There's concern in her eyes. But for what? It's clear that unless Mark is gone, she won't allow herself to give in to the connection we have.

I need to lay off the alcohol. My emotions are all over the fucking place.

Paige sets her hand on my chest and leans forward to place a gentle kiss on my cheek.

"I do care about you Declan. I appreciate everything you're doing for me. There's just too much happening for me to process, and I'm struggling," she whispers. I could listen to her talk forever. The rasp in her voice caresses my skin like a soft rose petal.

I raise my head from the arm of the seat to get a better view of her. Her jade-green eyes bring me the serenity I need. But also, the pain I can't escape. I need her to want me as I want her. I need her to let me in. I just don't know how to get her to do it.

"I'm the leader of a mafia. I can torture people to talk. Get them to spill their secrets to me as I carve into their skin. It's easy. Getting *you* to open up to me... now that's hard. I don't understand what you're doing to me. But I *want* you to want me, Paige. And it seems that no matter what I do. You don't want that."

Tears well up in her eyes, making them glossy and she looks away.

"I don't know how..." her voice cracks and the tears begin to slide down her face.

I let out a sigh and lean my head back. The world spins and my eyes feel heavy.

"Just... Go... Please," I whisper and close my eyes.

Paige sniffles and leans down to place a kiss on my lips. I hear the click of the door opening. Before it closes, I swear I hear a quiet 'I'm sorry' before I fall into a drunken sleep.

Chapter 25

Paige

Quietly shutting the door to his office, I leave Declan and walk somberly up the steps toward my room.

My being around is putting too many people in danger. I need to leave… alone. I can't take Sarah away from the life she's building here. She's been too happy for my bullshit to mess that up for her. I'm hurting Declan by not being able to share the feelings with him that I feel so deeply within me. My presence is causing more harm than good.

Entering my room, I head toward the closet to fill a bag of my belongings. Every article I place inside is a countdown to my leaving.

Packed with the bare minimum, I stare longingly at the room. I know what I said about not wanting to be here. But I lied.

I want to stay with him. I really do. I want to find a way to accept that I'm his as much as he is mine. That we're meant to be together for the rest of our lives. But my life has been and will always be too fucked up. Even for the mafia. He has an entire empire to run. He doesn't need my baggage to add to that.

Keeping my steps light, I sneak through the house. I can't risk being spotted and having someone tell Declan of my plans.

I hope he finds it in him to forgive me for this.

Every so often, I have to duck behind a vase, curtains, or a corner to hide from the ridiculous number of men walking around. I'm taking advantage of my petite size to the fullest and it's helping me in maneuvering through the mansion without being spotted. Instead of taking the front door, I sneak out the back. Hearing voices, I throw myself into the bushes.

Bad idea.

The twigs dig into my skin, and I hiss. My hair is wrapping around the thorns and getting stuck. The voices increase as the men get closer. I lower myself, ripping my hair out as I flatten my body so I'm lying on the dirt. I hold my breath as they walk past.

Once the coast is clear, I release my breath and rise quietly to my feet. I climb out of the bush and walk into the night.

"Alright, you can do this." My attempts at encouraging myself don't help at all. I'm a nervous wreck. If I'm caught, I don't know if I'll have another chance to leave. Declan will never allow me to leave his sight again.

Keeping to the shadows as best as I can, I scurry through the grounds like a mouse or squirrel running to its burrow.

Get to the trees.

I change my direction and make a break for the forest. It's so dense here that the starry night sky is essentially non-existent through the canopy. The darkness barely allows me to make out the trunks of the trees. Leaves crunch below my feet noisily and the air chills me to the bone.

Pulling my coat tightly around my body, I slow my steps as I continue my trek toward the wall on the East side of the property.

Heel-to-toe. Heel-to-toe. Heel-to-toe.

I end up getting turned around and I have no idea which direction I'm facing anymore.

"Who goes there?" A deep voice cuts through the forest and I take off on a sprint.

The tree just to my right splinters when a loud bang sounds.

They're fucking shooting at me!

Holy shit. Holy shit. Holy shit.

Blood pumping in my ears, heart racing, I stumble over roots and rocks as my adrenaline courses through my veins.

"Fuck! It's Paige! Quit fucking shooting!" someone shouts behind me. I don't turn to the voice to avoid falling.

"Paige!" another voice screams. *Don't fucking stop running.*

I've run so far and hard that my feet might fall off. My nose and cheeks burn from the cold. The voices of the men disappeared in the distance once they realized I wasn't going to stop. They've likely already told Declan that I left.

I have no idea how much longer I walk before I finally make it to the other side of the forest. I hide behind a tree and see more men walking around.

Fucking fuck.

The space is completely open so I can't hide anywhere without being spotted before I'm far enough to make it to the wall that borders the property.

Traveling on foot was a stupid fucking idea. I should have taken my car, *but* Declan probably put a tracker on it, so I guess it's a good idea to be walking.

Plopping myself on the ground, I sit with my back pressed against the trunk of the closest tree. And I wait.

I've studied the guards enough to find a very small window of time to make it to the wall. Do I have enough time to make it over? Probably not, but I made it this far and I'm not turning back now.

My window opens and I stay crouched low to the ground without crawling.

I feel like Black Widow or Catwoman.

I snort. Obviously, I'm delirious if that thought pops into my head.

I'm about twenty feet from the wall by the time my window of opportunity closes. Falling completely to the ground, I flatten myself again until the next window opens.

Someone upstairs must agree that me being gone is the best option because there is a fucking tree close enough to the wall and tall enough to climb that I can make it over.

The static of a radio interrupts my mini burst of happiness. "Any sight of Paige yet? She should be reaching the end of the trees soon."

I can't make out the reply but the men surrounding me are all on higher alert now that they have an official target to be on the look-out for.

Fuck it.

Throwing myself up, I put as much strength into my legs to dart to the tree.

"There she is!"

My breathing is shallow, my lungs burn, and sweat streams down my face, but I keep running.

Someone's hand wraps around my arm tightly once I reach the tree, but I spin around and kick him in the crotch with as much force as I can muster.

With a pained grunt, the hand releases me and I start climbing. My hands cut open with each rough grasp I make on the bark, but I'm too focused on escaping to feel the intensity of them.

I hear other people climbing below me. Once I reach the top, I don't waste any time to see how close they are before I jump.

My knees buckle and the wind is knocked out of me when I hit the ground. It takes me a moment, but I'm able to get up and run once again.

Multiple thumps of others landing on the ground after making it over the wall sound behind me.

"Paige, stop! What are you doing?"

I can't find it in me to feel bad for running. It's better this way. Once I'm out of the city, Declan and Sarah can move on. They'll soon realize that the carnage I threaten to bring is not worth their time and effort.

I'll find a way to maybe leave the country and I'll be free of Mark.

Rationality isn't my strong suit and I'm probably going to regret leaving, but right now I can't see another way around this. It's been *weeks* and Declan hasn't been able to find Mark.

It's only a matter of time before he catches up to me. Before he takes me and uses my body for his benefit. It's not a risk I'm willing to take.

I make it to the road when I'm suddenly blinded by headlights. I halt and hold my hand up to block out the brightness. A black van skids to a stop in front of me. The door swings open and *Mark* jumps out with two other men.

"Hello, Paige." His stance is menacing, and his eyes are filled with excitement.

My heart drops and my blood turns to ice. The temperature outside is warm compared to the temperature of my body.

I was so fucking close! NO!

When I try to make a run for it, I'm grabbed violently by my hair and a rag is placed against my nose and mouth. My eyes burn from the chemical vapors.

Don't breathe it in!

All my hopes of being free disintegrate when my eyes droop and my body relaxes.

Declan's men running at us is the last thing I see before I fall into pitch blackness.

Chapter 26

Declan

"Paige was taken." The world completely stops when the words leave Rhys's mouth.

When I woke up to find out that Paige had taken off, I sent everyone to search for her. How a small woman was able to outrun my men is beyond me. They were fucking trained to capture intruders for fucks sakes. And now she's been taken and will be auctioned off to be sent to fuck knows where.

"What happened?" I say quietly as I stare out of my office window. I'm struggling to contain the craving to slaughter every single one of my men for allowing this to happen.

"The men were able to find her running on the East side of the property. She climbed a tree close to the wall and jumped over. By the time the men made it to the other side, she was being drugged and dumped into the back of a van." I don't miss the sadness in Rhys's voice. He will have to inform Sarah that Paige was taken. That I failed to keep her safe.

If I hadn't been a fucking pussy and gotten shitfaced, I would have slept next to her. I would have been able to feel her body leave the bed.

"I don't want you going to Antonio's anymore. We need to find where they'll be doing the next auction before she's sold." I keep my voice calm despite the rage and panic I feel.

"You got it," Rhys nods.

"We also need to find out how they knew she would be running and how they knew where she would be. Someone in the ranks set this up."

I grab the bottle of whiskey on my desk and take three swigs.

"What are we going to do about Sarah? She's going to go apeshit when I tell her."

"I don't know Rhys. Her reaction doesn't fucking concern me right now," I hiss and take another swig.

"Get the men who were working the parameter she used. We're going to find out what happened and why she was able to get away in the first place."

Rhys squeezes my shoulder and exits the room.

I should have fucking taught her to defend herself when she begged me to. It shouldn't have been put off. If I would have pulled my head out of my ass, this situation wouldn't have happened. She would have felt secure enough to stay.

I lift the bottle to my lips but pause. Tilting it away from my face, I stare at the amber liquid swishing around inside.

If you're going to have any chance at finding her before it's too late, you need to be alert.

I set the bottle down on the desk and leave the room.

Entrails are littered on the ground of the cellar. I disemboweled the men who claimed she outran them in the woods. Their inability to do what they were trained to do makes them absolutely useless to me.

When I was told someone took a shot at her, I sliced his balls off and then shoved them into his throat before I cut him from his neck to his dick. His screams died out before I got to the bottom, but it was still satisfying to feel his skin slice open and watch his intestines fall to the floor.

I haven't found out any information that I could use to find her. Each passing second, I risk losing Paige forever. That is not something I'm willing to accept.

Rhys has been working with a few other men to get the details of the next auction but since we are not in good standing with the Russians, it's taking longer than it should.

My body is a raging inferno. I will burn everything in my wake until she's home.

"Does anyone else want to share how they were outrun by a five-foot woman in the woods when they're trained professionals?" I play with the tip of my blade and face the remaining men bound by their arms and legs on the ground.

I'm not sure if they can really even provide me anything, but right now I just want to carve into bodies until I can see Paige again.

The cellar door bursts open and Rhys walks in. Setting my blade on the table, I walk to meet him.

"The next auction is set to be in Mexico. I guess the Cartel has a lot of women they're wanting to sell," he says in a hushed tone.

"Get us on the next flight there," I order. Jackie's comment pops into my head and I freeze. Rhys arches a brow in question.

"Find Jackie and bring her here." I growl, "The cunt knew something was going to happen, and I'm going to make good on my promise."

Jackie is hanging from the ceiling and blood from her wrists slides down her arms from her despicable attempts at getting loose.

"Declan... please! I swear I didn't know what was going to happen!" Her cries only provoke my hunger to make her suffer.

She fucking *knew* about this.

I charge at her and hold the carving knife against her cheek. "Don't fucking lie to me. You knew something would happen to her and I promised to make you pay," I seethe.

Her makeup is streaked from the tears sliding down her face.

"I-I'll tell you anything, just *please* don't kill me." Her chin quivers as she pleas for life.

Rhys is watching from the corner of the room with a scowl on his face. Normally, I don't condone violence against women, but for *this* woman, I'll make an exception. She deserves what is coming to her.

"Where is Paige being held now?" I ask, circling her.

"I don't know that!" she screams.

"You're a stupid fucking cunt if you think I believe your bullshit," I spit.

"I swear!"

I backhand her and she swings from her chains.

"If you don't start giving me answers, Jackie, I will peel your face off right fucking now. I'm not above making you a pile of limbs and skin for your betrayal."

She blanches, "O-okay, I heard she was going to be flown out of New York as soon as she was taken. She's supposed to be in Mexico by the morning. But that's all I know! I swear!"

I peer over at Rhys who narrows his eyes at me.

"What are you going to do with her?" He flicks his eyes to Jackie, "Antonio will take this as a declaration of war."

"How about we call up Antonio? Make him help in the search for Paige in exchange for keeping Jackie alive?" I shrug.

I spin around to face Jackie and slice her from collarbone to collarbone. She shrieks out in pain and the sound bounces off the walls. "Can't say she'll still be pretty when he gets her back though."

My head tilts to the side as I watch the blood slide down her chest. It's exhilarating.

"Declan, are you sure about this?"

I glare at Rhys, but the fucker holds my stare. "I will kill anyone and everyone who stands in my way of getting Paige," I promise. "If Antonio wants a war, I'll give him one. Jackie will suffer for her role in Paige being kidnapped, regardless of if it was a large one or not."

A sigh leaves Rhys's lips and he runs a hand through his hair.

"I'll call him." Pulling out his phone, Rhys dials Antonio's number and leaves the room.

I look back to Jackie and she whimpers at the promise of vengeance in my eyes.

"Please Declan, I'll do anything," her voice breaks as she chokes out a sob.

Rolling my neck, I smirk at her and slide the blade lightly across her skin when I circle her.

I tisk, "Jackie. Jackie. Jackie. There is nothing you can offer that will save you from me."

She lets out her sob and bows her head.

Rhys returns and looks at me somberly. "He's on his way."

"Excellent."

I leave Jackie hanging in the cellar and don't bother changing my blood-soaked shirt from the murders I committed earlier. I sit calmly behind my desk as I wait for Antonio to come.

My door swings open violently and crashes against the wall. Antonio charges in, face red, fists clenched, and hackles raised.

"Where the fuck is my sister?!" he roars.

I slowly shake my head in disappointment "Antonio, have a seat."

He spits on the ground, "I will be doing no such thing. Where is Jackie? If even a hair on her head was touched, I will destroy you Declan."

"Sit. The. Fuck. Down," I growl through clenched teeth.

His nostrils flare and then he sits. He knows which one of us has the upper hand and which one will cause the most damage.

"Jackie is currently hanging by her wrists in my cellar," I reply with a smile on my face.

Antonio freezes and his eyes bulge. "What have you done to her?" he whispers.

I shrug nonchalantly, "Nothing too physically scarring. Her head might be fucked up though."

"What do you want? Why are you doing this?" he demands, his panic rising.

"I want your help," I say.

"You want my help?! You took my sister, likely tortured the fuck out of her, and you want my fucking help?" he roars.

Slamming my hands down on my desk, I rise and stand over him, "Your drug addict of a sister played a role in the love of my life being taken. Paige is days away from being sold by the Russians in Mexico. If you want your precious sister to remain alive, you will be helping me find her."

He takes and releases a deep breath. "If I agree to this, Jackie is to be set free."

"You think I'm an idiot? Jackie will remain in the cellar until Paige is returned to me. The state she is released in depends entirely on you." I sit back down in my seat and stare at him with my brow raised.

He growls as he glares at me but finally relents to my demand.

Six hours later, we arrive in Tijuana.

"Where's the auction going to take place?" I ask Rhys as we leave the airport.

"There is a mansion just outside the city. It's supposed to be there in three days."

"And you were able to get me on the list, right?"

Rhys chuckles and shakes his head, "when have I ever failed you Dec? Of course I got you on the list." I squeeze his shoulder, "Let's go get Paige."

Chapter 27

Paige

I wake with an unbearable drumming in my skull. My body feels sluggish and weak. I'm shackled by my ankle to a concrete wall that's stained with blood.

Unfortunately, I'm not the only one.

The smell of mildew, sweat, and urine saturates the air, making it difficult to breathe. There are at least thirty other *noticeably young* girls and women in this room with me. We're all dressed in raggedy dresses that are stained with God knows what. I don't know where I am. It doesn't help that everyone in this room speaks different languages.

After Mark drugged me, I woke up on a plane. He didn't rape me this time, but he did promise it would happen soon. Then I was drugged again when we landed.

I'm trembling as I scan the room. Taking in the faces of every person here.

A little girl, no older than ten, crouches in the corner with tears in her eyes. My heart hurts so much at the thought of what fate waits for her. This has to be some kind of human trafficking operation. That is the only thing that comes to mind at the number of girls here.

What is going to happen to me?

I try to rid that thought from my mind because I can't afford to fall into that horrific mindset. I need to find my strength to be able to survive whatever lies ahead.

The sound of a loud deadbolt unlocking echoes and the door to our prison opens. Distant cries of torment and anguish can be heard just outside.

A large man with scars on his face and long black hair stalks into the room. Everyone tries to crawl away, but it is no use. Our chains are too short.

He scans the room with a hungry look in his eyes. He's looking at us like we're a menu. It's sickening.

His eyes land on a Hispanic woman in the middle of the room and he walks toward her. "¡No, por favor no!" she yells, and she tries to pry the chain from the concrete floor. Her sobs cause chills to scatter over my entire body.

My heart breaks and silent tears slide down my face as I watch the man grab her by her hair, after removing her shackles, and dragging her kicking and screaming out the door.

The sound of the door closing and locking echoes in the now-silent room. Her shrieks dissipated the moment the door was closed behind them.

The other women start muttering and rocking back and forth. They're all praying to whatever God they worship.

There is no God. If there was, we wouldn't be here.

I scan the room and take in the depressing state of each woman and girl in here. Some have bruises on their faces. Some look like they haven't showered in months. Their faces are stained with tears. It's the most repulsive sight I've ever laid eyes on.

What kind of monster would do this?

The woman next to me is praying in English.

"Hey," I whisper, and she startles. I hold my hands up to show I mean her no harm.

She's a beautiful girl with red hair, pale skin, and freckles. Her blue eyes are filled with so much pain. *She looks remarkably familiar.*

"Do you know where we are?" I ask softly.

She nods "We're at an auction... in Mexico," she mumbles.

An auction... fuck.

"My name is Paige Henley," I offer her a sad smile.

"I'm Emily," she returns a smile equally as gloomy.

Emily? ... Nononono it can't be Declan's Emily... Can it?

"E... Emily?" my voice cracks. My heart threatens to come up my throat.

Please don't be Declan's Emily.

"Emily Moore."

My heart completely shatters. I study her face and *I see it.* Her resemblance to Declan. They have the same cheekbones. The same dimples. The same fucking eye color that makes every fiber of my being feel enveloped in love.

"Oh my God... you're Declan's sister, aren't you?" I choke back a sob and lift my hand to my mouth.

Her eyes widen and my question is confirmed.

"You know Declan?" she whispers-yells and leans forward.

"Y-yes... Oh my God... Emily..." I can't hold back my sob. He thinks she's in Ireland. This is going to destroy him when he finds out.

"How are you here? Declan said you were in Ireland visiting your mom."

She looks away for a moment before returning her gaze to me. "I was... I met a guy a few days into the trip, and he kidnapped me. I'm not sure how they're keeping my kidnapping from my family but... No one knows I'm missing."

I shake my head solemnly. How could this be our reality?

"How do you know Declan?" She asks.

"He's a very important person to me... He was helping me... keeping me safe. I was a fool and ran because I was scared of being with him. And look where that got me." I lower my gaze to the ground.

You're so fucking stupid... You should have stayed with him.

Her eyes fill with tears, and she reaches out to hold my hand. We intertwine our fingers. It's awful to say but I'm happy not to be alone in this. We can find a way to lean on each other and make it out of here.

I hope.

Hours pass and we all remain chained. Emily and I have shared as many happy stories as possible in an attempt to be positive in this shitty fucking situation. It helps as a distraction but the longer we're here, the harder it is to think we're going to make it out.

With nowhere to use the restroom, we have no choice but to pee where we sit. We're soaking in it. The smell of ammonia fills the air.

We haven't eaten anything, and no one has come back in to check on us. Some of the girls here are so malnourished, I can't comprehend how they're still alive.

More hours pass and the deadbolt sounds. We all hunch our shoulders to hide ourselves, so we are not picked next.

The woman who was taken earlier is dragged behind the same man who took her. Her head hangs low from her limp body. Dropping her to the ground, he re-shackles her ankle and exits the room, touching women as he goes.

Everyone is silent. The sound of my blood pumping fills my ears. We all wait, watching to see if her chest will rise. Giving us any sign if she's even fucking alive.

The silence is broken by her quiet whimper. And the room breathes a sigh in relief.

My stomach drops when she rolls onto her back. Her face is unrecognizable. It's swollen and covered in bruises and blood. Her dress is ripped to shreds and dried blood coats the inside of her legs.

Bile rises up my throat, but I swallow it back.

Another woman scoots as close as possible to her body and lifts her head to set it on her lap. She caresses the woman's hair softly and whispers.

"Estás bien. Estás bien. Todo va estar bien, vas a ver. Estoy aquí contigo." *You're okay. You're okay. Everything will be okay, you'll see. I'm here with you.*

Each of us watch with tears streaming down our faces as one woman tries to comfort the other. I squeeze Emily's hand tightly and she squeezes mine in return.

The hopelessness seeps out of each one of us and stifles any light in the room.

Hours later, the woman — Elena— succumbs to her wounds. The cries of the other women echo.

No other men come to visit. Elena's body stays where she died and we have no choice but to watch her decompose.

We're not going to make it out of here alive.

Chapter 28

Declan

Rhys, Antonio, and I walk into the mansion where the auction is being held. My body pulsates with impatience.

In the center of one of the rooms is a stage for the women to be displayed for the bastards buying them. Seats surround the stage which is a large crescent shape. Men fill the space, laughing loudly, and drinking their vodka and whiskey. My fists clench. I'm filled with disgust at how excited they are. Knowing they are buying women like cattle.

I'm struggling with my need to search the place for Paige. Knowing she may be so close and not being able to get to her is maddening.

We're escorted to a secluded area on the upper level of the room. My eyes dart around the area to see if I can spot her as we walk up the steps.

"What if she's not here?" Antonio asks with a whisper.

"She's here," I snap.

She has to be.

The lights dim and a spotlight is pointed at the stage.

Vladimir Solkolov, the Pakhan of the Russian Bratva, steps into the spotlight. "Welcome gentleman." He stretches his arms outwardly with a huge smile.

Don't shoot him in the face. Don't shoot him in the face.

"We have a wide selection tonight and I can assure you, you will be pleased with your purchases," he says smugly.

My blood boils and I suppress the growl threatening to leave my chest.

"A list of the women being auctioned tonight will be brought to you momentarily. So, relax and enjoy a drink of the fine alcohol we have here. We will be starting very soon."

The lights brighten, men clap, and Vladimir spins around and saunters off the stage.

My thoughts run feral as I scan every person in the room. There are criminals, politicians, and celebrities alike. Despicable.

A moment later, a man walks in and hands us the list of women. I rip the pages from his hands and flip through them as quickly as possible.

She's not on the list. SHE'S NOT ON THE FUCKING LIST!

"She's not here…" I whisper in shock and my fingers loosen their grip.

Rhys and Antonio take the pages from my grasp and comb through them.

"Declan…" Sadness fills Rhys's tone and he slowly lowers the papers.

I'm at a loss for words. She was meant to be here. My chest is cracking with disappointment and fear.

What if I've lost her?

No. Fuck that.

Antonio's whisper cuts through our silence, "She must be being sold in a private auction to high-profile buyers."

I turn to Rhys for help and his apologetic face enrages me.

She was supposed to be here.

The lights dim once more, and a woman slowly walks to the center of the stage. Her face is pale and sickly, her hair sticks to her face, and she is so skinny the bones of her shoulders protrude through the dress. Her body sways back and forth.

She's been drugged.

The three of us look at each other in shock at the horrific sight before us.

Drug trade? Fine. Weapons trade? Perfect. But Skin trade? It's an abomination.

Men shout out numbers as the auction officially begins.

Women are taken off the stage as quickly as they come. They're sold for thousands upon thousands. It's unbelievable, even as I watch it happen with my own eyes.

Vladimir returns to the stage. "I have saved the best for last. All have been confirmed to be untouched and innocent. Enjoy." he bows his head and walks off the stage.

"What the fuck does that mean?" Antonio's brows furrow as he stares at the stage.

"You don't think..." Rhys's sentence dies out when the first *child* comes into view.

The men instantly begin shouting their bids over each other before she's even made it to the center. There is no way this girl is older than ten.

Her appearance is no better than the women's.

I'm going to be sick.

I'm disgusted. *She's a fucking child.*

Child after child, they are sold for thousands. The emotions I feel for each of them shake me to my core.

Every one of them has tears in their eyes and blank, hopeless expressions.

"We need to stop this." Antonio tries standing from his seat but is stopped when Rhys grips his forearm.

"If we do anything right now, we will be killed. There are at least fifty men in here buying, not including the guards. Do you really think the three of us can take all of them on?"

"Then we need to find a way to dismantle these trades," he says through clenched teeth.

I wholeheartedly agree.

My stomach twists at the thought of Paige being in a similar condition. I feel like I'm being gutted.

Hour after hour, women and children are sold. My blood boils with each one displayed on the stage. Once the auction is over, the three of us quickly stride to the exit.

"Declan Moore," Vladimir's voice sounds from behind and we freeze.

I straighten my spine and lift my chin when I meet his gaze. He smiles wide and opens his arms, pulling me into a hug.

"I was incredibly pleased to hear you wanted to be in attendance tonight. It's a nice step in the right direction to end our differences, no?" He turns his gaze to Antonio and Rhys and bellows, "And you brought Antonio! What a wonderful surprise."

"Yes, thank you for having us. It was no doubt a.... Memorable experience," I say as calm as I can manage and Antonio nods.

"I couldn't help but notice that neither of you made purchases. Were my girls not to your liking?" The suspicion in his tone is evident.

"We were just getting acquainted with the whole process," Antonio says with a pleasant but fake smile.

"Ah, well, I can assure you my women are all examined for absolute high quality," Vladimir says proudly. "You won't find such excellence with anyone else".

I imagine myself peeling the skin from his face and I wish so deeply to make it real.

"When will your next auction be?" I ask. My jaw tightens painfully as I wait for his response.

Vladimir claps his hands once.

"We will be having another public auction in a month."

My stomach falls.

A month? Too much can happen in that time. She can be sold in a private auction by then. She could be fucking dead by then.

"You wouldn't happen to have any private auctions happening soon, would you?" Antonio masks his hopefulness as best as he can but I can still hear it.

I shove my hands into my pockets to hide the tightness of my fists and shift my weight to appear relaxed.

Vladimir's eyes flick between the three of us. "Since you're new to trading, you won't be invited to any private events in the near future." There is something in his face that I can't decipher.

His posture has stiffened. His jaw ticks.

What are you hiding Vladimir?

My eyes slightly narrow and he lifts his brow when he notices.

"Well, that's unfortunate. We had hoped to see what kind of women you deem special enough to keep from public auctions."

I'm grateful that Antonio is leading this conversation. I'm barely containing myself from digging his eyes out and feeding them to him.

"It's a good thing there is never a shortage of women. After a few public auctions, we can discuss an invitation to a private one." Someone calls out to Vladimir, and he leaves us standing by the front door.

Shutting the door to the car, I repeatedly punch the dashboard until it dents from the force of each hit.

"Fuck! God fucking damnit!" I roar, running my fingers through my hair before pulling on the strands.

Rhys and Antonio are silent as I seethe. My soul feels like it's caving in. My Paige will no longer be the same woman I've fallen for. This world will destroy everything good about her.

"Declan, we'll find her." Rhys tries to sooth me, but nothing can calm the storm raging through my body.

"I'll do whatever it takes to find her. If I need to kill every person on my way there, then so be it," I promise when I meet Rhys's eyes.

"I'm sure Vladimir keeps a record of all the girls they have, right? Maybe we can hack into his files and see if there's anything that can give us a one up about where she is." Antonio looks between Rhys and me.

Nodding sternly, Rhys says "If there is a file, we'll find it."

Chapter 29

Paige

My joints throb with an overwhelming pain. My lips have ripped open and scabbed over repeatedly despite being allowed water every few hours. Every so often, we're rounded up and taken to use the restroom and like a prison, we have to shower together while being watched.

Beady eyes watch our naked flesh with so much hunger it's nauseating.

We've been down here for days, and each day, women and children are taken and returned beaten and bloodied. Some never return. Three others have died. Two girls and one woman. Despite not knowing any of them, my heart fills with agonizing grief.

Emily and I haven't been taken yet. I'm not sure if that is a good thing or if that means whoever does take us will be worse than the others.

The deadbolt unlocks and we all whimper in fear. Two men stalk into the room. "Everybody up," they order.

With wobbling legs, we stand and wait.

The door opens wider and an older man with a bald head and an expensive white suit saunters in.

“Hello ladies,” his voice is thick with a Russian accent and his smile is anything but welcoming. “Apologies for not coming to introduce myself sooner. I am a very busy man.” He chuckles as though talking to shackled and beaten women is a normal occurrence.

He must be the man in charge of this, so I guess it is.

“My name is Vladimir Solkolov, Pakhan of the Russian Bratva. Prepare yourselves, as we will be leaving for your next home.” His eyes scour over all of us before they come to a stop on me. My throat tightens and my blood runs ice cold.

He tilts his head toward one of the men and whispers in his ear. His eyes never stray from mine.

A dry swallow travels down my throat.

More men enter the room and begin hauling everyone out.

Emily is taken before I am, and we clutch onto each other until the very last second. Her worried eyes widen as she takes in the fact that I‘m the last one shackled to the floor.

Vladimir and the two men close in on me like a pack of wolves. I raise my chin slightly but the tremble in my body betrays my nervousness.

“Now… you are a very beautiful woman.” His eyes rake hungrily down my body. My heart feels like it is seconds away from bursting out of my chest and sweat rolls down my back.

He caresses my cheek with the back of his hand, and I wince when his skin slides across mine. I’d vomit if I had any food in my system.

Stepping back and adjusting his coat, Vladimir juts his chin outwardly toward me and the men move to remove my shackles. Both of my arms are grabbed tightly as I’m hauled away.

I'm so weak that I cannot fight them. My legs drag behind me and I feel the skin from my feet peel away from my body. My cries of pain are ignored by everyone we pass.

This place is a soul-sucking horror house.

The entire building screams of never-ending torture, oppression, and death. I peer into the doorways of each open room we pass. They're all empty except for a select few. Those have women being beaten or gang raped.

Whatever pieces of my soul remained completely disintegrate when we pass a room with a little girl being tied to a bed. She's naked and her body is nothing but bruises. Tears fall into her hair as she stares up at the ceiling.

Her gut-wrenching cries echo down the hall after we've passed the door.

All hopes I had of finding a way out of here diminish with each passing second.

It's been five days since we were moved from one hell to another. Everyone has been separated into groups and placed into rooms together — except for me.

I've been placed in a broom closet-sized room that has a dirty, stained mattress on the ground and a bucket in the corner. There's a camera mounted to the wall by the door.

The red light mocks me as it blinks.

Vladimir has sent men in to bring me food and water. None of them have raped me, but their lingering stares make my skin crawl.

Unlike the other place, which had heavy steel doors to block out sound, this place has doors with small windows in them. I can hear the banging of doors opening and closing and the cries of women in the distance.

Two days ago, they started injecting us with heroin. Some have died from overdoses. Unfortunately, I haven't been blessed with that escape.

The men are much more careful with my doses since Vladimir has declared that I receive 'special treatment'. *Barf.*

My door unlocks and opens. *Viktor,* my 'assigned bodyguard' comes into view when the bright light shines behind him.

"Let's go," he grunts and steps aside for me to exit.

"Where are we going?"

My face whips to the side when he slaps me.

You shouldn't have said anything!

"You don't get to ask questions, shlyukha. Now move."

I've come to learn that *shlyukha* means whore. That's comical since it's their fault I'm here in the first fucking place.

Viktor leads me up a long flight of steps that opens up to a mansion.

We're under a fucking mansion.

I scan the room to check for any possible escape routes, but the sheer number of men around here puts a stop to that.

We walk down a long hallway. My bare feet patter against the cold marble flooring.

I hope the dirt from them stains.

Viktor unlocks a room and I step in. It's an office with a giant fireplace. There are four men sitting in expensive suits smoking cigars. They all stop when they see they're no longer alone.

Vladimir stands from his seat and walks toward me. "There she is," he hums, and I'm thrown back to being that scared fourteen-year-old girl in Mark's kitchen.

I feel light-headed and my vision tunnels.

This can't happen again.

I whirl around to try and run away but smack right into Viktor. He wraps his hands around my shoulders roughly and turns me back toward Vladimir, who is stalking my way with a menacing glint in his eyes.

"Now, Paige," he pouts, "I was beginning to think you would have been grateful for the treatment you've been receiving. After all, you have a private bedroom." He offers me an evil smile.

My eyelids flutter and I fight to hold my tears. This bastard isn't going to see me cry.

When I don't reply to him, his smile disappears, and anger fills his features. He slaps me across the face. The large ring on his finger slices through my cheek on impact and I fall to the ground.

I choke back my sob and try to rise but a shoe is placed on my back, and I'm pushed down. Vladimir kneels beside me and growls under his breath, "You will not disrespect me, Paige. I own you." He grips onto my hair and pulls me up.

I scratch at his hand, trying to pry his grip from my strands.

He drags me toward the men grouped in a circle around the fireplace and throws me in the center. The area rug burns my knees and the palms of my hands.

"Get up," he grunts.

I bite down on my tongue as I fight to keep my emotions under control and push myself to my feet.

My mind continues to switch back and forth between the past and the present. My panic is rising and I'm having a harder time containing my emotions.

Clear your mind, Paige.

The men assess me with hooded eyes and some of the sick fucks get hard.

One of them stands and walks toward me. He pulls out a pocketknife and my body goes rigid. He grips onto the collar of the ragged dress and cuts it down the middle and I gasp.

My breasts bounce with the force of him ripping it away from my body. I'm fully exposed to these men and their eyes darken in lust.

The tip of the knife is placed in the center of my chest and the man pushes it in. The sting of the blade cutting into my skin causing me to wince. I feel the skin break and blood slide down my stomach. The taste of copper fills my mouth as I bite down on my tongue.

"Hmm, you look so good covered in blood," the man hums.

At this point, it's getting too hard to hold back the tears. The first one falls, and his eyes brighten.

Clear your mind. Clear your mind.

I repeat the chant over and over, but it doesn't help.

The prick of a needle hits in my neck and I feel the burn of the heroin entering my system. It's pure bliss.

I begin to relax, and the men stand to crowd me.

I'm laid down onto the floor and hands roam over my flesh.

This is it.

I close my eyes and fall into the effects of the heroin.

This will be over soon.

The man who I've learned is named Aleksei slices into the underside of my breast and presses into the wound.

I groan but my body is too listless to make any effort to move away.

My legs are pushed open, and fingers slide up my thighs. The callouses scratch me like claws from a cat. Nothing like the euphoric feel of Declan's callouses touching me.

A pinch is applied to my clit and the nerves scream. The room tilts like I'm on a boat rocking-side to-side in an ocean storm.

"Please... stop," I say in a muffled, cloudy voice.

A bite to my thigh makes me whimper, followed by a sharp pain as another slice is made to my stomach.

"Enjoy, boys," Vladimir's voice says from somewhere in the room, followed by the click of the door closing.

The clinking of belts being undone, and clothes being removed fills my ears. My heart rate is slow and sluggish but pounds hard against my chest.

Fingers dig into my cheeks when someone grabs my jaw. My face is jerked to the right and Aleksei's hazy face comes into view.

The promise of crucifixion is emanated in his black eyes.

"You will be mine," he whispers.

A whimper escapes my lips as he bores into me.

"Let's get to it, men," Aleksei says when releases my face. He begins undressing, revealing a body covered in a variety of scars.

The other three men begin closing in on me and they reach hands out to touch my skin. I jerk with each touch of their fingers and curl into myself.

Despite the heroin, I can feel the panic in my body. Someone slaps my ass and I yelp. The burn is instant, and I know it has already welted. My hair is moved – exposing my shoulder – and a kiss is placed at the hollow of my neck. I shiver at the disgust that fills my blood.

Aleksei studies my body, taking his sweet fucking time. The look in his eyes is evil. A mixture of lust, anticipation, and vile thoughts. I'm struggling to hold the contents of my stomach.

"Your skin is far too flawless, my pet. We will need to remedy that." He steps closer to me and slices across my stomach diagonally. I gasp and press my hand against the cut. It is deeper than the cuts he's already made, and the blood doesn't slow as it oozes.

Another set of hands cup my mound before dragging a finger through my dry slit. It burns and I bite down on my tongue to avoid crying out.

Chapter 30

Declan

Paige has been missing for six weeks.

I am losing myself to the demon inside. I've given up the idea of attending auctions to try and buy her.

I have teams working tirelessly to locate where a private auction is being held so we can target it.

I've begun torturing anyone and everyone who would possibly know any information about Vladimir's operation. So far, not a single one has given me shit to work with. My cellar is stained with gallons of blood, it might as well be painted red. Anger and panic flow through my veins unchecked. I don't know how much longer I can continue, not knowing when I'll be able to see her again.

"Declan you need to try and rest. You're working yourself into the ground," Ingrid pleas.

"There will be no resting until I get her back. Every day she's gone is another that I could lose her forever."

Her eyes fill with sympathy.

"I didn't realize she meant this much to you," she whispers and walks to me where I stand overlooking my property.

We were able to find out that the women were moved to another location but can't find where that location is. I shot four men that day.

Ingrid rubs my back with her withered hand, but it doesn't provide any comfort. Nothing will supply any comfort.

I need Paige's touch. Her rainy smell and her enchanting jade-green eyes.

Rhys and Liam burst into the room panting like they ran here.

"We found where the private auction is going to be," Rhys says quickly.

I perk up.

"Where?" My adrenaline is already pumping, and my heart is galloping.

"Saint Petersburg. Tomorrow."

"Let's go. Tell Antonio to continue searching for other private or public auctions from everyone associated with Vladimir in case she's not in this one either." I don't spare Ingrid another glance as I run out of my office.

As we're making our way outside to the car, Sarah comes flying down the road.

"Fuck," Rhys mutters.

Her car skids to a stop and she jumps out.

"I'm done waiting around while you guys look for Paige. This is bullshit. She was mine before she became yours, Declan," she huffs in anger.

"Baby —"

"Don't 'baby' me, Rhys! You either include me in whatever plans you have, or you both can fuck off and I'll find her myself."

"That's not happening," Rhys growls.

"Why the fuck not?! I can help!" she screams, eyes wild in anger.

I interrupt when they begin yelling over each other.

"Sarah, you need to understand that we cannot take you anywhere near where Paige is. It will put you at risk and we can't do that."

Her glare flicks to me but disappears when she sees the hurt in my eyes.

"You know where she is, don't you? What's happening to her..." she whispers, and the tears begin to form.

"We don't have an exact location, but she's been trafficked."

A sob leaves her lips and Rhys wraps an arm around her. "No! You said she was taken by Mark!" she pushes Rhys away from her.

"She was. But Mark sold her to Vladimir Solkolov. He traffics women and children," I inform her. My voice, empty.

"We're doing everything we can to find her, baby." Rhys rubs his hands up and down her back.

Watching the two of them together guts me and I become angry at myself. I know I shouldn't be upset with them for having each other, but I don't have the option to be with Paige.

"Stay here with Sarah," I turn and walk toward the car.

Rhys runs up to my side, "What the fuck do you mean? I'm not letting you go in there without me."

"I'm not going in. I'm going to fucking torch the place and bring them out."

"Are you sure that's a smart idea?"

"If it increases my chances of bringing her back, I'll do anything." My steps don't slow.

I pull the door on the driver's side open and hop in. Just as I'm shifting the car into drive, Rhys opens the passenger side and climbs in with me.

"What are you doing?" I grunt.

"You're not going alone. We didn't plan on taking anyone in the first place so it's just the two of us."

I look out of the window to see Sarah unloading a bag and walking into the house. I turn my eyes to Rhys.

"She's staying here with Ingrid," he explains.

Nodding to him, I shift the car into drive and peel out of the driveway.

We arrived at our hotel in Saint Petersburg without being detected by any of Vladimir's men. Since this is supposed to be a private auction, very few people know anything about it and Vladimir doubled the men posted in the airport.

"What is the plan aside from torching the place?" Rhys leans forward in his seat, resting his forearms on his knees.

"What do we know about the building?" I ask.

"It's a warehouse just outside of the city that's made out to be abandoned. We know that there are three levels, including a basement. The auction is being held on the main floor. The other floors are being used for whatever the men want to do with their purchases."

"Were we able to get a list of who is being auctioned?" My heart speeds up with the thought of seeing Paige's photo on the list.

"Ivan sent me an email. I haven't opened it yet."

Reaching over to his bag, he pulls out an encrypted laptop and opens the file.

We sit side by side as we scan through the photos of women and children. It isn't until we reach a page labeled 'Prized Purchases' that I completely freeze.

No. FUCK NO.

"Declan..." Rhys stiffens, the shock in his voice matching mine.

"There is no fucking way. No fucking way. She's in Ireland with my ma."

I rip my phone out of my pocket and dial my mother's number.

"Hel—"

"Where is Emily?" I bark out before she can greet me.

"What do you mean? She left for the US over two months ago. What is going on?"

The phone slips from my hand and falls to the floor.

Rhys picks it up and begins speaking to my ma in hushed tones.

I run back to the computer. There she is. Her blue eyes have lost their brightness. Her red hair no longer shines, and her cheekbones have hollowed. But it's her.

It's Emily...

"Your ma said Emily left while she was out at the market but sent her a text that she needed to return home for some photoshoots," Rhys says and sets my phone on the table.

I scroll through the next two pages and spot her. Paige.

Paige and Emily are both going to be in this auction.

"How the fuck did this happen?" I say more to myself than Rhys.

His hand clamps down on my shoulder and he gives it a tight squeeze.

"I don't know but we need to work out a different, clearer plan if we are going to have any chance at rescuing them both."

My mind is in shambles. Emily and I haven't spoken in a few weeks but that is nothing unusual when she's in Ireland.

"Vladimir never planned to have us attend a private auction," I conclude. He knew he had my sister and was going to sell her privately.

The fucker had her this whole fucking time!

I squeeze my hands into fists and dig my nails into my palms.

"Call Finn and Antonio. I want them and as many men as they can bring on a plane and in Saint Petersburg, *tonight."*

I reach for my phone and dial my uncle.

"What are you going to do?" Rhys asks.

"I'm calling my family in Ireland. We're wiping Vladimir and his men off the face of this fucking earth," I growl.

Once our army is on its way, Rhys and I sort through the weapons we brought for ourselves.

I'm going to gut Vladimir like a fish.

We sharpen the knives that need sharpening and ensure the guns are cleaned and working properly.

Hours later and deep into the night, Finn and Antonio arrive with at least fifty men each. My uncle promised to be here and ready to go by morning.

The Russian Bratva will cease to exist once we're through with them.

Chapter 31

Paige

Is Heaven real? I know Hell is. I've been living in it.

The last few days have been the worst of my life. My childhood torture pales in comparison to the abuse I receive here.

The men Vladimir allowed to rape me, visit daily. Some of them come multiple times a day, and with others.

Aleksei's fetish of slicing my body has reached new levels since that night.

Sometimes he cuts me just for fun. He makes sure I'm bound to the bed so I can't fight or get away when he comes in to 'play' when I'm lucid and not doped up on heroin. My body looks like it's been through a woodchipper from the number of slices he's made at this point.

I've needed stitches a few times but when Aleksei spots them, he ensures they're reopened by the time his visit is over. The cuts are deep and wide. They're never going to fade like the ones Mark and Mom gave me.

Every day, Viktor comes in to inject me with more heroin. I've become addicted. It's my only escape from this nightmare. Every time he comes in, I wish it would be the day I die of an overdose.

Unfortunately for me, Viktor still makes sure to dose me correctly.

Vladimir says I'm one of his 'prizes'. I'm not sure what that means, but I definitely don't feel like a prize. I've always assumed that women would be required to have unblemished skin when they're being sold, but that clearly isn't the case with Vladimir. The men he sells to are sadistic fucks and Aleksei wants to buy *me.*

"Stop! Please!" My voice is hoarse from screaming.

My *wonderful* friend, Aleksei, is here to visit and my skin is coated in blood. He's carving into me, only this time… It's between my legs.

He's refrained from cutting me there, but I guess today is the day his restraint breaks.

"Oh, come on, baby. You bleed so beautifully. I can't stop now," he muses, and he licks the blade of the knife. He moans in pleasure when his tongue slices open.

My arms and legs are bound so I'm spread eagle on the mattress with nowhere to go.

I'm an animal carcass lying on a butcher's table.

Blood soaks the mattress and tears flow down my face and into my hair.

The pain is agonizing. Adrenaline and heroin are fighting in a war to take control of my mind. Everything is heightened and muted simultaneously.

He leans back and admires the mutilation of my body. "Perfect. Let's see how they stitch *that* backup."

He slaps my pussy, causing me to shriek and thrash against my confines. He chuckles darkly under his breath and does it again.

Standing up, he unbinds me, and I curl into myself. My body screams in agony with the movement. I hear the bang of the door close behind him.

Viktor comes into the room a moment later and lifts me into his arms. Each step to the makeshift 'hospital' causes piercing pain throughout my entire body. My blood soaks his shirt but he seems to enjoy it. A smirk is plastered on his face.

I'm set on the hard metal bed for the third time this week. The exhaustion begins to set in after a few minutes of lying here and I close my eyes. Viktor's steps fade when he exits the room.

I don't open them when I hear heavy footsteps return or when I hear the creak of another person being set on a bed.

"Paige?" a voice whispers.

Opening one eyelid, I see Emily on the bed opposite me. Her face is swollen and littered with cuts and bruises.

"Hi," I croak.

"What happened?" her voice cracks as her eyes scan my body in a panic.

"Just another day," I wince when I try to make a small shrug.

"We need to find a way out of here," she says quickly. Her eyes flick side to side, making sure we're alone.

"The only way we're getting out is when they sell us or kill us, Em." I shake my head solemnly.

"We need to try."

"How do you expect us to try? They keep us locked up like dogs," I grit.

She examines me once more and her face pales.

"You're losing a lot of blood, Paige. Has no one come to help you?" The panic rises in her voice.

I don't answer. I'd much rather not alert anyone that I'm still lying here so I can just bleed out.

"Help!" Emily yells.

"That's pointless. They hear that word every single day and do nothing about it," my dejection made clear.

Emily continues to try and get someone's attention. After several minutes, large boots stomp on the ground, and Viktor returns. He looks at both of us and then leaves the room.

See, pointless.

He reappears with one of the newer doctors on their payroll and pushes him toward us.

"Fix them. They're going to be sold tonight," he growls and then stomps away.

I'm in such a weakened state that I can't even summon enough fucks to give about what he said.

Emily's soft sobs and the clinking of surgical instruments mildly drown out the other cries in the background.

The doctor steps into my view and looks down at me in sympathy.

"Declan is going to get you out, Paige," he whispers.

Tears build in my eyes at the sound of his name. I'd give anything to be with Declan, but I'm worse off than I was when I met him.

He'll never want me now.

Leaning in closer, the doctor says, "He's coming tonight."

"What?" Emily says.

The doctor spins around to her and nods, "He's coming. He's in Russia."

"Who are you?" I ask.

He gives me a small smile, "I am a friend. I've been sent in here to make sure you're alive and we are ready to run when Declan and Rhys come in."

His eyes scan down my body and widen when they reach the apex of my thighs.

"Paige..." he whispers and the sadness in his voice *hurts.*

I grip onto the arm of his shirt and his eyes return to mine.

"Please... make the pain stop," I beg.

He nods and reaches for the lidocaine to numb the area. I shake my head and pull him in closer.

"I want all the pain to go away... permanently." I stare unblinking into his eyes hoping he gets my point.

His stare bounces between my eyes and he shakes his head. He must see the resolution in my gaze because he takes in a deep breath and looks away.

"I can't do that. They will be here tonight. You will be rescued, *tonight."* His face is set in determination.

I lean back against the bed, and he begins working on my wounds.

I don't let him see the determination in my eyes. He'll try to stop me.

Once he's finished, he moves on to Emily. He's left the surgical instruments next to me, so I quickly grab the morphine and a syringe and slip them under my bandages.

I can't allow myself the hope that what he said is true. Declan isn't coming.

And even if he does. I'll be long gone.

Chapter 32

Declan

Dressed in tactical gear, my men, along with Antonio's and my uncle's, all congregate near the location of the warehouse.

I'm buzzing with anger and desperation.

Knowing my sister and Paige are both in there — so close — is making me ravenous to burst through those doors and slaughter everyone inside.

We've determined the different entrances we will be using to infiltrate the building.

Antonio's men will enter through the back, my uncle's through the front. My men will remain outside to surround the area and kill anyone who exits.

Rhys and I will be entering through a set of outside doors that lead down to the basement.

That's the only logical place they'd use to harbor all these women.

The plan is clear and simple. I can only hope it works out that way.

We are all stationed throughout the vicinity as blacked-out vehicles arrive with the *guests.* We take photos of every man and woman who exits and makes their way into the warehouse so we can track anyone who manages to escape.

We wait long enough to confirm no other cars will be showing up while we move in.

"We're set to go," Antonio's voice comes in through our earpieces.

"Aye, we're ready too," my uncle confirms.

"We're ready boss," Finn says.

I take a deep breath to calm my nerves.

This needs to work out perfectly.

"Good. Let's move," I say through the microphone.

Rhys and I move quietly to the door to the basement. We nod to each other, and I begin working on unlocking it.

Creeping quietly inside, I look around. It's only a concrete staircase leading down to a hallway.

My uncle's voice sounds through the earpiece, "Are you in place for us to start killing these fuckers?"

"Ten seconds," Rhys replies.

We move quickly down the hallway, and we begin hearing the sounds of painful cries. I stiffen and peek over my shoulder to Rhys, whose face is filled with panic.

A loud boom echoes and the building shakes.

Men yelling in Russian start running down the hallway in our direction. When they spot us, they're momentarily confused which gives us enough time to draw our pistols and start shooting.

Sounds of screaming, bullets flying, and bodies hitting the ground bounce off the walls.

I shoot a man in the shoulder, but the fucker comes at me like a freight train. We fall onto the ground and the gun falls from my hands.

He pins me and lands a punch to my cheek. My nose begins to bleed, and he hits me again. I jab him in the throat with my fingers causing him to choke and fall back on his ass.

Flipping over, I grab the pistol. Coming back, I shoot him between the eyes, and he lands with a *thud.*

Once the hallway has a clear path, I run down and turn into another hallway that opens to a space filled with doors. Rhys comes up behind me and we both stand frozen for a moment. Taking in the sheer amount of fucking *jail cells* in this place.

It reeks of blood, piss, and sex. The atmosphere is suffocating.

"You take that side, I'll take this side," I order, and we quickly split up.

Each room I push open is filled to the brim with women and children. They all cower when they see me fill the doorway.

"Go! Run, we're getting everyone out!" I leave each of the rooms as soon as the sentence is out of my mouth.

I hear the patter of bare feet running away from me and toward the hallway.

"There are women and children coming up through the halls, make sure you don't shoot them!" I yell through the microphone, and everyone confirms they've heard the order.

I lift my gun to shoot another man in the face but am met with a *click.*

Before I get a chance to reload, I feel a slice to my arm.

I pull out my own blade and we scramble to the ground. He slices my arm again and tries to go for my throat, but I stab him in the side repeatedly, blood coats my hand with every jab but I don't stop until his body slumps.

Panting, I push his body off me and stand.

My panic rises with each door I open. There is no sign of either one of them.

"Paige!" I shout "Emily!"

"Declan!" Emily's shriek echoes and I take off on a sprint.

"Where are you?!"

"Down here!" she cries.

My eyes dart around until they land on a fucking *hole* in the ground with a grate over it.

Emily's hands whip around frantically through the metal bars.

She's in the fucking ground?!

Bodies lie scattered and more fall as our men enter the basement and begin shooting.

I run to the grate and see my sister's tear-stricken face. She has bruises and cuts everywhere.

"I'm going to get you out, Em, just hold on." My voice is tight with emotion.

Grabbing onto the bars, I use all my strength to pull it up and toss it to the side.

Emily reaches for me, and I hoist her up by placing my hands below her armpits. She's lost so much weight, I'm worried I'll break her.

We wrap our arms around each other, and she sobs into my chest. I set my cheek on the top of her head and stroke her hair.

"Do you know where a girl named Paige is?" I ask after a few moments.

Her cries grow in pain instead of relief.

"Oh Declan," she wails.

My relief at finding my sister is replaced with terror of what she is going to say.

"What's going on?"

"Paige is... Paige is d-dead," she chokes out.

My blood turns cold, and my chest feels like it's caved in.

"What do you mean? What the fuck happened?"

"Declan!" Rhys's shout cuts off her response and I whip around to him.

In his arms is Paige's small limp body.

Nonononono.

I hand Emily over to Liam and bolt to Paige.

When I reach her, I push her hair away from her face. She's so pale. Her small body is cold and covered in dried blood, bruises, and stitches.

I pull her away from Rhys and fall to my knees.

Cradling her lifeless body in my arms, I let out a scream that can be heard over all the noise.

"Paige... Please... Mo ghrá. Come back to me." I whisper through my tears.

I'm not sure how long I sit there with my forehead pressed against hers. The carnage surrounding us has long since faded into the background.

I refuse to live a life without Paige.

With a newfound determination, I set her body down on the ground and start performing chest compressions.

"Declan," Rhys's voice is filled with remorse.

"No! She's not leaving me. I won't let her. She's *mine.* She doesn't get to leave me like this," I growl through gritted teeth.

"Emily, how long has it been since this happened?" Rhys asks.

"It hasn't been long, but I don't know how long a person can go being *dead,*" she replies quietly.

I alternate between chest compressions, breathing air into her lungs, and checking for a heartbeat.

You're not fucking leaving me, Paige. Not after I've just found you.

Sweat covers my brow and I'm panting but I continue.

I lean down and press my ear to her chest.

Thoomp-thoomp. Thoomp-Thoomp.

My heart hammers in my chest at the sound of hers restarting.

"She's alive!"

Emily's relief-filled cry fills my ears.

"Paige. Baby. Can you hear me?" I ask quietly.

Color starts returning to her face, and I see her chest rise with each slow breath she takes.

She doesn't wake but she's alive and right now, that's all that matters.

I scoop her up and stand.

"Get Vladimir and any other person who hasn't been killed yet to the cellar at the estate," I meet Rhys's eyes before striding to the hallway with Paige in my arms.

Chapter 33

Paige

The sound of steady beeping slowly fills my ears. I can't move my body or open my eyes. Panic floods my system and the beeping increases.

"She's waking up," someone's deep voice says. *I know that voice.*

"Paige, honey, can you hear me?" another familiar voice.

"I'll go get the doctor." The sound of shoes hitting the ground fades as a person leaves.

A large hand envelopes mine, "Mo ghrá."

Declan.

My fingers twitch as I work to get my body to move.

"That's it, baby, come back to me," he encourages softly.

I'm able to move my hand enough to wrap my fingers around his. He gives it a small squeeze and continues to encourage me.

My eyes slowly open and my blurred vision steadily clears.

Rhys and Sarah come into view. Sarah's eyes are red-rimmed and swollen. A river of tears flows down her face, but she smiles. Rhys gives me a small smile.

I sweep my gaze to Declan and my stomach flips with panic of being in his proximity again.

"Hi," he whispers. His eyes are filled with relief, pain...and love. So much love.

It won't last.

"Where am I?" I croak. My throat is so dry, it hurts to swallow.

Sarah quickly grabs a cup filled with water and lifts the straw to my mouth. Once my throat is lubricated, I pull away. She sets the cup down and moves back to Rhys.

"You're in a hospital in New York," Declan says.

My face scrunches in confusion.

How am I back in New York?

"How?" I ask quietly.

"We found you, baby. We came and rescued you."

The last thing I can remember is injecting myself with morphine. *A lot of fucking morphine.*

I should be dead.

"How am I alive?" I peer up at Declan who furrows his eyebrows and looks down. When he lifts his eyes to mine, they're filled with pain.

"You weren't when we got there," he whispers. "I brought you back."

I swallow the lump in my throat.

"Why?"

"What do you mean why?" Sarah's voice rises. "You died, Paige!"

"I wanted to die," I say calmly when I turn toward her.

She is stunned silent, and her brows rise to her hairline. Devastation covers her face which pisses me the fuck off.

"I FUCKING KILLED MYSELF, SARAH!" I scream and she rears back.

"We should give them some privacy," Rhys says quietly, and he leads Sarah out of the room.

The doctor steps in a moment later.

"Hello Paige, I'm Dr. Stephens. I'm glad to see you're awake."

"I'm not." His smile drops at my reply and his eyes quickly flick to Declan.

"Um," he clears his throat, "I'm very sorry to hear that, but you do have many people who are very relieved you're here."

I stare blankly at him.

"When can she be discharged?" Declan asks.

Dr. Stephens flicks through my chart on the computer. "Well..." he says with a sigh and runs his hands through his gray hair.

He watches me for a moment before continuing. "Because of her current mental state, she will need to be admitted into the psychiatric ward."

Oh great.

"No. She won't be admitted. When can I take her home?" Declan's voice is rough.

"Mr. Moore, I understand that you wish to take Miss Henley home, but you need to understand that she is in a very delicate state."

"I understand completely. Which is why she needs to be home. Sticking her in a fucking room with cushioned walls won't do shit for her."

The doctor quickly glances at me. "How about we discuss this outside?" he gestures to the door.

Declan bends down to kiss the top of my head but I jerk back.

He pulls away and a sad smile covers his face.

The two of them exit the room, leaving me to listen to the mocking beep of my heart beating.

My entire body instantly fills with an untamed rage at the unbearable beeping telling me that I'm alive. I rip off the monitors from my chest and the IV from my hand. I shove the monitor onto the ground, and it breaks. I let out a scream in anger.

Declan and Dr. Stephens rush into the room and see me curled up into a ball with my hands over my ears.

"What happened?" Declan asks as he takes in the destroyed monitor and hanging cords.

"Make it stop! Make it stop!"

Declan comes to my side, and when he attempts to touch me, I shriek and move as close to the side of the bed as possible.

He puts his palms up and steps away.

"It's okay, you're okay," he whispers.

"No! I'm not okay! Why couldn't you just let me die?!"

His face steels and he stands upright, "I refuse to let you leave me, Paige. You're meant to be with me."

My limbs shake aggressively, "No! No! No!" I shriek. "You should have fucking let me die! I *want* to fucking die!"

He looks defeatedly at the doctor and slowly nods. "Okay..."

Sarah is standing in the doorway with a horrified look in her eyes and a hand over her mouth.

"Let me fucking die!" my scream echoes through the open door.

"Paige, we need you to calm down," Dr. Stephens says soothingly.

I throw the pillow across the room, and it hits the whiteboard on the wall, causing it to fall and break.

"Get out!"

"We're going to need to sedate her," the doctor says to Declan.

I try getting up from the bed but am hit with a blinding pain between my legs and I fall to the ground.

Dr. Stephens and Declan scramble to me.

"Don't fucking touch me!" Despite my pain, I kick my legs outward in an attempt to hit them.

"Paige, honey," Sarah's sad voice says quietly. "You're okay... I'm here." She steps slowly to me and kneels.

"Don't let them touch me," my voice cracks and I begin to sob.

"I won't, babe. You're safe." Her lips quiver.

A hand is lightly on my shoulder, and I jerk back. Sarah puts her palms up and bows her head slightly.

"It's me. It's just me," she whispers.

She reaches for me again and then pulls me into her arms.

I relax into them and let go of my tears.

Chapter 34

Declan

I was forced to leave Paige's side after she was admitted into the psych ward. The panic I feel at not having her home mixes with the anguish and rage inside my soul.

Her appearance was worse than I could have imagined. Her frame was skeletal. Eyes bloodshot — crazed. Her beautiful face... tormented.

It's been five days and it's just as hard to breathe as it was the day we found her dead. Seeing her lifeless body in Rhys's arms killed a piece of my soul.

When we returned, I released Jackie back to Antonio and haven't heard from either of them since.

With her gone, we moved in ten men, including Vladimir, who survived our attack on the warehouse.

My phone vibrates in my pocket. When I pull it out, Rhys's name fills the screen.

"What?" I grunt when I answer.

"Come to the cellar. I have something you'll want to see." The cheerfulness in his voice pisses me off.

How can anyone be cheerful when Paige is lost to her suffering? I don't know how to bring her back from that.

I open the cellar door and see Rhys standing in front of someone who is bound to a chair.

When he sees that it's me whose stepped inside, Rhys stands to the side and reveals *Mark* is who is bound and gagged.

The thrill of retribution runs through my veins. I stalk over to him and land a punch to his face. It jerks back and blood falls from his nose.

I'm trembling with rage. This man will suffer for his part in all of this. For the pain he caused a young Paige to experience. For the torture she felt.

Rhys points to the table and I see my instruments lined up.

I don't say a word as I stride over and pick up an enucleation spoon. Making my way back to a bound Mark, his face pales and he begins screaming through the fabric wrapped around his mouth.

With one hand, I violent pull his head back by his hair and with the other, I shove the instrument into his eye socket. His screams are muffled, and he shakes uncontrollably as I scoop out his eye. When I finish, the eyeball plops onto the ground and I stomp on it.

The tissue squishes beneath my shoe and pops. I do the same to the other eye.

I step back and admire the two holes I've created in his face as blood runs out from the sockets and he screams.

A manic smile grows on my face, and I stride back to the table.

Grabbing a set of surgical retractors, forceps and a scalpel I walk back and remove the gag from his mouth.

"Please! I will do whatever you want!" Mark begins begging for his life.

"I don't want shit from you other than your blood to drain from your body," I say calmly.

He whimpers, the river of blood continues to flow down his cheeks. "Why are you doing this?"

"Paige Henley," I state and the color drains from his face.

"Listen man, I don't know what she told you, b-but whatever it was, was a lie."

An animalistic growl breaks through my chest and I squeeze his jaw tightly. "Don't insult me by spewing ridiculous lies. I know *everything* and I will take deep pleasure in ripping you apart for the pain you've caused her."

I shove the retractors into his mouth — destroying teeth in the process — and pry it open. Locking them in place, I grab the forceps and pull out his tongue. I waste no time slicing through the flesh and tossing it to the ground.

Blood fills his mouth, and he howls in pain. Without removing the retractors, I move to grab a set of pliers and work on removing the remaining teeth in his mouth.

When his face is hollowed out, I slice off his ears. Then his arms, his legs, and his dick. His head falls to the ground when I saw through his spine and rolls under the chair.

By the time I'm finished, Mark is nothing but an empty torso on the seat. His organs are scattered on the floor. My clothes are soaked in his blood, and I haven't felt this alive since Paige took her first breath in the warehouse's basement.

"Bring me another," I say to Rhys, and he leaves to grab another body for me to carve into.

I've killed half of the men that were brought in by the time my bloodlust is sated enough for me to stop.

It's been a month since Paige was admitted into the psych ward. Paige didn't want to speak to me until just a few days ago. It was so amazing to hear her voice. She sounded hesitant for a while, but I'm hoping that changes when we see each other in person.

I haven't killed any of the other men yet. Something inside me told me to wait.

I'm sitting out by the Palomino— Lily. She reverted back to her isolating ways after Paige was taken. She and I have bonded over our mutual pain of losing her. But she still doesn't interact with me the way she did with Paige.

The school stopped calling after two weeks. I couldn't draw attention to her abduction without drawing attention to myself by the FBI.

My crimes severely limit my chances of making a deal with them.

Paige is supposed to be discharged today. Sarah will be picking her up and bringing her here. Sarah never returned to their apartment. Instead, she moved in with Rhys.

Paige agreed to move back here after I talked about Lily still being here and Emily moving in.

The doctors mentioned that some normalcy may help Paige after some time but not to expect that to change for several months.

If we pressure her too much, she will likely lash out and regress.

I watch as Lily eats the apple I gave her. I talk with her just as I heard Paige do, and surprisingly, it helps. Her gentle eyes comfort me.

After Emily was discharged from the hospital, we moved her to the estate and sold the penthouse. It's safer here and Ingrid helps with her nightmares. My ma has since returned to Ireland after she spent the month being with Emily.

When she asked Emily to move there permanently, Emily panicked. She locked herself in her room and refused to leave or eat for days.

It doesn't seem that she will be taking a trip to Ireland any time soon.

I hear the sound of tires driving down the road. Patting Lily on the side, I leave to the front of the house.

Sarah's car pulls into the driveway.

Walking over, I open the door for Paige and reach a hand out to her. She watches me closely as she places her hand in mine.

The electricity I felt the first time our hands met strikes us both and we suck in a breath.

She avoids meeting my eyes as she climbs out.

"Do you want to see Lily before we go inside?" I ask her quietly.

She still doesn't meet my gaze, but she nods.

Sarah watches from the car as I walk Paige to Lily. I send her a wave when we're far enough away and she drives off.

"Lily, look who came to see you."

Lily's ears perk up and she lifts her head. When she sees Paige, she stands taller, like she can't quite believe her eyes.

"Hi, Lily girl," Paige says softly and walks toward the pen.

Lily meets her halfway and they bring their foreheads together.

Paige's tense shoulders relax immensely and I breathe out a sigh of relief.

We're going to be okay. Paige is going to be okay.

We stand outside with Lily for several hours before Paige asks to go inside.

The two of us walk quietly to her room.

"It's the same way you left it. If you want to change anything, we can." I reach for the door and open it.

Paige's eyes are lifeless as she takes in the room.

"Mo ghrá?" I croak.

Her eyes finally meet mine. They're so hollow.

“Can you tell me what that means now?” She asks quietly.

I smile softly at her, “It means ‘my love’.”

Her eyes glisten as tears begin to form and she takes in a shaky breath.

“You’ve called me that since the day I met you.”

“I have,” I confirm.

“Why?”

“Because you’re the love of my life. My heart doesn’t beat without you.”

She doesn’t say anything. A single tear slides down her face.

I slowly reach out a hand and she stiffens. Pausing, I wait. When she doesn’t pull away, I move my hand again and gently wipe the tear away.

She closes her eyes and sighs.

“Paige... I love you,” I say.

She chokes on a sob, “You won’t.”

Before I can ask her why she would ever think that, she runs into the room and slams the door shut.

Chapter 35

Paige

'Paige... I love you.'

Those three little words are supposed to bring you so much happiness. Instead, they bring me a sense of mourning.

Declan hasn't seen the scars. The hideousness of my body. The one he caressed and loved is gone. A monstrosity has taken its place.

Just like my soul.

He won't love me once he's realized my mind, heart, and body are destroyed.

I sit staring blankly out of the window wrapped in a large blanket. I'm wearing leggings and an oversized hoodie. The mirror in the ensuite was removed when I came back. I can't look at myself without breaking down.

Every scar is another reminder that who I was is not who I am anymore. It's a thousand times worse than when I was a child.

When those scars started to fade, I felt some weight lifting off me. These scars though... They're too large and deep. They'll never leave. Hiding my body is the only way I can cope with them.

A light knock on my door startles me and I yelp.

It opens slowly and Emily peers in.

I jump to my feet and plow into her, holding onto her like she's my lifeline. My tears stain her shirt and I feel hers fall onto my hair.

When we pull away, we both work to clean each other's faces with sad smiles.

"How are you feeling?" She asks.

"I don't," I answer softly.

Her face fills with sadness. "Yeah... I get that."

I pull her toward my bed and we lie there together in a tight cocoon.

Emily is one of the only reasons I agreed to come stay here. It was hard not being with her after what we've been through together.

"What are you thinking?" she asks after a while.

"Nothing. Everything," I mutter.

"It feels weird being home." She squeezes me tightly.

I nod against her chest.

"We'll be okay," she whispers.

"I know you will."

She lifts her head to look at me. "You will be too, Paige."

I blink rapidly to push the tears away before they fall.

"I don't think so, Em." My voice cracks when I feel my throat tighten.

Her brows curve inward as her face saddens.

She holds my hand tightly. "We're going to get through this. Together."

I let out a deep sigh and turn over onto my back. Staring at the ceiling, I think of how I could possibly be okay after everything. Trying to be okay after what I experienced with Mark was hard enough.

"Have you spoken with Declan?"

I tense slightly at the sound of his name. I'm pushing him away. I know I am. But I have to. The sooner he accepts we can no longer be, the sooner we both can find a way to move on.

I shake my head without saying anything.

It's Emily's turn to sigh and turn to her back.

We lie side by side staring at nothing.

"He does love you," she whispers.

"He might now, but he won't," I say sadly.

I can't see a man like him ever loving a woman as damaged as I am. He needs someone to stand by his side. A strong woman to rule the Irish mafia with him. I can't be that.

"What makes you say that?"

I shrug, "You've seen my body, Em. They ruined me. I'm just lucky that the only thing on my face is the cut from Vladimir's ring. I can't even let him touch me without flinching when he lifts his hand."

"You're wrong, you know? Declan doesn't love you for your looks, Paige. And if he did, you're still beautiful."

I snort humorlessly.

"I'm serious. And with time, you'll be able to touch him. I know it."

"How can you be so positive about this whole situation?"

Her smile is tearful, "If I don't then I fall into a hole I won't come out from."

We sit in silence for a long while.

Another knock comes from the door, and we jump from the bed and cower in the corner.

"Paige?" Declan's voice sounds from the other side.

I look to Emily who gives me an encouraging smile and nods toward the door.

Taking a deep breath, I stand and make my way over.

When I open it, Declan stands with his hands in his pockets. He looks so handsome. He's wearing dark jeans and a white V-neck. His hair is a mess, as though he's been running his fingers through it.

"Can you join me for a walk?"

"Um..." I peek over my shoulder and Emily nods enthusiastically.

Turning back to Declan, I give him a small nod.

He offers me his hand and I stare down at it.

Take it.

I can't...

"I'm sorry," I whisper and lower my head.

"It's okay, *mo ghrá.* I can be patient," he says with a smile and puts his hand back into his pocket.

My love.

I step out of the room, and he leads me outside.

We stroll through the grounds in silence. Declan maintains a safe distance and doesn't attempt to touch me again.

"Paige," he says and stops walking.

Stopping, I turn to him.

"I want you to know that I'll wait however long I need to, for you."

"But —"

He holds up a hand, stopping my retort. "I need you to understand that you're *it* for me. You always have been."

I pull my eyes away from him and scan the grassy area around us.

"It's not fair to you to have to wait, Declan. You need a strong woman at your side. And that's not me."

He takes a small step toward me, and I tense.

"I won't ever hurt you, *mo ghrá*. I mean, not unless you want me to but that's not something we need to talk about any time soon." A smirk plays on his lips, "You're one of the strongest women I've ever known, Paige. You're meant to be by my side."

Not unless I want him to.

Maybe... No. That can't happen. You can't even let him touch you.

"I need to leave for Ireland for a few weeks to handle some weapon shipments. Mark has been handled. He won't be bothering you ever again."

"And Vladimir?"

He smiles at me, "He's being taken care of."

I let out a deep breath.

That's good. This is good.

"When will you be back?" I raise my eyes to his.

"I'm not sure. But you can text me or call me anytime you want to."

Chewing on the inside of my lip, I nod.

He gently swipes a loose strand of hair from my face. I squeeze my eyes closed and breathe in a shaky breath.

"I love you," he whispers.

My lip quivers.

"Let's go back inside. I'll be leaving tonight."

We walk back toward the estate.

I know the light at the end of the tunnel will never come into view.

Chapter 36

Declan

The flight to Ireland feels excruciatingly slow.

As much as I wanted to stay with Paige, I have an empire to run, and she needs space.

Emily has made some improvements with her own trauma. We were able to sit down and talk with a therapist and she's phenomenal. Emily has been able to open up to me about what she went through. And fuck was it hard to hear. I will ensure the remaining men die much more painfully than the previous ones.

"Sarah said she was going to the mansion to be with Paige and Emily," Rhys says from his seat across from me. He's staring down at his phone.

"Good."

I never knew how deep the relationship Sarah shared with Paige was. After she was brought home, it was clear their bond is soul deep.

When Sarah is at the estate, Paige is more willing to be out of her room. More willing to eat.

Once landed, we head to my uncle's estate.

"Declan, my boy! Welcome!" My uncle pulls me into a tight hug.

"Hello again, Uncle. Thank you for your help in rescuing Paige and Emily," I say as we separate.

"No need to thank me for rescuing family, Declan." He waves his hand in dismissal. "Rhys, how are you?"

Rhys dips his chin in a nod, "I'm doing well, Cormac."

My uncle claps his hand against my back and leads me to his office. He pulls out a cigar and lights it. Rhys and I decline when he offers one to us.

"The weapons production has been going on without a hitch." Smoke bellows from his mouth.

"That's good to hear. With the stop on our warehouses after they were attacked, we need to replenish that supply."

Vladimir and Mark had been working together to try and distract me while they had taken Emily and worked on their plans for getting Paige through attacking my warehouses. The Italian I tortured was a man from Antonio's team who was working with Vladimir under the table.

I have my suspicions of who in my team betrayed my trust and worked with Mark on capturing Paige. I've been watching his every move closely. Waiting for him to slip up and prove he's guilty. So far, he's been very careful with his movements.

"How are the girls?" my uncle asks.

I let out a sigh and run my fingers through my hair. "As best as they can be, Uncle. Emily has been making some improvement, but of course, she has a long way to go. Paige seems to be sinking into herself. Her friend Sarah is the only person she can interact with aside from Emily."

My uncle nods solemnly, "I had heard that she was in the hospital for quite some time."

"Yes. There was no other option but to have her admitted. She was a danger to herself."

"And now?" he blows out another cloud of smoke.

I lower my head and shake it slowly, "She's... quiet. She refused to attend therapy due to past experiences. I can't touch her without her seeming in pain."

"She's been through a very great ordeal. Vladimir's trading is a very brutal place to be." He rubs his thick peppered beard. "Give her time."

That's exactly what I plan to do.

After discussing the weapons, we make our way to my uncle's warehouse.

We enter through the large garage door. Inside is filled with conveyor belts and hundreds of men loading the guns and ammo into boxes and trucks. The system works impeccably well.

We came to Ireland to learn from our mistakes regarding the security of our own warehouses.

I refuse to be bested again.

My phone vibrates in my pocket, and I remove it to see a message from Paige.

Paige: Did you make it okay?

Me: I did. How are you feeling?

The dots appear and disappear multiple times before stopping.

Me: I love you, mo ghrá.

She doesn't reply after the message is opened.

Give her time.

I place my phone back into my pocket and walk alongside Rhys and my uncle through the warehouse.

The next few days are hectic, to say the least. We've been collecting enough weapons to fill three of my warehouses. Rhys has been working on getting the information for our security system to be set up to the levels they are here.

Paige hasn't communicated with me since the day we arrived. I've sent her messages, but each has gone unread. I know she will come back to me. I just need to be patient.

I'm not sure how long it will be before I can return to her. But when I do, I will find a way to save her, even if it's from herself.

Chapter 37

Paige

I've spent the last two weeks wandering the inside of the mansion, reading, or spending time with Lily.

Sarah has been hovering over me and Emily like a fly and it's been suffocating. I appreciate how much she wants to help, but I don't think I need it.

I think I need to save myself from my demons.

Sarah was becoming a crutch. As much as I needed her help in the beginning, I needed to learn to stand on my own.

Walking through the estate, I find a door in the office that looks very out of place. I try tugging it open and pushing against it, but it doesn't budge.

Hmm.

I dig through the drawers and find a key.

Bingo.

The door unlocks with a soft click. Opening it, I see a set of concrete steps that lead down.

Following the steps, I stop in front of a big metal door.

You shouldn't go inside. Don't go inside.

I'm going inside.

I push my shoulders back and take a deep breath then push the door.

A large empty concrete room comes into view. It smells very strongly of bleach.

Entering the room, I scan around and see a utility sink and a metal rectangle table. There's a black bag on top.

Walking over to the table, I unzip the bag. When it's opened, I see a bunch of surgical and hardware tools inside. My eyebrows knit in confusion.

I take in the empty room once more. The atmosphere is thick with an ominous feeling.

What is this place?

Re-zipping the bag closed, I walk around. My light steps echo through the empty space. The walls are bare.

I pause in the center of the room and look down. There are dark stains on the ground.

Blood.

My heart rate increases as flashes of my time with Vladimir and Aleksei run rampant in my mind.

If you're going to save yourself, you need to do this.

But fuck, I'm scared.

The memories become more vivid, and it becomes harder to breathe.

Fuck this.

I sprint through the door and take the steps two at a time.

Once I reach the office, I slam the other door behind me and lock it.

My forehead rests against the wood as I work to control my breathing.

"Fuck," I hiss and slam my fist against the door.

My eyes fill with tears, and they spill down my face. I don't want to let this trauma dictate my life like I allowed the others to do.

I want the life I was meant to have. Not the one that was forced on me.

I push away from the door and leave the office without a second glance.

Declan has been gone for five weeks.

I guess the saying 'distance makes the heart grow fonder' is true because I *miss him.*

I mean, I missed him when I was in my prison, but this is a different kind of longing. I fell so deep into despair that the only way for me to survive as long as I did was to no longer feel.

Now, I want to see him. I want the comfort of his sandalwood smell. I want to drown in his blue eyes again. I want his help to take my pain away.

I hope that doesn't change when he comes back.

"Are you okay?" Sarah asks from my bedroom doorway.

I'm lying in bed with a romance book from the library. Shutting the book and setting it on my nightstand, I pull the blankets back and motion for her to join me.

When she slides in, I lay my head on her lap, and she strokes my hair.

"I will be," I whisper.

And this time, I'm starting to truly believe it.

Another month goes by, and Declan finally returns.

I'm a ball of nerves at the knowledge that he will be here soon. I'm also scared that I won't be able to handle being close to him. Those initial days after being rescued were awful. Declan was my safe space and Aleksei obliterated that.

I can't let him win. I am stronger than the trauma I've suffered.

A soft knock sounds and my door creaks open. I take multiple calming breaths before I turn toward it.

"Hi," Declan whispers. His eyes are warm.

"Hi," I whisper back.

He closes the door behind him and walks slowly toward me. I work to refrain from flinching or tensing.

"How are you?" he asks as he watches me carefully.

"I'm... better."

He smiles softly, "That's really good to hear, baby."

I love you.

I can't let the words out. I want to so badly but if I do and I'm not able to love him how he deserves, it will ruin me further.

"Declan, can I.... can I ask you a question?" I fold my arms around my middle.

He smiles wider.

"Why are you smiling at me like that?"

He lets out quiet a chuckle, "Because you said almost those exact words the first night we met."

Warmth fills me.

"Well, my next question won't be the same one... I want your help."

He sobers but stays quiet.

"I want you to help me not be scared anymore."

He steps closer and this time, it's easier to keep calm.

"I won't make the same mistake twice, Paige. I was a fool not to show you how to defend yourself in the past and I will never forgive myself for it. I'll teach you everything you want to know, weapons and all."

Over the next several days, Declan and I meet for an hour, and he shows me how to shoot. We tried some hand-to-hand fighting, but I wasn't able to handle having him on top of me. It was too much.

His touches no longer make me feel like I'm being scalded. In fact, I *want* his touch.

I say that's progress.

When I was discharged from the hospital, they prescribed me some heavy-duty sleeping meds, so I don't really dream. But I don't want to need them for the rest of my life.

I don't know how to figure out a way past that without destroying all the progress I've made.

"Hey, Declan?" I say while stroking Lily's mane.

"Yes, mo ghrá?"

"While you were gone, I found a doorway in your office that leads to some underground room. What is it?"

He stiffens and his eyes flick to mine. "It's my cellar."

"And what do you do down there?"

I have a pretty good idea considering the stains I saw but I want to hear it from him.

"It's where I take care of people that need to be taken care of."

"So cryptic," I mumble.

"Paige, what did you see when you were down there?"

I exit Lily's pen and walk toward him. His addicting smell fills my nose and butterflies flutter in my stomach.

"Just a sink, a table with a bag on it with tools inside, and... blood stains," I say, whispering the last part.

He lets out a heavy sigh and runs his fingers through his hair.

"Do you trust me?" he asks quietly, eyes searching mine.

"Yes." I don't hesitate to answer. I trust Declan beyond any comprehension of the word.

"I want to show you something that's down in that cellar, and I need you to trust me when I say, *nothing* will happen to you."

Swallowing the lump in my throat, I nod and follow Declan into the estate.

The walk down to the *cellar* is nerve-wracking. I do trust Declan, but I'm scared of what he wants to show me. My stomach tightens in anticipation.

He glances over his shoulder at me before he pushes the door open.

Everything is just as it was when I left. The table and bag remain in their same positions. The bleach smell is still as strong. As is the atmosphere.

Declan walks to the far end of the room where another door is. I didn't notice it when I was here last time.

"Still trust me?" he says with a worried gaze.

I nod and take a deep breath.

The hinges creak and echo throughout the space as he pushes the door open.

There are cells.

I gasp and begin to tremble. My breathing shallows.

Declan intertwines his fingers in mine, "I'm here with you, mo ghrá. We're home."

My eyes flick back and forth between his.

You can do this. You can do this.

I continue the chant in my head when I nod and when we continue our path down through the cells.

There are no torturous cries of women and children echoing through the space. I'm not bound to a mattress. I'm not being sliced into. Beaten or raped. I'm not in pain.

This is fine. You're fine.

Declan doesn't let go of my hand once. His thumb rubs over my wrist every so often in reassurance and it helps ground me.

He stops in front of one of the cells. His grip tightens slightly, pulling my eyes to his. "You're safe with me."

The cell opens and Vladimir lies chained to the wall.

My eyes widen. My entire heart falls.

I try tugging my hand out of Declan's but he squeezes tighter. "You can do this, Paige. You're stronger than you think."

I shake my head as I continue to stare at Vladimir. He's unconscious and looks like he's been starved.

Has he been down here the entire time?

"H-How many people are down here?" I stutter.

"I have five men remaining."

"Remaining?" I lift a brow.

"I killed the other five we captured from Russia as soon as I was able to," he says matter-of-factly.

"What are you going to do with him?" I say, pointing a trembling finger to Vladimir.

He shrugs, "That depends on you."

"Me? Why me?" My brows furrow and I look between Vladimir and Declan.

"I want to help you overcome your demons. I want to watch you overcome them," he says with a smile.

I look back at Vladimir's unconscious body.

Overcome my demons…

I chew on the inside of my lip for a moment. "Can you show me the others?"

He kisses the back of my hand and nods.

When we walk out of the cell, I feel… hopeful.

The other men in the cells are in the same conditions as Vladimir. Each unconscious and malnourished. Reaching the final cell, panic suddenly floods my body. The hairs on the back of my neck stand erect and my breath becomes labored.

My hand shoots out and I grab onto Declan's forearm tightly. He pauses before pushing the door open and furrows his brows.

The blood has drained from my face, and I feel clammy.

But why?

"Who is in this cell?" I whisper through a shaky breath.

"A friend of Vladimir's— Aleksei."

The air is sucked out of my lungs. Dizziness takes over and I struggle to stay upright.

"What's going on?" Declan's concerned voice begins fading from my ears as my vision darkens.

I press my hand against my chest.

I can't breathe!

"Paige," Declan's hands wrap around my shoulders, and he pulls me tightly against his chest.

"I'm right here, baby. You're with me. You're safe," he mutters against my hair. He rubs his hand up and down my back in a soothing motion.

His scent fills my nose and I breathe him in deep. Grounding myself.

You're safe. Aleksei can't hurt you. Declan is here.

He holds me until my heart no longer races and I'm not gasping for breath.

Cupping my face, Declan tips my head upward to look at him. "You're safe with me, mo ghrá."

"I'm scared," I whisper in a broken voice as my eyes fill with tears.

His eyes fill with sadness as they scan over my face.

"It's okay to be scared. But know you're not in this alone."

I give him a small watery smile. "Okay..."

"Are you ready?" he asks.

"No. But I want to do this."

"That's my girl," he says with a huge smile.

My heart expands at him calling me his girl. I've always been his. It's time I embrace it.

Chapter 38

Declan

Wrapping my hand around Paige's I use the other to push open the door.

She tenses as Aleksei comes into view.

I squeeze her hand to reassure her that I'm still here.

Just like the others, Aleksei has been starved since he's been locked in here. Only receiving enough food and water to stay alive.

I was not anticipating her reaction to Aleksei. Vladimir? Yes. I'm going to have to find a way to get her to talk with me about what happened. Once I do, I'll enjoy ripping his intestines out through his throat.

We remain just outside of the doorway, watching an unconscious Aleksei.

"When do you plan to kill them?" Paige asks quietly. Her hand trembles in mine and she fidgets in place.

"After I spoke with you."

She lets go of my hand and faces me. Turning toward her, we meet eyes, and I can't figure out what hers say.

"I want to do it," her voice is strong despite the fear in her posture.

My brows rise to my hairline. "Kill them?"

She nods quickly and turns back to Aleksei. "You said you wanted to watch me overcome my demons. Well, the only way I can overcome them is to destroy them."

Okay, Declan. Now is NOT the time.

My body has a mind of its own and it catches Paige's attention.

"Declan... I'm not sure I'll ever be able to, you know." She shifts uncomfortably.

I cup her face. "Baby, I would wait a lifetime for you if that's what you needed."

"You shouldn't have to," she whispers sadly.

I caress the scar on her left cheek. "There is nothing in this world or the next that would keep me from waiting for you."

Her eyes close and she presses further into my hand.

My phone chimes, interrupting us. I take it out of my pocket to see a message from Rhys.

Rhys: Shipments are here.

Declan: I'll be there soon.

Putting my phone away, I meet Paige's eyes again. "Whenever you're ready to take care of your demons, baby, I'll be there."

Her eyes soften and she nods with a small smile on her lips.

I feel lighter than I have in months as I drive toward the new warehouse by the docks.

Paige is going to be okay. I can't wait to watch her realize the strength she's always had. The strength I admire so much.

Parking in front of the warehouse, I exit the car and meet Finn and Rhys outside.

"Boys," I greet.

"Boss," Finn grunts.

"Hey, Dec," Rhys says.

The three of us enter the warehouse where there are men unloading the trucks filled with guns and ammo we sent from Ireland. We have enough merchandise here to earn back the money lost with the fires and theft.

My uncle has a team tracking our stolen weapons since we weren't able to locate them in any of the locations Vladimir owns.

"I showed Paige the cellar," I tell Rhys under my breath.

He freezes and whips his head in my direction, his eyes are wide, and his brows are to his hairline. "Now, why the actual fuck would you show her that?"

"Technically, she found it on her own while we were in Ireland. I simply showed her the men in the cells."

"Again, I ask, why the fuck would you show her that?"

I roll my eyes and then give him a pointed look. "Because she asked what it was, and I will give her anything she wants and answer any questions she asks." I smirk, "She asked to kill the bastards."

Rhys's face is stupefied at that information.

"She said the only way she can overcome them is by destroying them."

His shoulders relax and he nods in understanding.

"Well, shit. I wasn't expecting that."

"Neither was I. My dick got hard when she said it."

Rhys and I laugh loudly.

"Have you guys —"

"No," I say sharply. I breathe deeply, "She's barely starting to let me touch her hands and face. She hides everything else."

Rhys slaps a hand on my shoulder and gives it a squeeze.

"Have you talked with her about what happened? Like you did with Emily?"

I shake my head. "I don't know if I'm ready to know the full story. Hearing what Emily went through was hard."

"I get that. But maybe you can help her heal in more ways than one." He shrugs and then walks toward one of the trucks.

Several hours later, our shipment has been unloaded and organized in the warehouse. The weapons going out to the other warehouses have been sent off. The ones that have been sold have also been distributed.

I park in the driveway of the estate. Shutting off the ignition, I sit back in the seat and stare blankly out of the windshield.

'You can help her heal in more ways than one.'

I need to stop thinking about myself here. Paige needs to move forward and if letting out what happen to her helps, then I need to figure out my own shit about dealing with it.

Taking a deep breath, I pull the key from the ignition and step out of the car.

Staring at Paige's door, I wriggle out my hands to calm my nerves and knock lightly before turning the knob.

She's sitting in bed with a book in her lap. Offering me a small smile, she closes the book and sets it aside.

"Would you mind if I stayed tonight?"

Her smile falls and she sits straighter. "In here?"

"Yeah. I would like to stay with you. If that would be okay," I say softly.

She chews on the inside of her lip as she flicks her eyes between mine.

Her answer finally comes after several seconds of silence. "Okay."

My heart sores and a huge smile covers my face.

"I'll go get some clothes to sleep in and be right back," I say and head for the door.

Entering my room, I rummage through my drawer to find some sweatpants and pull a white t-shirt from the closet. I quickly change and make my way back to Paige's room.

She's in the same position as when I left her. Only this time, she's more tense.

When I walk toward the bed, she shifts over, and I pull the blankets back. Sliding in, I lie with one arm behind my head and the other resting on my stomach.

I feel her eyes on my profile as she lies facing me on her side.

"Goodnight, Paige."

"Goodnight," she whispers.

I close my eyes and fall asleep listening to the sound of her soft breaths.

The sun shines across my face through the window. I lift my arm to block it, only my arm doesn't move. When I open my eyes and peer down, Paige is pressed against my body.

Trying not to wake her, I gently wrap my arm around her body.

She continues breathing softly in her sleep. She looks so peaceful.

I study her face. The scar on her cheek wasn't there before she was taken. It's long, but thin and sits on her cheekbone.

I desperately want to run a finger across her skin, but I know she will wake to that.

She begins to stir, and I lower my arm from her body, so she doesn't feel trapped.

Her face scrunches and she rubs it against my chest and breaths deeply.

She's breathing me in.

After a second, she must remember that I'm truly lying with her because her eyes shoot open, and she stiffens.

"Good morning, mo ghrá," my voice gruff with sleep.

She looks up at me and her brows furrow. "Morning."

Pulling the blankets back, she sits up and fusses with the sweatshirt she is wearing to cover her body properly.

"Paige," I say to get her attention.

She stops with her fussing and looks over her shoulder.

"You don't have to hide from me," I whisper when I prop up on my elbow.

Tears rim her eyes, and she looks away from me. "Yes, I do."

"Why?"

She shakes her head quickly.

"Baby, look at me," I plead.

Her shoulders rise and fall as she takes a deep breath. When she turns around, the tears have slid down her face. She looks in so much pain.

"You never need to hide from me, Paige. Let me see you. All of you. Not just your body, but your mind, your heart, everything."

She sniffles and tilts her head to the side. "You won't want me the same if I do."

"I got fucking hard when you said you wanted to kill men, Paige. I will always want you."

The corner of her lip tips upward.

I rub my hand softly up and down her arm. "Show me. We aren't going to do anything, just please show me," I beg quietly.

She continues to stare at me in hesitation and then slowly reaches the hem of the sweatshirt.

Her moves are guarded as she lifts the fabric from her body.

The skin on her stomach is covered in white scars of every length and thickness and in all different directions.

My chest constricts with each scar exposed. My throat tightens and I feel my blood rushing to my ears.

The scars continue up onto her breasts, chest, and arms.

I hurt *for* her. For me, I feel rage. Her reaction to Aleksei begins to make sense.

He did this to her.

She shifts uncomfortably at my assessment of her body.

Reaching over, I caress the scars on her collarbone and down her arms.

"These don't change the way I love you." Whispering, I continue my gentle touches across her stomach and sides.

Her chest rises and falls rapidly with each movement of my hand. I can feel her heart racing against my fingers.

"Are there more?" I ask quietly and look up at her.

She gives me a small nod.

"Can I see?"

Tentatively, she tucks her thumbs under the band of her leggings and slides them down her thighs.

The skin there is also littered with the same type of scars, but these appear deeper. More manic in pattern.

"Will you tell me what happened?" I whisper as I move to caress her skin.

She tenses lightly when I touch her upper thighs.

"W-when Aleksei..." She takes in a shaky breath. "When he would visit me, he would bind me... and cut me."

My heartbeat booms in my ears as my blood increases. My jaw ticks as I work to control my anger.

"How often would this happen?" I ask, caressing her skin gently.

"Every day." Her voice reflects the shame she feels about being forced to endure this torture.

I wrap my hand around her bicep and gently pull her toward me. She allows me to tuck her between my legs and pull her against my chest.

Wrapping my arms around her body, I breathe her in. Her rainy scent fills my nose and I relax at the weight of her body against mine.

She's here, alive, and she's letting me hold her.

"We'll make sure he suffers for what he's done to you, mo ghrá," I whisper against her hair.

Her heart continues to race in her chest, but her body slowly begins to relax against me.

"Thank you," her voice is so soft, I almost miss it.

"You don't need to thank me, Paige. I'd burn the world and lay the bodies of all those who have wronged you at your feet. You only need to say the words."

When I place a kiss on her head, she doesn't tense.

This intimacy might be what she needs.

We've stayed in bed all morning; it's now late into the afternoon. I've been working in my office and Paige has been sitting opposite me reading a book.

I meet her eyes over my desk to see her staring at the cellar door.

"Do you want to go down?" I set my pen aside and close my laptop.

"Yes," her voice is shaky, but she sits taller and lifts her chin.

"Then let's go." I stand and hold out my hand to her. She places hers in mine, and that electricity once again travels between us.

Her eyes soften when she meets mine and she squeezes my hand. The once-broken path between our hearts is mending and becoming stronger. The Paige I knew is still in there. She's a little dented and rough around the edges, but she is still the woman I fell madly in love with the day I laid eyes on her.

We enter the cellar door and make our way to the cells.

"Do you want to see all of them?" I ask as I take the keys from my pocket.

Her eyes travel down the hallway. They're distant. When they clear, she turns to me and shakes her head.

"I want to save Aleksei and Vladimir for last," her voice comes in more confident.

"Are you saying you want to start today?" I can't hide the surprise on my face or in my voice.

"I do but I want Emily to help me."

Emily has always been a gentle soul. I'm not sure she would be willing to do this.

But the Emily you have now, is not the same Emily you knew.

I nod and quickly send a message to Rhys to bring her down here. She's very aware of what the cellar is and what goes on down here.

Placing my hand on her lower back, I lead Paige back to the main room to wait for them to arrive.

Ten minutes later, the door opens and Emily walks in hesitantly. She looks around the room and slightly relaxes when she sees Paige standing in the center.

"Will you help me?" Paige says before Emily can get a word out.

Emily furrows her brows and scans the room again. "With what?"

"To repay the men who hurt us." Paige's voice is very calm.

She's really going to do this.

The silence in the room is tense, Emily shifts continuously from one foot to the other and twists her hands in front of her.

"How?" she finally asks.

"How ever you wish," I say.

She flicks her gaze to me, and I can see the battle raging in her eyes. She's fighting between her old, gentle self and the new vengeful one.

Rhys wraps an arm around her and pulls her into him. "You don't need to do this, but it might help you release the emotions you're holding inside," he says softly.

Lowering her eyes to the ground, Emily chews on the inside of her cheek. She releases a deep breath and then straightens her spine. Looking to me and then Paige, she says in a strong voice, "Let's do this."

Chapter 39

Paige

Declan and Rhys have Emily and I stay in the open space as they walk to the cells to get the first man.

My heart feels seconds away from bursting out of my chest. I feel clammy and I'm vibrating with anxiety.

You can do this. You need to do this.

You will do this.

The sounds of pained grunts and feet dragging echo through the room.

They drop the barely conscious man into the chair in the center of the space. They tie his hands behind him, and his feet are tied to the legs of the chair.

Seeing this evil man bound in front of me makes me feel something I can't describe. Adrenaline courses through my veins as a bucket of cold water is thrown on his body.

He fully wakes with a gasp and rapidly scans the room with wide eyes.

The four of us stand directly in front of him.

Spotting Declan and Rhys, he attempts to squirm in the restraints.

That's the emotion. I'm absolutely ravenous at the prospect of causing this person even a fraction of the pain I suffered alongside Emily.

"Where would you like to start, mo ghrá?" Declan watches me as I take in the man in front of me.

"Where would you start?" I move my eyes to his.

He smiles wickedly and strides to the metal table. I follow and stop next to him. Unzipping the bag, he begins organizing the instruments neatly along the surface of the table.

His movements are precise. Every tool has an assigned place.

Once he's finished, Declan studies each tool meticulously. He checks the sharpness of every scalpel and knife. It's fascinating to watch this side of him.

"There are many options of how we can start. Considering this is your first time doing this, I think we should start out slow."

Lifting the meat tenderizer, he lifts it up and twists it in his hand. "We can crush his hands for touching you."

He hands it over to me and I test the weight in my hand.

I look over my shoulder at Emily and see her watching us closely.

"Do you want to start?" I ask her and she shakes her head.

Taking a deep breath, I straighten my shoulders and lift my chin. I spin around and face the man in the chair.

My steps are calculated and confident as I walk toward him.

He shakes his head repeatedly the closer I get. I tilt my head and I'm sure I look predatory.

My heart is steady in my chest.

"Hold his hands down."

Rhys and Declan walk over to move his hands from behind him and retie them to the arms of the chair.

"Please. Please don't do this," he begs.

My pitiless eyes rise to his and I lower myself to his level, "How many times did we scream those exact words as we were gang-raped?" my voice is calm.

"I'm sorry," he whispers through quivering lips.

"Wrong fucking answer," I growl with untamed fury.

In one swift motion, I swing the meat tenderizer and smash it against his hand. The crunching sound of his bones breaking is instant.

Ruthlessly, I continue crushing his hand until it appears more like ground beef than a hand. Blood splatters on my face and I feel... *good.*

I feel so damn good at letting this pain and agony out. The suffering at the hands of so many people in my life. The resentment and hatred toward my mother. The torment I've endured through my nightmares. The mourning for the childhood I never got to have.

Every. Fucking. Emotion.

My animalistic shouts echo off the walls and mix with his screams of pain.

He has blood droplets scattered across his face, snot and tears flow down from his nose and eyes.

Panting from exertion, I look down at my work and a cruel, satisfied smile spreads across my face.

"So much for starting slow," Rhys mutters behind me.

I spin around and look at Emily again. Her eyes are wide, but she doesn't look afraid. Her pupils are dilated. She looks hungry to enact her own revenge.

Lifting the weapon in her direction, I motion for her to take it. She wraps her fingers around the handle and then slowly strides closer to our current victim.

Emily wastes no time in bringing the weapon down on his other hand. Again, the crunch is instant as well as his crying.

Her eyes turn wild, and she brings it down over and over just as I did. I feel so much pride in watching her take what is owed.

Turning my head, I see Declan standing with his hands in his pockets and a smirk on his lips. He feels me staring and his eyes meet mine. He shoots me a wink and then resumes watching his sister.

Emily and I move to the table together and browse for our next instrument. I stop on a large kitchen knife and Emily picks up a set of pliers.

"His tongue?" I ask Emily.

She nods and we spin around and walk back side-by-side to the man.

He closes his mouth tightly and shakes his face to avoid having his tongue pulled out.

"Here," Rhys says, and he brings over a clamp-looking tool.

Declan walks over and forcefully grabs the man by his hair and jerks his head back. When his mouth opens in pain, Rhys shoves the tool into his mouth and forces it open. The click of him locking it in place sounds and he steps away.

The man's mouth is open wide, tongue fully on display.

Declan doesn't remove his grip from his hair. He holds him steady as Emily reaches the pliers into his mouth and grabs hold of his tongue tightly.

His panicked-filled screams make me feel elated. This is a high I've never felt. I could easily become addicted to this.

I quickly walk over and slice the muscle clean off. Blood instantly pools and falls from his mouth onto his clothes and lap.

"Leave his mouth open," Declan says and then he takes the pliers from Emily and begins ripping teeth out.

I had initially assumed killing someone would send me into a panic or bring back flashes of what I went through. Instead, I feel like I'm flying. I could do this forever.

It wasn't long after cutting his tongue that our *friend* died.

His body is slumped over and blood coats the ground.

"How are you girls feeling?" Rhys asks.

"Lighter," Emily responds at the same time I say, "Ready for more."

He chuckles and shakes his head in disbelief.

"Let's let you process what happened before we make a serial killer out of you, yeah?"

The first real smile in months spreads over my face and I nod in agreement.

Declan and I walk toward my bedroom in comfortable silence. His hand is placed at the small of my back and the heat feels *nice.*

Showing him the damage Aleksei created was nauseatingly difficult. But his words about his love for me not being any different helped calm my nerves slightly.

He hasn't seen the most intimate part of me and I'm a wreck about what his reaction will be.

I had to have reconstructive surgery to fix the extensive damage Aleksei made. I haven't spent much time looking at myself there but from what I have seen, it's very different than before.

"I can hear your mind working, Paige," Declan mumbles.

"I'm sorry... I just have a lot on my mind," I say.

"About what happened in the cellar?"

I shake my head as we reach my door. Facing it, I stare at the wood grains, gathering my thoughts. Declan is everything I could have ever wanted in a partner. He's seen me at my worst and still loves me fiercely. He's a man I know I can depend on.

I turn around to Declan who gives me a small encouraging smile.

He looks at me with so much love. Even after seeing my body and watching me torture a man to death.

"I want to try something," I say and open the door to my room.

He follows me inside and closes the door behind him.

"What do you need, mo ghrá?" he asks quietly.

My heart pumps wildly in my chest. If I can do this, then I know my future will be okay. If I can do this, then *I* will be okay.

I take a deep breath and steel my shoulders. "Kiss me."

His face shows no emotion and his eyes flick between mine.

"Are you sure?"

"I don't want to fear your touch anymore, Declan." My voice cracks. "I want to crave it again. I want to crave being with you," I plead.

He steps into me and cups my face. I lean into his touch and my eyes flutter closed. His thumb gently rubs the scar on my cheek.

I feel him shift slightly and his breath skates along my lips.

Chills travel through my body causing goosebumps to scatter over my skin. My chest rises and falls rapidly with each second that his lips hover just above mine.

In the softest touch, Declan places his lips against mine. I release the breath I didn't realize I was holding and press into his mouth.

Our lips part and our tongues dance slowly together.

This is not a kiss of seduction but a kiss of promise. A promise that I'm okay and that he will be here. A promise that he will love me with every fiber of his being.

I grip onto the fabric of his blood-stained shirt and pull him closer. His hand moves from my face into my hair. Tears slide down my face from the intense emotions coursing through me. I'm free falling and it's the most exhilarating experience of my life.

With one final peck to my lips, we pull away from each other.

Declan's eyes slowly open and meet mine. His shimmer with unshed tears.

"Are you crying?" I ask in surprise.

He gives me a shaky smile. "I've missed you," he whispers and then pulls me into his chest.

We stand holding each other. Holding onto the fact that despite what we've been through, we are stronger.

Chapter 40

Declan

I release Paige and walk her toward the ensuite. Turning on the shower, I test the water then step back.

"Go ahead and get cleaned up in here. I'll go to my room and shower in there," I say to her and pivot to the door.

"Declan," her soft voice halts me in my tracks. Turning around, Paige has her arms wrapped around her center as she studies me.

"Yes?"

"You can stay, if you want." She chews on the inside of her cheek, and she flushes, seeming unsure. I shake my head softly and give her a small smile. "You don't need to say that because you think that's what I want, mo ghrá. I will move at whatever pace *you* want."

"I-I want you to stay. But will you promise me something?"

"Anything."

She lowers her arms to her sides and steels her face.

"Promise me that you'll be careful."

Careful? With that?

"I promise." When she sees the confusion on my face she smiles sadly.

"You'll understand soon enough." Her voice is reverent as she begins undressing.

I stand still as her scarred body is revealed. Her soft curves have filled in since returning home, but she's still very frail.

She stops once the only article of clothing remaining is her panties. Standing straight, she takes a deep breath in and meets my eyes.

My brows furrow. I don't understand what I need to be careful of and her actions are confusing.

Her fingers tremble vigorously when she tucks her thumbs into the band and slowly slides her panties down.

When she stands, she shrinks into herself and watches my reaction.

Along her pelvis is a large and jagged scar that lowers down into the apex of her thighs. The scars from where stitches were placed span along a few other scars. She has hyperpigmentation from where skin grafts were performed.

He mutilated her.

The back of my eyes burn as tears begin to form.

"Paige, my beautiful, sweet, Paige. I am so sorry that I failed you. That my incapability to reach you in time caused you so much pain."

The first tear falls from my eye and Paige tracks the movement as it slides down my cheek.

I step closer to her and reach out my hand to caress her skin.

"I will never forgive myself for the pain you've endured. I hope *you* never forgive me," my voice cracks.

Her bottom lip trembles and she curls into me. My arms wrap around her small frame.

"I will spend the rest of this life and the next reminding you how much I love you. Your body, your heart, your soul. I will never stop loving any part of you." The first sob breaks through my lips.

"Now… you understand," she says quietly as her arms wrap around my waist and she squeezes.

"Please never question my love for you. My soul lives for you. It will only ever live for you as my heart will only ever beat for you," I whisper.

With a final squeeze, I release her and she steps away from my body. I lightly grip onto her chin with my thumb and forefinger and tip her head. Tears have slipped from her eyes and slide down her face. Her eyes are filled with relief and flickers of happiness.

Kissing her on the forehead, I step back and begin undressing.

We step into the shower and stand under the spray of water. The blood washes down our bodies and flows down the drain.

"What are you thinking?" Paige asks softly.

I smile at her and cup her cheek to caress the scar once more.

"Thank you for allowing me in," I whisper.

Grabbing the body soap, I lather it into my hands and rub it onto her skin. She relaxes into my touch as I massage her muscles. I move her into the water to rinse the soap and then grab the shampoo.

Once her hair is cleaned, I put some conditioner in it and then begin cleaning myself.

Paige stops me when I rub the soap against my chest. Taking it from my hand, she lathers her own and then rubs the soap on my skin.

My traitor of a cock decides at that very moment to become hard. This is the first time she's touched my bare skin in months and my body is heated beyond comprehension.

It presses against her hip and she freezes before looking down.

I offer her a sheepish grin. "Sorry," I mutter.

Her entire face blazes crimson but her eyes show amusement.

"You don't need to apologize, Declan. It actually makes me feel really good to see that I still have that kind of effect on you," she teases quietly.

I thumb her bottom lip and peer down at her with hooded eyes. "You will always have this effect on me."

She lowers her face from mine and continues to clean my upper body.

When she begins rubbing the soap onto my abs, they tense, and I suppress a groan. Her movements are deliberately slow.

"Mo ghrá," I warn.

She smiles innocently at me and then bites on her lower lip. "Yes, baby?"

I pull her into me. "Baby, huh? I like the sound of that."

She chuckles under her breath and the flush of her cheeks returns.

We finish getting cleaned up and exit the shower. Wrapped in our towels, we walk back into the room.

"I'll be back after I get some more clothes to sleep in," I say and stride to the door.

"Wait."

I pause and turn to face Paige and raise my brow in question.

"Stay...please." She rubs her toes together.

"I don't have any clothes here, Paige."

"I know. I just thought... well, I just thought that maybe we can lay together? I've missed your touch and with what happened today and the shower, I just want to feel you."

Say no more.

I unhook the towel from my waist and toss it aside. Paige's eyes leisurely travel down my body and stop at my cock that hasn't softened in the slightest. Her eyes quickly flick to mine and she licks her lips. I track the movement.

I clear my throat and place a kiss on her head then walk toward the bed. Pulling the blankets back, I slide under and motion for Paige to lie with me.

She removes her towel and slowly walks over. When she lies down, I pull her back to my front.

Her skin still feels velvety, even with the scars, and having her with me calms the demon deep inside.

"I love you," she says quietly.

I freeze.

Did she really say that?

She shifts to turn around and face me. I gaze down and her eyes glisten, making the green seem translucent.

"I love you, Declan," she says again.

A big toothy grin spreads across my face and I let out a relieved laugh. Shaking my head slowly, I run my fingers through her damp hair.

"I love you more than I can even explain, Paige."

She presses her chest against mine, her pebbled nipples rub against me and I groan. She rubs her small hand against the stubble of my cheek and then presses her lips against mine.

I wrap my arms around her and deepen our kiss.

She parts her lips and I take the invitation. My tongue slides into her mouth and clashes against hers.

My hands travel down her body. Cupping the back of her thigh, I bring her leg up and wrap it around my waist. She gasps but doesn't tense.

This is good. This is really good.

"Is this okay?" I ask between kisses.

"Yes. This is more than okay," her voice is breathy and husky.

Fuck.

"Tell me if you want to stop." My hand caresses her thigh.

"Mmm," she moans softly into my mouth.

Her hands travel across the span of my chest and move lower.

She lightly touches the tip of my cock with her fingers and my hips jerk.

"Paige," I say when I pull away from her. "Please try not to force yourself into something you're not ready to do. I can wait."

Her eyes roam over my face slowly and a small smile forms over hers. "I'm ready."

Pressing her lips against mine, she teases with her tongue, coaxing my lips to part. Our kiss is slow and sensual.

We move our hands slowly, rediscovering each other's bodies.

When I place my hand on the inside of her thigh, she sucks in a small breath. I pause and look into her eyes to make sure she's okay. Hers flicker between mine for a moment but she nods and parts her legs.

My fingers caress her scars as they move upward in a slow pace. Paige's breaths are labored, and her body language tells me she's hesitant, but her eyes tell me she trusts me to stop if she says the words.

I reach the apex of her thighs and her eyes flutter slightly with uncertainty. "I love you," I whisper. I reach a finger out and make contact with her scarred skin. She hisses and my eyes shoot to hers.

"It's okay. It doesn't hurt." she shakes her head.

I move my hand closer and touch her again, maintaining eye contact with her the entire time.

Her eyes close when I touch her clit lightly. A soft moan escapes her lips.

I press my lips to her neck. "You're doing so good, baby."

She runs her fingers up my chest and into my hair. My fingers circle her clit, adding a little pressure at a time as I watch her face etched with ecstasy.

"That's it, feel my fingers touching your beautiful pussy." I whisper in a husky tone.

Her mouth falls open. I suck her bottom lip into my mouth and nip lightly. The hand she has in my hair clenches, and I smirk.

"How does that feel, mo ghrá?"

"So good," she moans.

I nip at her shoulders and then suck her hardened nipple into my mouth. I groan when she starts to slowly roll her hips into my hand.

I slide a finger down into her pussy, her wetness coats me. It's otherworldly to see the trust she is allowing me to have.

"Fuck baby, your delicious cunt weeps so beautifully for me."

"Only you," she sighs.

I press the finger inside and pump in and out slowly while rubbing circles on her clit with my thumb. She moves her hands to my biceps and digs her fingers into my flesh. I welcome the sting of her nails drawing blood as they claw downward.

Her back arches as she rides my hand and moves her hips in unhurried rotations.

"That's it, Paige. That's it." I press a second finger in and speed up my thrusts when I feel her pussy starting to clench.

"Oh *God*," she moans, eyes rolling back.

Her body stalls and then she lets out a deep throaty moan before her cum spills from her pussy and coats my hand. She slumps into my chest. Her cheeks are flushed, and she has a radiant glow on her face.

I slip my fingers from her pussy and suck her juices off them. A deep groan escapes my lips at the sweet taste of her honey.

"Thank you." Her watery eyes meet mine.

"For what, mo ghrá?" I ask, pushing a strand of hair behind her ear.

"Loving me," she whispers.

My heart expands in my chest at her sincerity.

"Loving you is as easy as breathing, Paige." I place a gentle kiss on her nose.

I pull her into my chest and breathe out a sigh of contentment. Her hands press against me, and I pull back to look at her.

"What about you?" she asks with her brows drawn in.

A soft smile plays on my lips, and I shake my head. "No need to worry about me. This was for you."

She looks remorseful as her eyes study the features of my face. I move my hand up to the side of her neck and brush my finger along her bottom lip. Her eyes soften and she smiles up at me with such admiration.

Her face turns away from me and she bites down on her lower lip. Her stare becomes contemplative. Her lips purse and then her eyes return to me.

"I want to try. I want you to remove their touches from my body so all I feel is you."

Gripping onto her hips, I lie down on my back and pull her body to straddle mine. Since she's unable to have me lie above her yet, I want to make sure she has complete control of this situation.

"Take what you want from me. Use me how you wish."

Her throat bobs as she swallows. "Really?" she whispers.

My hands slide up and down her thighs tenderly. "You have the power here, Paige."

With shaky hands, she moves mine up her torso to cup her perfect raindrop-shaped breasts. I knead them causing her head to fall back and she presses her chest into my touch. She rocks her pussy up and down my cock, spreading her juices. I'm delirious with arousal.

I moan, "Oh fuck."

She hums and brings her hands up, placing them on mine. Using her forefinger and thumb, she pinches her nipples.

Leaning back, she grips my length in her hand and lines me up. I watch as every inch of my cock spreads her pussy when she lowers herself. My eyes pinch tightly, and I grit my teeth.

Fuck I'm going to come already.

"Shit, baby, your cunt is gripping me so fucking tight. I'm going to come before I'm fully inside you," I say through clenched teeth.

She pushes my hands down and I wrap them around her waist. My fingers dig into her flesh when I'm fully seated in her mouthwatering pussy.

I drop my head down onto the pillow and stare up at her. Her cheeks are tinted pink, and she watches me with hooded eyes. Licking her lips, she rises to the tip and then slides down slowly.

"Fuck. Fuck. Fuck," I groan.

Her hands settle on my chest, and she rides me. Each roll of her hips sends me into absolute bliss. I'm drunk on the feeling of her warm cunt sliding up and down on my cock. Her gorgeous tits bounce with each of her movements.

"That's it, baby. Fuck, I love watching your delicious pussy take my cock. She's so fucking greedy."

She wraps her hand around my throat and squeezes.

That's new.

"I own you. *You are mine,*" she growls.

Fuck I'm going to combust.

I lift my hips to press deeper inside, and she tuts, stopping her movements.

"You're not in control, remember? I am. So, stay still while I fuck you, Declan," She rasps in a mocking tone.

Lowering my body, I remove my hands from her hips and place them above my head. "Do your worst, mo ghrá."

A seductive smirk spreads across her face when she begins rolling her hips again, and a moan spills from my lips.

"Oh *God,*" mouth falling open, her head tips back. The ends of her hair tickle my thighs as she rides my cock.

She leans forward and bites down on my lower lip. I groan when the copper taste of my blood touches my tongue. She licks the blood from my lip and then covers my mouth with hers. Our tongues collide and we lose ourselves in the moment. Savoring this connection that was taken from us.

The hand on my throat tightens. “Look at me,” she orders, and I immediately obey. “Come for me.”

The base of my spine tingles, my balls tighten, and then I’m exploding into her pussy.

So that’s how that feels.

“Good boy,” she praises and then smashes her lips against mine.

Congratulations Declan, you have a praise kink.

My cock becomes hard again as she continues to ride me.

Chapter 41

Paige

I stand panting and sweating. Blood is dripping down from the strands of my hair that escaped my hair tie. My skin tingles from the high I'm feeling. I feel strong. *Alive.* I cannot name a single moment in which I've ever felt this way. It's exhilarating.

My blood-soaked knife falls from my grip and clatters on the ground. The screams from the men still ring in my ears. I hope they embed themselves in the walls so I can hear their lullaby whenever I wish.

I lift my eyes to the door in the corner that leads to where my final two monsters are being held. The anticipation of standing face-to-face with them has been hovering over me like a dark cloud. I haven't had the courage to see them again.

After Declan let me have the control with our sex life, I've been thriving. We no longer sleep in separate rooms. He follows my lead and boy do I love it. I can now have him hover over my body without feeling the suffocating weight of what Aleksei has done to me.

My insecurities have diminished. Declan worships my body like I'm a Goddess. He takes every opportunity to kiss each of my scars, and whispers loving words every night. My heart swells each time. The love and devotion he shows me is such a contradiction to his authoritative side he shows with his men or associates.

And he's all mine.

Lily has started coming out of the pen and has been interacting with the other horses in the pasture. It's been extraordinary to watch. Her personality has blossomed as well; she's gentle, kind, and quirky. I spend a few hours with her every day. Talking to her, lying with her, and sometimes reading to her. Her soul mingles with mine effortlessly. Over the last few months, she's been a cornerstone in my recovery.

I have no plans to return to my job in the near future. Leaving the property has been something I continue to struggle with, but I have spoken with Declan about Sage's situation. Being the amazing person that he is, Declan had 'a few words' with the case manager and she was removed from her abusive home. She was adopted by an amazing couple that cannot have children of their own. They fell madly in love with her story and opted to adopt her versus a newborn.

I cried for hours when I heard the news.

Declan has mentioned in passing wanting children. I'm still unsure where I stand with that. I become terror-stricken whenever it's brought up. The memory of the cold tile flooring soaked in blood and the days following are so ingrained in my psyche. It's hard to just let that part go. I do see myself having a family with Declan. I know he'd be an amazing and loving father. It's just *getting* to that point that's the problem.

The cellar door creaks open, and I look over my shoulder.

Finn stands in the doorway watching me with calculated eyes. My eyebrow arches in question. And I turn to face him.

"Can I help you?" I ask cautiously.

The mood in the room changes drastically and the hairs on the back of my neck stand up straight. My stomach twists with unease.

My interactions with Finn are extremely limited. And even then, Declan or Rhys are always with me when he's around. But this time, I'm completely alone.

His hand disappears behind him, and I hear the twist of the lock engaging.

"I just wanted to have a few words with you," he says in a peculiar tone that I can't decipher.

My heart rate reaches dangerous speeds being in his proximity.

My fingers rub against each other, tingling with the need to reach down and grab the knife.

I steel my face so he cannot see how uncomfortable I am. I refuse to let another person control me or my emotions.

"What about?" my voice gives nothing away, but he still smirks as though he is calling my bluff.

"We need to discuss you disappearing." He steps further into the room.

"Disappearing?" I parrot, taking a step back.

His eyes become dark, and his smile grows. "Yes. You see, your involvement with Declan has become... a problem."

I pivot with each step he makes, avoiding him taking the opportunity to stand behind me. "How so?" My eyes narrow when he stands next to the chair and slides in fingers along the back.

"You make him distracted," he says and his eyes flick to me. "He's become sloppy. He pushes off meetings or trips to the shipment yard. It simply won't do."

"So, what? You plan to get rid of me?" I ask in a snarky tone.

He shrugs innocently, "I did once before."

And then it hits me like a damn bus. *He* is responsible for my abduction. For my suffering at the hands of Vladimir and Aleksei. For the mutilation of my body. For *everything.*

I sweep the knife from the ground at the same time he lunges at me. He fists my hair before I get a chance to pull away and throws me to the ground. The knife falls from my hand and slides across the floor. The back of my head slams down against the concrete and I'm instantly dazed.

Straddling me, Finn wraps his hands tightly around my throat and squeezes. My hands claw at his forearms and face, but he continues to choke me. When I try to slam down onto his elbows to loosen his grip, it is no use. He's too strong for me.

I buck and twist my body around and then he lifts my head and crashes it back down. The pain reverberating throughout my entire skull.

"I promised his father that he would lead this organization perfectly. *You* stand in the way of that. He is losing focus on everything his father built. I refuse to let him be controlled by cunt," he seethes.

I slide my hand around frantically, hoping to find the knife that I dropped.

The handle brushes against my fingertips and I extend my fingers as far as humanly possible. The muscles in my digits strain and my head becomes fuzzy from the lack of oxygen.

You can do this!

The sound of the lock disengaging echoes just as I grip onto the handle. Declan steps into the room — momentarily distracting Finn and I plunge the knife into his neck. His hand flies to the gushing wound, his mouth opening and closing in short gasps.

Declan runs into the room. "Paige!"

But I'm already straddling Finn and stabbing him in the face, neck, and chest repeatedly.

"FUCK. YOU!" I roar with each plunge of the knife into his body. I'm filled with so much untamed, barbaric rage that I can no longer hear Declan's shouts behind me.

The bones crunch and the sensation reverberates through the handle and up my arm. His gasps quickly change into gurgles as he chokes on his blood. It splatters across my face, in my hair, and on my clothes. I have no doubt the scene resembles a horror movie.

I'm so agonizingly angry. If it weren't for this man, I wouldn't have been taken by Mark. I wouldn't have been sold to Vladimir. I wouldn't have been raped, or mutilated by Aleksei, or drugged, or fucking tortured. I wouldn't have had to stay in a box with the rotting corpse of a woman who didn't deserve what had happened to her.

After I've stabbed his lifeless body at least seventy times, I fall onto my back. My breaths are labored, my heart pounds against my eardrums, and my brain feels as though it is banging against my skull. The adrenaline continues to flow freely in my bloodstream causing me to tremble.

My eyes stay focused on a small black dot on the ceiling until my breathing stabilizes and my vision becomes clearer.

Declan's hysteric face hovers over me. "What the fuck happened?!"

I groan as I pull myself to sit with his help. I stare blankly at Finn's body, watching the blood spread under him like lava oozing from a volcano. "He was responsible for Mark taking me," I say in voice devoid of emotion.

Declan lets out a sigh, "I had my suspicions, but he was good at covering his tracks." I look up at him. His eyes are filled with so much anger and guilt. "He wasn't supposed to be here, Paige. I sent him out to check on a shipment."

His eyes move down to my neck and his nostrils flare, no doubt seeing his handprints on my skin. My throat burns from the pressure and it's difficult to swallow.

"I'm done," I croak.

"With what?" Declan asks nervously.

"I'm done being a damsel in distress. I'm done feeling weak. I'm done letting awful people dictate my life. I'm fucking *done.*"

Declan glances at Finn's body and then back to me. A smug smile spreads across his face. "I'd say you've done a very good job not being a damsel in distress, mo ghrá."

I snort and wince when a sharp pain shoots from the back of my head. I press my hand against it and feel the squelch of wetness on my hair.

When I look at my hand, it's covered in blood. "Well, shit," I giggle.

I feel light-headed and unsteady. My eyes get droopy, and I start to lean to the side. Declan scoops me up.

"Let's get your head taken care of, baby," he mutters, and we leave Finn's corpse behind.

After fifteen staples, about thirty stitches, and a bandage being wrapped around my head, I'm finally able to find a moment to take a breath.

Declan disappeared after the doctor finished patching me up to take care of Finn's body, along with the two other men I killed. He hasn't quite told me what he does with them other than cutting them into pieces. I plan to ask him about it as soon as possible, especially since I apparently developed a knack for murder.

Sarah: Why THE FUCK did Rhys tell me you killed not one, not two, but THREE fucking men today?

Me: ...

Sarah: I'm coming over.

Oh great.

Sarah has always been a fucking psycho but she's reaching astronomical levels now. Emily and I told her about the two of us killing one of the men Declan and Rhys captured. Let's just say, she was very offended that we didn't offer to have her join.

I'm not prepared to deal with her wrath about the murders I did today.

Technically, one was self-defense.

A knock comes from my bedroom door.

"Come in," I shout then wince because I'm a dumbass and thought yelling with a concussion was a fantastic idea.

Ingrid steps into the room with a small mug cradled in her hands. She smiles warmly at me.

What the fuck?

She doesn't interact with me unless she has to, and her face is always stoic. I'm a little wary of this newfound emotion she's sharing with me.

"I brought you some peppermint tea to help with the headache." Setting the cup down on the nightstand, she straightens and just… stares at me.

"Thank you," I say with a small smile, unsure of what to do with her watching me so intently.

"I want to apologize."

Thrown by this sudden statement, I look up at her and arch a brow "For…" my sentence strays off.

"I passed judgment on you that was not warranted, and it was severely inaccurate. When I initially saw you, I deemed you weak and unable to be the woman Declan needed at his side." She furrows her brows and shakes her head. "That is farthest from the truth as a statement can be."

I stare at her in bewilderment. This was *not* anything I would have conjured in my wildest dreams.

"Your strength is beyond measurable. Your resilience, tenacity, and perseverance are exactly what Declan needs in a woman— in an equal. I may not be a woman of many words, but I am very observant." She levels me with a look. "And *you, mo stór*, are a force to be reckoned with."

My mouth gapes. I'm floored by what she just said. Completely at a loss for words.

"I— I don't know what to say," wide-eyed, I stutter.

She smiles softly, lifting my hand in hers and patting it lightly. "You don't need to say anything, *leanbh*."

Her chin juts out, gesturing toward the tea. "Drink. I will have Niall prepare your meal to be eaten in bed. Now rest."

She sets my hand down and walks out of the room.

Did that just fucking happen?

Chapter 42

Declan

"Paige has turned into a perfect little Mike Meyers," Rhys says, taking a bite from his apple. The crunch it makes with each chew makes me feel seconds away from scooping his eyes out. It's infuriating.

"Stop fucking eating that Goddamn apple," I growl with a glare.

His chewing stops and he raises his brows, "What the fuck is wrong with my eating?" He takes another bite.

I rip the apple from his hand and chuck it into the harbor. Rhys watches as it flies through the air and splashes into the water.

"Now that was just unnecessary," he says, swallowing the piece in his mouth and crossing his arms. "What the fuck is your issue?"

While I suspected he was behind the obstacles I was experiencing, Finn's betrayal hit me harder than I was anticipating. He had been a part of my life for many years, and I had trusted him with my life.

"Just processing Finn's betrayal," I say quietly, looking over the water. Paige had told me about his promise to my father which just enraged me more. My father was a family man and loved my mother with all he had. So, for Finn to think removing the love of my life was acceptable, made no sense. Not only that, but he was also responsible for everything Paige went through.

If she hadn't killed him, I would have but I'm unbelievably proud that Paige is letting her fire burn. She's eradicating her demons and it's a sight to behold.

"Vladimir and Aleksei are the last two men that Paige needs to eliminate for her to heal. I'm not sure when she plans to handle them."

"And you think she'll be okay? I mean, they're the ones who have caused her the most trauma."

I place my hands in my pockets and nod my head. "I know she will be okay. She needs this."

"Boss,"

Rhys and I turn around to the sound of Liam's voice. "Antonio is here."

Antonio reached out about a week ago. The terms of our initial agreement are still valid, so I requested he meet us here to discuss his shipment.

Antonio stands inside the warehouse, assessing the new process of operations. He nods his head appreciatively with his lips pursed.

"Thank you for coming Antonio." His head turns to me, and he offers me a smile.

"Of course," his hand gestures to the machinery and men working. "This is very impressive."

"We flew out to Ireland to get some suggestions for improvement." Our hands clasp together, and we shake. I take a step back and return my hand to my pocket.

I play with the little velvet box that holds the ring I got the day after Paige's first night with me. As I said, she was mine the moment I laid eyes on her. Now I just need to make it official. I want her to share my last name in addition to this empire.

The plan is to propose after she is no longer haunted by her trauma. I can't help but keep the box close to me in case the perfect moment presents itself before that time.

There are still a few secrets Paige hasn't shared with me. There's one in particular that I want to know about related to children. She retreats into herself when we tread near the subject. Her eyes become distant, and I know she's reliving a past that weighs heavily on her soul. At times, her eyes show a hint of guilt which I don't understand.

I'm unable to muster any explanation outside of the possibility that she placed a child up for adoption. That is the only justification for any guilt she may feel. Hopefully, she trusts me enough to carry that burden for her.

"How are Paige and Emily?" Antonio asks as we walk through the warehouse.

Rhys chuckles under his breath and I elbow him in the rib causing him to grunt.

"Emily has been doing well overall. She's been going to therapy, and it's been a significant help in her recovery. Paige... Well, her recovery involves some acts that many would consider unconventional." A smirk plays on my lips and Antonio's brow rises.

"Oh?" he presses.

"She's recently discovered an interest for blood."

His steps halt and he spins to me which a shocked expression, "Care to elaborate?"

"Over the last few weeks, she's killed four men," I state.

His jaw becomes lax, and then he laughs loudly. "Well, it appears Paige was carefully curated to be your perfect match." His grin widens.

I pat his back. "I knew that before she started slaughtering people, Antonio."

"Yes well, now you crazy fucks can torture people together."

My cock bounces in delight. Maiming and dismembering alongside Paige would be a foreplay unlike any other. I will *of course* be working on getting her on board with that.

Fucking when you're full of adrenaline is the best fuck you could experience. I can't wait.

We stand in front of one of our trucks that was loaded with approximately eighty boxes. The doors slam shut, and the locks are placed.

"Double the weapons you requested, as agreed upon."

"Excellent,"

"Care to share what you need all these weapons for?" I ask with a slight rise of my eyebrow.

Antonio's eyes flare. "I'm going to take down the Valenti family."

The Valenti's are another Italian mafia, but they're in Detroit. Their rivalry with the Romano's has been ongoing since Antonio's grandfather was Don. It's not clear how it started, but I assume it's over territory. Any attempts at a merger have failed as Jackie is the first Romano daughter in generations. Last I heard, Massimo — the son of the Don, refused to arrange a marriage with Jackie because of her drug use. It would affect her ability to bear children and the Italians are all about large families.

"How is Jackie?" I bite down on my tongue to avoid smiling. The last thing I need is for Antonio to see how much I enjoyed hurting her to get my vengeance for Paige.

His eyes narrow and he lets out a frustrated sigh. "I set her to rehab after your little *stunt.* Her drug use became out of control, and she was becoming violent."

"Well, let's hope the program helps this time around." I didn't use to hate Jackie, but after what she did to Paige, I loathe her. "Just make sure she stays clear of me and Paige when she's released."

"I'll be sending her to Italy."

"Good."

I nod to the truck, "They will follow you back to your home. As usual, it was a pleasure doing business with you." I pat his back and stride toward the door.

Rhys stays behind to ensure Antonio leaves without any extra merchandise.

When I pull up to my home, Sarah's car is in the driveway.

Well fuck.

There goes my plan of sinking into Paige. Sarah is the crazy sister I thought Emily would grow up to be. Her intensity can sometimes be overwhelming, but she is a perfect match for Rhys's laid-back personality.

I walk through the front door and am greeted with the sound of Paige's laughter. A grin spreads over my face and I quickly walk toward the sound.

Paige, Sarah, and Emily are seated at the kitchen island watching Niall prepare food. Paige's eyes brighten when she spots me and my heart melts.

She hops off the stool and walks over to me. My eyes slide down her body and a blush spreads over her face. I tip my head down and rub my thumb back and forth over my bottom lip.

"You look absolutely edible, mo ghrá," I rasp.

She bites down on her lower lip and peers at me through her lashes. She's wearing a yellow sundress that gives her olive skin an amazing glow. It stops mid-calf and flows down her soft curves in a way that has my cock throbbing.

"You don't look too bad yourself." She places her hand on my chest and stands on her toes to place a kiss on my lips. My hand immediately cups the back of her head. Teasing the seam of her lips with my tongue, she opens for me and I waste no time in deepening our kiss. I groan when she sucks on my tongue. I press into her so she can feel just what she's done to me, and a soft moan escapes her lips.

The kiss slows and then stops. Pulling away, I see the undeniable lust in her hooded eyes. I shoot her a wink.

Looking over her shoulder, I see Emily roll her eyes with a smirk on her lips and Sarah gags as though she's disgusted. She's really trying to hide her own lust since Rhys isn't present to help her. I'm surprised the two of them haven't popped out any babies with the number of times they fuck.

I chuckle, "Ladies." I nod to them and then greet Niall.

"The women have requested steaks for dinner tonight, sir," Niall says as he prepares a garden salad.

"Sounds delicious." I place my hand on the small of Paige's back and rub my thumb against her spine. She smiles up at me with those eyes that I can't resist.

Fuck. I love this woman.

"What have you ladies been up to, today?"

Sarah flicks her eyes to Paige before meeting mine. "I came to interrogate Paige."

My brows crease and I look down at Paige who simply shrugs her shoulder, completely unbothered. "She wanted to know why I killed more people without her."

I burst into a fit of laughter and press my hand on my stomach.

"What have I gotten myself into with you two?" I look over to Emily whose face is void of emotions. And I immediately sober.

"Are you okay?" I ask. She straightens her spine and points to herself.

"Me?"

"I am looking right at you, Em."

"Psh, yeah I'm completely good." She flicks her hand out in dismissal.

Paige wraps an arm around my waist and squeezes lightly, catching my attention. She gives me an odd look before letting go and walking back to her seat. When I look back at Emily, she's staring distantly at the counter.

What the fuck?

"Em?" I ask but she doesn't respond.

"All done, boss," Liam says, and Emily's trance is instantly broken. Her cheeks flush when she sees Liam walk into the kitchen. I narrow my eyes slightly and when she notices my stare, she quickly averts my eyes.

I turn to Liam, who is watching Emily with longing in his eyes.

"Liam," my voice is tight. His eyes steel and he looks at me. "Meet me in my office."

With one last glance in Emily's direction, he follows the order. Paige purses her lips and widen her eyes, silently scolding me.

"What?" I whisper.

She rolls her eyes in exacerbation and turns to watch Niall season the steaks.

I close my office door behind me. Liam stands just in front of my desk with his back to me. His shoulders tense when he hears the lock engage.

"Care to explain," I say as I walk to the wet bar and pour us both some whiskey.

"Sir?"

"Don't insult my intelligence, Liam. Not unless you want to end up in the cellar."

His face blanches and his throat bobs. His throat clears, "Uh... I care for Emily."

I narrow my eyes and watch him. He shifts uncomfortably at my eyes boring into him. "Have you touched her?" my voice hard.

His eyes widen and he holds his hands out, shaking his head. "No. No, sir. We haven't done anything. We just sit and talk."

I hand him the whiskey, which he takes with shaking hands. I tip mine back and continue to watch him over the rim of the glass.

"How long?" I ask when I lower the whiskey.

He takes a deep breath. "When she returned home."

"It stops now."

Sadness fills his eyes and his shoulders slump. Lowering his head, he nods solemnly. "Yes, sir."

"Emily has been through enough. She doesn't need to get involved with you. Have I made myself clear?"

"Yes, sir."

"Good. Get out."

He sets the glass on my desk and leaves the room.

Paige enters a moment later and raises her brow. "What did you do?"

My eyes pivot between hers. "You knew about this?"

She crosses her arms and pops out her hip. "Don't answer my question with a question, Declan. What. Did. You. Do?" Her demeanor remains stoic as she watches me closely.

"I put a stop to it."

Her fists clench and she releases a deep breath. "Why? What makes you think you can do that?" Her brows furrow, and her eyes begin to fill with anger.

"She is my sister. I have to protect her from fuckers who will take advantage of her," I growl.

Hackles rising, she shouts, "You don't get to dictate who she falls in love with, Declan."

I rear back, "She's not in love with him."

A humorless laugh escapes from her lips, and she shakes her head, looking at me with disappointment. I'm shot in the chest with that look.

"Why do you think she's been making such amazing improvements? Because of Liam. He is the sole reason she has continued to go to therapy." She holds her hands out in frustration. I hear the words she's saying to me, but I don't believe them. Emily cannot be in love with Liam. I refuse to accept that. He is not good enough for my sister. No one is.

"I forbid it. He's not good enough for her, Paige."

She jabs a finger into my chest. "That is such fucking bullshit, Declan. So, what? You're good enough to be with me but Liam — who truly loves your sister — isn't good enough for her? Why? Because you're the boss and he's not? He loves her and takes care of her just as you do me."

"I stand by what I said. It's not happening," my voice unwavering.

"Emily will get worse. You'll see. And it will be entirely your fault."

The walls of my office rattle when the door slams.

Chapter 43

Paige

Declan and I didn't speak a word to each other throughout dinner. The tension put Emily and Sarah on edge, and they disappeared as soon as they finished their meals. I'm so angry that he thinks forbidding Liam and Emily to see each other is appropriate.

I know Emily will lose the progress she's made. Declan simply does not understand the hurdles she has overcome with the help of Liam.

I enter our room and make my way to the ensuite. I turn on the shower and begin stripping my clothes. Entering the shower, I tip my head back and allow the warmth of the water to pour down onto my face. I hear the bedroom door open and close. Seconds later, the sound of Declan's shoes entering the restroom comes.

"Are you going to refuse to speak to me for the remainder of the night?" he asks in an annoyed tone.

I grunt in response.

The shuffling of his clothing fills the silence and then the shower-glass door opens and closes behind me. Declan wraps his arms around my waist and sets his chin atop my head. My shoulders rise and fall when I take a deep breath.

"I can't stand behind Liam being with Emily," he whispers.

"I understand your desire to protect her, but you're going to cause more harm than good." I twist around to face him. The water drops down from the strands of hair that have fallen over his forehead.

You know that scene in *Man of Steel* where Clark Kent is soaked and helping at the oil rig? Yeah, well that's the energy Declan is giving off right now. My harlot of a pussy refuses to accept the memo that we are - in fact - pissed at him.

His thumbs rub the base of my spine softly and goosebumps spread like wildfire across my body. He's very well aware of my body's reaction to his, so the bastard has a smug smirk on his face, to which I narrow my eyes.

"If you think we're going to fuck after what happened today, you're sadly mistaken." I raise my brows in challenge.

"Is that so?" he drawls, tugging me closer. My nipples press against his warm body, and I tremble. I raise my chin, feigning the confidence that I *know* he can tell is fake.

He presses his nose against the side of my jaw and maneuvers my head to the side. His lips caress the column of my neck. My head falls back – allowing him more access - and I moan when he kisses the sensitive area behind my ear.

He hums and the vibrations travel from his body into mine. I feel them down to my toes.

"This isn't going to work." My argument isn't even remotely convincing.

Declan nips at my earlobe, eliciting an involuntary shudder from me. His hands slide down my body so slow it's painful. I am completely wanton to this man, and he knows it.

"I love how responsive you are," he whispers as he kisses my neck and then my shoulder. My hands caress his hard biceps as I make my way up to wrap my arms around his neck. He groans when I run my fingers through his wet hair and tug.

"Tell me to stop and I will," he says, knowing full and well that there is no way in Hell, I will tell him to stop touching me. The tip of his nose lightly rubs against mine as he waits for the answer. His lips hover over mine which are slightly ajar, waiting for him to kiss me. When I lift onto my toes, he pulls back, denying me.

I whimper, "Please."

A self-satisfied smirk grows on his face. "Please what, mo ghrá?" he teases. His eyes are hooded, and his pupils are dilated. I look down at his mouth and his tongue slides out to wet his bottom lip.

"Kiss me, Declan. Please kiss me," I beg.

"Hmm, baby, you know how much I love to hear you beg."

But the bastard still doesn't kiss. He simply keeps his lips centimeters from mine. My pussy is pulsating, my body is hyperaware of his every move, and I'm blazing in an arousal so intense, I might just catch fire.

I trace every mountain and valley of his muscular body as I make my way lower. When I reach his hardened cock, I wrap my fingers around it and pump. He hisses and his precum drips into my palm.

Giving it a couple more pumps, I lower myself to my knees and peer up at him through my lashes. He bites his bottom lip.

"Maybe I'll deny you," I tease.

"Don't you fucking dare," he growls and runs the back of his fingers gently down my cheek.

I flick my tongue out and roll it around the head of his cock, tasting the slightly salty precum. My eyes flutter closed, and I moan.

Declan scoops my hair into a loose fist.

"Open that exquisite mouth of yours, baby, and suck my cock."

His dirty mouth sends a jolt to my clit. I shift my hips to relieve the ache. His fist tightens ever so slightly, and I open my mouth.

His length slides in, and once he's reached the back of my throat, he pulls back and begins fucking my face. My hands wrap around his hips, and I squeeze his ass, encouraging his thrusts. Drool leaks from the sides of my mouth and falls onto my breasts. The water from the shower continues to rain on my back. I'm in sensory overload and I never want it to end.

Hollowing out my cheeks and pressing my tongue up against the underside of his cock, I create a vacuum and suck hard.

"Fuck, Paige. You look so fucking amazing sucking my cock. You're such a good girl for me, aren't you?"

I hum in delight at his praise.

"Rub your pussy, mo ghrá," he lets out in a throaty voice, and I know he's close. My hips jerk the moment my fingers touch my clit. My eyes roll to the back of my head when I apply pressure and move my fingers in a circle.

"That's it, baby. Fuck, you're absolute perfection." His thrusts increase as does the amount of drool that spills from the corners of my mouth. My hips rock back and forth – riding my hand. I plunge two fingers into my pussy and pump furiously – chasing my orgasm that is moments from crashing into me.

Declan pulls out of my mouth with a *pop,* "Stick out your tongue."

Tipping my head back, I stick my tongue out and stare into his eyes as he pumps himself intensely.

"Fuck!" he roars as stream after stream of his cum jets out and covers my face and chest. I scoop up some of his delectable seed and suck it off my fingers.

Declan is panting hard, and his pupils are completely blown. The water now runs down my face, causing his cum to mix and run down the rest of my body. He quickly shuts off the water and lifts me into his arms. He grips my ass with both hands tightly and my legs wrap around his hips. We exit the shower, and he leads us to the room.

He throws me onto the bed before kneeling in front of me. He spreads my legs and immediately feasts on my pussy. I take his hair in a tight grip and ride his face. The need to come leaves no room for any other thought.

"Oh my God! Yes. Yes. Yes," I chant repeatedly.

He shoves two fingers into my pussy. The stretch is enough to send me over the edge. My hips lift and the dam that was holding my orgasm breaks. Fluid pours from me like a broken fire hydrant. My thighs shake uncontrollably as he continues to devour me. Declan doesn't stop until my pussy relaxes around his fingers and I slump into the bed.

He sits up and reaches for my hips. "I'm not through with you yet, Paige." Flipping my body around, Declan pulls my hips up, so I'm now on all fours. His hand comes down on my ass cheek and a loud *smack* echoes through the room. I yelp and he spanks me again.

His cock is hard as steel when he thrust into me. Fingers dig into my hips as he fucks me. I scream his name over and over. He spreads my ass cheeks, peaking over my shoulder, I watch Declan looking at his cock disappearing into my pussy with every roll of his hips.

“Shit, baby, I could die inside your sweet cunt.”

“Spank me again,” I moan, and he obliges. “Yes, Declan. Fuck me. Own me.”

He fists my hair and does just that.

My pussy is swollen and sore by the time we’re done losing ourselves in oblivion. I’m now lying on his chest, listening to the steady beat of his heart, and feeling the rise and fall of his chest with every breath he takes. I cannot even begin to describe the peace I feel. Everything about this man brings me a tranquility I didn’t know I would be able to reach. He silences the demons that whisper in my ear, the destructive thoughts that plague my mind, and replaces them with unquestionable love and blissful happiness.

“For the record, I blame you,” I pout.

“What for?”

“It is without a doubt your fault that I can’t control my pussy when you’re around.”

Declan’s boisterous laugh fills the room. Pulling me in close, he kisses the top of my head. “I’m not complaining.”

Rolling my eyes, I tease, “Of course you’re not.”

Burrowing myself closer to his warm body, I let out a content sigh.

“Marry me,” he whispers, and I freeze.

Propping myself up on my forearm, I gawk at Declan with a slackened jaw. “What?”

His eyes soften and he cups my cheek tenderly. “Marry me, Paige.”

My eyes bounce between his, searching for any signs that he's joking, but his gaze is unwavering. "Are you serious?" I whisper.

He slides out of bed and walks to the bathroom. I hear the sounds of his clothes rustling for a moment and then he returns with a *fucking velvet box* in his hand.

Climbing back into bed, Declan pulls me into his chest and opens the box. My hand flies to my mouth and I gasp.

A pear-cut moss agave stone is set in the center of a rose-gold band. It's simple and elegant – perfect. Tears immediately form in my eyes, and I look up at Declan. A soft smile curves over his face.

"The moment I laid eyes on you, I *knew* you were meant to be mine. Everything about you draws me in. Your eyes, your smile, your sassy attitude, your amazing rainy scent that I love so much. I meant it when I said that loving you is as easy as breathing. It comes naturally. When I look into my future, I see you. *You*, Paige, are my entire life. My heart and soul don't exist without you. This life – this empire — means nothing if I don't have the other half of me by my side. So, what do you say, mo ghrá? Will you allow me to worship you for the rest of time's existence?"

I choke out a sob and nod rapidly, "Yes. Of course, yes."

The ring fits flawlessly on my finger as Declan slides it into place. My heart is bursting at the seams in my chest. My soul is dancing on cloud nine. The happiness is endless.

"I love you, Declan. So much," I whisper and kiss him.

"I live for you, Paige."

Chapter 44

Declan

"Are you sure you're ready?" Days after I asked her to marry me, Paige decided it was time to finally purge the last of the demons from her life. So, here we are, standing in front of the door leading to the cells where Vladimir and Aleksei are being held.

"Knowing the next chapter of my life includes a lifetime with you? Definitely."

The hinges groan as I push open the door. Paige and I walk hand in hand to Vladimir's cell. She nods at me when I look at her for confirmation that she wants to start with him.

"Go wait in the main room. I'll bring him to you," I say, and she leaves.

I unlock the door and push it open. Vladimir sits propped against the far wall with a forearm resting on a bent leg. His eyes narrow when he sees me enter the room.

"Get up," I order.

Vladimir slowly lowers his leg and then begins lifting himself from the ground. He stands facing me with his shoulders back and his chin raised. "Let's get this over with," he says, showing no emotion.

I step to the side, and he passes by to exit the cell. We move to the main room where Paige stands by the table, examining the instruments I had laid out for her. I push Vladimir's shoulder down and force him into the seat. Paige doesn't turn around as I bind his arms and legs against the chair.

Once I finish, I walk to her and set my hand on the small of her back. "Ready when you are, ghrá. Do you want my help?"

She continues to inspect each of the knives, hammers, and clamps just as I do whenever I'm ready to torture someone in this room. Her movements are vulture-like. Predatory. Her transformation into this remarkable force of nature is outstanding to witness. She is in her element and I'm just a spectator.

She ignores my question, settling on a circular saw, spinning on her heels and facing Vladimir.

His eyes flare in surprise at the woman standing in front of him, then he looks at me.

"You're going to allow this meek little woman to handle your business?" he says with a tisk.

"You speak to me when you're in that seat," Paige growls and my cock hardens at her commanding presence. Vladimir's eyes slowly turn to her, and he raises a brow.

"What do you think you're going to achieve with that?" he dips his chin, gesturing to the saw.

A malicious smile spreads across Paige's face and she steps toward Vladimir. Recognizing this woman as being unlike the one he knew, Vladimir tenses and his jaw ticks slightly as he becomes uncomfortable.

The saw whirls to life and Paige begins severing his limbs from his body. The sounds of his shrieks excite her, and she goes into a frenzy. She laughs manically and her pupils are dilated. Blood sprays every close surface as she dismembers him piece by piece. Rather than simply cutting his head off, she saws vertically down his body. Cutting him completely in half. The bones crunch as the saw breaks through them and his organs spill from his corpse.

She is a sight to see, and I fall deeper in love with each cut she makes to his lifeless body.

The silence is deafening when she shuts off the saw. She drops it to the ground and walks to the table. I tilt my head to the side as her hand hovers over the table in search of another tool. She picks up a skinning knife and then stands behind Vladimir's body. She fists the hair on one side and then shoves the blade above the exposed flesh. His skin separates from the rest of him as she slides the knife downward.

She slices pounds of flesh from his corpse which slap onto the ground when she tosses them aside to move on to the next. She continues to butcher him until she has scrapped each bone clean of any meat or tendon.

When she's finished, she stands over the carnage like the Goddess of death. She is covered in blood and gore and has never looked more beautiful.

Striding over to her, I cup her face and smash my lips against hers. Our kiss is ravenous, like a starved animal finally being fed. We rip each other's clothes off and within seconds I have her on the ground in Vladimir's blood, thrusting into her. She gasps as I stretch her pussy and fuck her viciously.

"Yes! Yes!" Her moans echo off the walls.

"Fuck, baby, you look so gorgeous covered in the blood of your victim," I rasp. Her walls tighten around me, choking my cock in a vice so delicious, I never want it to stop.

"Don't stop. Fuck, don't stop."

I wrap my hand around her neck and squeeze. Her eyes roll to the back of her head, and she arches into me. Our bloodied bodies slide against each other with each of my hard thrusts.

"Harder, Declan. Fuck me harder," she begs.

I move my hips in punishing thrusts and soon she's squirting all over my cock.

"Good fucking girl. Squirt all over my cock. You're such a good fucking girl for me, aren't you?"

"Yes! Yes, I'm your good girl," she cries.

"Your cunt is squeezing me so tight, mo ghrá. I'm going to fill her with my cum."

The base of my spine tingles just as her walls tighten further. With one final brutal thrust, I come deep inside her. Stars dance in my vision as I spill into her cunt. Her nails scratch at my back and she comes with my name on her lips.

I fall to the side, collapsing on the floor next to her. We both are panting, coming down from the high we just experienced.

Paige giggles and turns her head in my direction. I meet her eyes and they're dazzling. Bright with such clarity. She leans in and kisses me.

"That was unexpected," she chuckles.

I smirk and place another kiss on her lips. "I can't wait to do it again," I drawl and wink at her.

She sobers slightly and then peaks at the door where her final monster lies in wait. She meets my eyes once more and she studies me.

"What is it?" I ask.

"He's a sick fuck who will likely enjoy me cutting into him, Declan. I refuse to let him take that from me."

"I have other ways we can torture him that don't involve dismemberment, mo ghrá." I stand and reach my palm out to her. The same electrical current flows from her to me as it always has and we smile at each other when it happens. "Let's get showered, have some men get this cleaned up, and then we'll come back to dispose of Aleksei."

I walk over to the small space we use for extra clothes and grab Paige a set of sweatpants and a T-shirt as well as a blanket. Grabbing myself a set of sweatpants and a T-shirt, we leave the cellar.

Reaching our bedroom, we make our way to the ensuite. I turn on the shower and turn around to Paige. She has already started removing her clothes, exposing Vladimir's dried blood on her skin. When she sees me staring, she smirks.

"Like what you see?" she purrs and wiggles her brows.

"You know I do, baby. You're exquisite." She blushes, and a shy smile spreads over her face. I always knew this woman would be mine, but seeing her standing in front of me now? It feels like a dream. A dream I could spend eternity living in.

When she's completely undressed, Paige saunters over to me and curls her fingers at the hem of my T-shirt. She slowly raises the material up my body, and I help her pull it over my head. She tosses it to the floor and then pulls the band of my sweatpants down. My cock is hard and as much as I would love to sink into her again, right now, I just want to hold her.

I grab hold of her hand and we step into the shower together. The spray washes away all the remnants of Vladimir's slaughter and her olive skin is left unblemished by his existence. Pulling her into my arms, I set my chin on the top of her head, and she hugs my center.

It's simple things, such as holding Paige and breathing the same air that she breathes, that mean the most to me. The connection I feel with her is something you read about but think never truly exists.

"I want Sarah here when we kill Aleksei." Her voice is calm, almost peaceful.

"We can televise it and show the entire world what happens when they fuck with you, if that's what you want," I suggest.

She snorts and shakes her head. "I want Sarah here to see me finally rid myself of the cloud that has been hovering over me since the day I met her."

I pull her into a hug and kiss her forehead. "Then have her come, baby."

"Is it weird that I'm hungry after just butchering someone?" she asks.

I chuckle, pulling her tighter to my body. "Not at all my murderous little phoenix. Let's finish so we can go get you fed."

"Little phoenix?" she parrots.

"They may have burned you down, but you rose from those ashes and came back stronger, brighter, and fiercer. You're a phoenix, mo ghrá."

Her eyes soften and she cups my cheek. I hold my hand against hers and lean in to kiss her palm. "You're my life, Paige," I whisper.

"And you are mine," she whispers back.

Chapter 45

Paige

Sarah walks into the kitchen with Rhys and rubs her hands together wickedly.

"Alright, who are we killing?" she says with a smile.

Rhys rolls his eyes playfully and kisses her temple. "Down, girl," he mutters.

She giggles under her breath, biting her lip.

I hop off the stool at the kitchen island and pull her into a hug. When I let go, her eyes quickly move to my hand and widen.

"Are you shitting me?" she gawks and swiftly takes my hand in hers. She twists it side to side as she examines the ring Declan gave me.

My cheeks heat and I bite my lip. "He asked a few days ago."

She furrows her brows and narrows her eyes at me. "And you didn't think to tell me? I am insulted."

"We've been a little busy," Declan says with a smirk. When I turn to him, he winks, and my blush deepens.

Emily walks in and sees our positions. Her eyes light up and a wide grin spreads across her face. Running over, she stands next to Sarah and looks down at the ring.

Her face morphs to sadness and her eyes water.

"What's wrong?" Her reaction is confusing.

She looks up at me and then glances over to Declan. "This was the ring my father gave to my mother the day they met. He said he knew the moment he saw her that she was going to be his wife." A tear slides down her cheek and she swipes it away.

Declan's eyes are soft when I meet them, "I did say I knew you were mine the moment I saw you, mo ghrá."

"That's so fucking romantic," Sarah says. The three of us are a blubbering mess of runny snot and tears.

My heart and soul are so full of exhilarating happiness. The light at the end of the tunnel is right in front of me now. The darkness is behind me. Now, all I need to do is walk into that light and close the tunnel.

The five of us walk down to the cellar. Sarah's head is on a swivel as she surveys everything. "So, you mean to tell me, you kill people below your house?" she asks Declan.

He shrugs. "Once the adrenaline disappears, you either get hungry, horny," he winks in my direction, "or sleepy."

She cackles and then turns to Rhys. "Do *we* have a cellar that I don't know about?"

"Torture is more of Declan's sort of thing. I like beating people to death; you know that." He spanks her ass lightly.

Emily watches the four of us with longing in her eyes, which Declan catches, and his brows furrow slightly, a small frown playing on his lips.

He takes his phone out of his pocket, sends a message, and then puts it back. I raise my brow when he looks at me, but he doesn't say anything; just smiles innocently.

Hmm.

Rhys and Declan leave us three girls in the cellar to get some *additional supplies*. We stand in the center of the room and Sarah continues to scan everything.

"The room is pretty much empty, Sarah. What are you looking at?" Emily teases.

"I want one," Sarah says plainly.

"A cellar?"

"Yup," she replies, emphasizing the "P" with a *pop.*

"Why does that not surprise me?" I laugh.

She shrugs and then smirks at me and Emily. "I need something to give me some more dopamine."

We all burst out in laughter.

Rhys and Declan return with Liam. I glance at Emily who stands straighter and a blush spreads across her face. Liam looks at her and smiles softly.

I look at Declan who is already watching me and he sends me a wink. My stomach flutters.

Just when I didn't think he could get more perfect.

The three of them set down bottles of hydrofluoric acid on the ground and then leave to collect Aleksei. When they return, my flutters have twisted into agonizing nausea. Aleksei saunters into the room and when he spots me, an evil smirk forms on his disgusting face.

I shift nervously in place as I watch him. Declan sees the change in my behavior and hits Aleksei on the back of the head with his gun, knocking him unconscious. While Rhys and Liam suspend his limp body from the chain attached to the ceiling, Declan walks over to me and cups my face.

His thumbs caress my cheeks as he looks into my eyes. "Remember, you are safe. You are not alone with him. I'm here. We are home. And you are a formidable force. A phoenix," he whispers. I nod and he places a kiss on my forehead.

I watch Aleksei's body swing from the chains for a split second then I twist around to the family I have standing in this room with me.

"What's the plan?" I ask Declan.

"Well, seeing as the fucker has a kink for knives and torture, I thought it would be fun to have acid rain down on him and burn him until he dies."

I look up to see how acid is supposed to *rain down on him* and see a network of tubes and hoses that I hadn't noticed before. A literal showerhead is in the center. I nod in appreciation of the system they have set up.

"Wake him up," I say, keeping my voice as steady as possible.

Liam walks over to the bottles of acid and pours one into a bucket. The liquid sloshes when he lifts the bucket and then heaves its contents at Aleksei. He screams when he wakes. His skin immediately bubbling where the acid had touched.

"Morning sunshine, glad you could rejoin us," Liam teases. When I look over at Emily, she is biting on the side of her lip with her cheeks crimson.

Aleksei glances at everyone, halting once he's reached me. His pupils dilate.

"I've missed you, pet," he drawls.

Declan growls and lands a punch to his face causing the chains to clink as his body is jolted. Aleksei lets out a laugh and spits blood onto the ground. Then he meets my eyes again.

"You know, I really want to play. How about you unchain me, and we can have a little fun, just for old-time's sake?"

I bite down on my tongue until my mouth fills with the taste of copper.

"Can we gag him? His voice is making me want to jab a needle in my eye," Sarah says.

Aleksei's stare turns to Sarah, and they flare with lustful interest. "Now, I bet you bleed beautifully," he purrs.

Rhys picks up a metal pole and shatters his kneecaps. "Don't you fucking look at her, you disgusting fuck."

Declan rests his hand on the small of my back and whispers in my ear, "The hoses are filled with acid, just say the word and we can open the floodgates." I nod and then take a deep breath.

I walk slowly to Aleksei.

"That's far enough," Declan says.

I look over at him and raise a brow.

"You don't want to get splashed."

I nob and stay just a few feet away from Aleksa. I stare into his eyes. Despite his kneecaps being broken and his face already swollen and bruised from the punch, he looks thrilled about his situation.

He's not worth it.

"Burn him," I tell Declan, still looking into Aleksei's eyes. The sound of a lever being pulled echoes. Seconds later, acid pours from the ceiling and onto Aleksei.

I stand, unmoving, as his skin bubbles with each drop that meets it, and he roars in pain. His flesh begins to melt off his body and fall to the floor in clumps. The smell of his burning body fills my nose and I choke down the bile that threatens to climb up my throat. Even in his last moments, his stench is retched.

It's not long before his screams die, and his body is nothing more than liquid on the ground at my feet.

Without a word, I walk out of the cellar. Closing that tunnel behind me.

Chapter 46

Declan

Paige lies fast asleep next to me. I watch the moonlight dance across her face, highlighting her high cheekbones and the slight tilt of her nose. Her lips lay slightly ajar as she breathes softly.

She shifts and a strand of hair falls onto her face. I gently tuck it behind her ear, causing her to stir. Her eyes flutter open, and she looks at me through sweet, tired eyes.

"What are you doing?" her natural rasp exaggerated from sleep.

"Just watching you," I whisper, caressing her cheek softly with the back of my fingers. She hums as she leans into my touch.

"Why is that?" she asks softly.

"You're just so damn beautiful, I don't want to miss a single moment." She smiles sleepily.

I cup her face and kiss her lips tenderly. I lick the seam of her lips – coaxing – and she opens. Our tongues move in a romantic slow dance as the kiss becomes heated. She whimpers into my mouth, and I move to hover above her.

Nudging her legs to fall open, I settle between them and press into her. She runs her fingers through my hair when I move to kiss the sensitive spot behind her ear. A breathy sigh falls from her lips.

I continue placing gentle kisses along the column of her neck, her shoulders, and her collarbone. My hand slides up her body, pushing the silk material of her sleep shirt up. The feel of her velvet soft skin causes a groan to come from the back of my throat.

She moves her hips, grinding into me, and I follow her lead. Our hands explore each other as our lips brush along lips and skin.

"I love you, Declan," she whispers through kisses.

"I live for you, Paige," I respond and then lift her shirt. Her beautiful breasts fall free, and I cup one in my hand and take her dark nipple into my mouth. She arches her back and moans my name.

Neither of us changes our leisurely pace. Simply staying completely captivated and lost in each other. Her hands travel over my shoulders and my neck and back again before she reaches down and slides my boxer-briefs down.

My hard cock leaks precum on her thigh as we continue to grind against each other. There is a distinct dark spot on her sleep shorts, showing just how wet she is.

I caress her thigh when she lifts it to wrap around my waist. Reaching the apex, I pull her shorts and panties to the side and glide a finger up and down her pussy. She moans at the contact and rolls her hips – trying to seek out more pressure.

"Always so wet for me," I rasp.

Tucking my fingers into the band of her shorts, I pull them – along with her panties – down her legs. She lets her legs fall open, leaving her glistening pussy exposed, and my mouth waters.

"You're perfection, Paige." I bend down and lick her pussy from bottom to top then I circle my tongue around her clit.

"Oh my God," she moans, her hips roll over and over as I lap at her pussy deliberately slow, savoring her honey taste.

I sink a finger into her, and her walls grip it tightly. "Fuck, baby, do you feel how tight you're holding onto my finger?" Her eyes are shut firmly and she's biting her lip, but she nods rapidly.

A low chuckle leaves my lips and then I add a second finger. I keep my pumps slow – teasing. Every so often, I curl my fingers to rub that perfect soft spot that drives her wild.

"Declan, I need you," she begs. I place a kiss on her pussy and then position myself at her entrance. I gradually sink my cock into her, watching myself disappear into her body inch by inch. Her back arches when I slide back out and then sink into her again. Her walls grip me so delectably.

My thrusts are unhurried. This isn't fucking. This is making love.

"Look at me, ghrá." Her sea-green eyes meet mine. "Keep your eyes on me, baby."

With each slow thrust, her eyes threaten to roll into the back of her head but because she's such a good girl, she keeps my gaze. Our ragged breaths and moans fill the room. I'm drowning in Paige's ecstasy.

I move my hand to rub her clit. Her walls start to tighten, and her moans get louder.

"Oh fuck. Declan, I'm going to come," she whimpers.

"Come for me. Paige. Lose yourself in me." Her pussy chokes my cock and then she comes with a loud and throaty groan.

"That's it, baby. That's it." I fuck her through her orgasm, continuing to rub her clit as she falls into her bliss.

Her body relaxes after she comes down from her high. My thrusts start to speed up – chasing my own orgasm that is ready to hit me. My jaw is slack and I'm panting as I watch myself pump in and out of her. Cream covers my cock and it's one of the best sights in the world.

Soon my spine tingles, telling me of the impending orgasm making its way. I grab hold of Paige's hips and my thrusts become more forceful. She digs her nails into my ass cheeks, pulling me into her, meeting me thrust for thrust. My balls tighten. I pump into her one final time. Body vibrating and heart racing, I spill my cum into her pussy with a deep groan.

She kisses the top of my head when I slump onto her chest. Her fingers trace little circles on my back. I listen as her heart thumps rhythmically beneath my ear. I know I wouldn't have survived if I never had the chance to hear this sound again.

After I've caught my breath, I push myself from her chest and walk to the ensuite. I take a washcloth from the shelf and run warm water on it. Striding back into the room, Paige is sitting cross-legged in the center of the bed, peering down at her hand.

"Everything okay?" I ask.

She looks up at me with eyes that show hints of apprehension.

"I want to tell you about why I struggle when talking about us having kids."

I pause in the doorway and wait for her to continue. The very few times we've remotely danced around the subject of future kids, Paige closes off. This is the one subject she struggles with telling me the most and I'm anxious to know why.

She looks out at the night sky through the window, her eyes become distant – haunted.

"I was seventeen when I was forced to get pregnant with Mark's baby." I suck in a sharp breath. She turns to me with watery eyes.

"I was four months pregnant when I started having really sharp pains in my stomach and then one day, I started bleeding, and it wouldn't stop. I was home alone for hours without a way to make it to the hospital. But after a while, I realized that I didn't *want* to go to the hospital. I hoped that I would just bleed out on the floor and die. Mark showed up and was banging on the bathroom door, screaming at me to let him in, but I was so weak that I couldn't. I laid there in my own blood on the tile floor until he broke the door down. He took me to the hospital and when I woke up, they told me that they performed some type of procedure to help remove the *tissue* from my body.

"I had hemorrhaged, which is why I bled so much. When I was released from the hospital, Mark took me home and raped me by the front door as soon as we got inside. He beat me for losing the baby and then raped me multiple times a day after that to try and get me pregnant again. It went on for months and each time I took a test that came back negative, he would beat me and then let his friends take turns raping me," she chokes out a sob and I scoop her up in my arms and set her in my lap. I stroke her hair softly.

"I became so suicidal that I took off and was standing at the top of a ravine that had to have been a hundred feet below me. I stood there and decided *this is it. I can't do this anymore.* Dying was my only way to escape the hell I was in," a gentle shaky smile plays on her lips, "that was the day I met Sarah. She stopped me from killing myself that day and we ran here to New York."

She looks up at me with such sad eyes, it cuts through my heart.

"I hated that baby, Declan. I didn't even name it. I hated that I was growing the product of my rape inside my body. I wanted nothing to do with it. I didn't mourn the miscarriage. I begged to whatever God that would listen to take that child from me. To make it disappear. *I* did that. What kind of person does that make me? I would have turned out exactly like my mom. Hating a child for simply existing."

I cup her face. "That baby died because they weren't meant for this earth. Not because you prayed for a greater force to take them. You're nothing like that woman who raised you. You wouldn't have hated that baby once you laid eyes on them. Your heart is too pure for that, Paige. Would you have raised them? There's no telling, but I have no doubts that you have ensured they lived a good life — away from that fucker and the evil he was letting into this world."

"I want to have babies with you, Declan. I do. But I'm *scared.* I'm so fucking scared that because I hated an innocent life so deeply, some force will refuse to gift me with one that I can truly love. I'm scared because I *know* I don't deserve the sort of love and happiness a child can bring into this world, but fuck I want it so bad."

The tears steadily flow down her cheeks. I wipe them with my thumbs. "You deserve all the happiness in the world, Paige. Maybe once you've truly let go of all the emotions and trauma you have bottled up inside, you will be able to see that. Maybe then you'll be free."

She closes her eyes for a moment. "I hope I can be."

Chapter 47

Paige

I sit in the front room, listening to the sounds of Sarah, Rhys, Declan, Emily, and Liam laughing from the kitchen. The last several days have been...draining. Since the oppressive weight of my demons has been lifted... I just feel so tired. I no longer feel like I'm constantly in a fight-or-flight situation, or that a shadow will creep up on me, but I just feel different.

I don't know what to do. A new weight feels like it's settling on me, but this weight is a faceless one without a name. It's teetering on the edge waiting to be pushed, waiting for its chance to explode. It's been building and building like a storm-cloud collecting water vapors.

I've been disassociating more frequently, feeling more agitated, and wanting space. Declan and Emily keep encouraging me to find ways to release this energy within me. They keep telling me that letting go will be the only way I can truly leave that tunnel closed.

Talking with Declan about my miscarriage helped, but also caused damage. It helped me deepen my connection with Declan and helped him understand how I'm feeling, but It's also made me feel things I didn't when I miscarried.

I never truly processed the loss – I wouldn't let myself. Back then, it felt asinine to mourn the loss of a child that was forced on me. To mourn a life that I didn't think I could love. Now? Now I feel like I *should* have mourned them. It wasn't their fault that they were conceived the way they were. It wasn't their fault that I was in a place that I begged for a way to escape from.

I think I would have found a way to give them a family and a life I was denied. Even if that meant it that life wasn't with me.

"Are you okay?" Sarah's voice is soft.

I turn from the window, and she is sitting in the seat across from me. I hadn't heard her walk in.

"Do you remember when I told you about my miscarriage?"

She grimaces but nods. "Of course I do. I remember everything you told me. Why do you ask?"

My eyes search hers. For what? I don't know.

"I spoke with Declan about it since he's asked about kids. I told him how much I hated that baby and how I know I don't deserve the love one can bring."

"Paige, you were a child when you became pregnant. You had so much trauma at that time, you're allowed to feel a certain way about whatever you were going through. But if there is anyone in this fucked up place that deserves that kind of pure love, it's you," she gives me a sad smile. "You don't need to even think about having kids right now, Paige. Allow yourself the time to process everything you've been through. Allow yourself to be in love with Declan and to have his love in return."

I nod. "You're right. I don't really even know what I'm trying to say about the whole situation, anyway." I wave my hand out in dismissal.

"Maybe a change of scenery is what you need?" I raise my brow at her. "You haven't left this mansion since you came back. I think it would help if you left and just processed everything away from the intense atmosphere here."

"I agree," Declan's voice says, and we startle. I look over and see him leaning against the wall with his ankles crossed and his hands in his pockets. He smiles at me and then strides over.

Sitting next to me, Declan places his hand on my thigh and rubs circles with his thumb. "I promised that I would take you to a better place than our Florida trip a few months back. I think now that there is no longer a threat to you, we should leave for a little while."

Sarah claps her hands excitedly. "Yes! Take her somewhere she can focus on healing and finding peace."

Declan glances at Sarah and then back to me. "How do you feel about going to Ireland? You can meet my ma."

I smile and nod. "Okay."

The week passes in a blur. Declan and Rhys haven't been around often since they need to ensure everything is going to run perfectly without Declan being here. We're going to be in Ireland for at least a month and Declan doesn't want to be interrupted unless things are being burnt down.

Emily won't be traveling with us. She hasn't quite gotten to the point of trusting she will be okay if she travels to Ireland, since that is where she was taken. So, she will be staying with Liam in the mansion. Seeing Emily happy outweighed Declan's hesitance about her being with Liam. She's told him how she loves him and he's the one she sees herself spending the rest of her life with. So, Declan let go, and Emily is glowing.

I've been rummaging through our closet, trying to decide what to pack. The clothes here are all new and designer. Declan insisted on buying me a new wardrobe, but I didn't realize how much shit it would be. There are hundreds of blouses, dresses, skirts, pants, and lingerie. Don't even get me started on the shoes. Emily found my reaction hilarious when I saw the clothes and told me that I better get used to this because Declan is going to spoil me for the rest of my life.

"Still staring blankly at the clothes?" Emily teases when she walks into the closet.

"I can now understand why celebrities have stylists," I grumble.

Emily lets out a snort, "I'll help you pack.". She wastes no time in tossing different articles of clothing in my arms. I'm drowning under a mountain of different colored outfits by the time she's finished.

"Will I really need all of this?" I huff.

"You're going for a month and chances are, Declan will not keep you at my mom's house. He will take you all over the place. So, yes. You need all this."

Declan's Ireland home is incomprehensibly gorgeous. It might be similar to the one in New York, but this is a literal castle. It's phenomenal.

"Like it?" I can hear the smile in Declan's tone as I stare, awestricken, at the structure in front of us.

The land around us is a vast forest of *green.* Everything is a flawless emerald color. The large front door opens, and a *beautiful* woman with long, wavy red hair and deep blue eyes steps out.

"*Dia duit*, mam." Declan's tone is loving and gentle as the woman walks down the steps.

"*Dia duit,* mo pháiste." Her voice is angelic as she pulls Declan into a tight embrace. When they separate, she meets my eyes with a sweet motherly smile.

"And you must be, Paige. I'm Caetlin."

"Hello," I smile shyly. When I attempt to shake her hand, she pushes it away and then pulls me into a hug.

"There is no handshaking in this family, my dear." Her perfume is light and floral.

My throat tightens at her referring to me as family. It's something I've wanted to be a part of my entire life. To be surrounded by people who care for me and my well-being, rather than what I can do for them.

"Let's get you both inside and settled, shall we?" She loops her arm through mine and leads us to the door.

The inside of her home is warm and welcoming. The décor includes numerous photos of Declan and Emily. The kitchen is large but, where Declan's is massive and professional restaurant-appearing, this one is very homey. Everything about this home radiates love. I never would have guessed a mafia family lived here.

"How is Emily?" Caetlin asks as she sets down three coffee mugs on the dining table.

"She's been doing well, still not ready to travel here but I think with the help of Liam, she will be," Declan says.

"That boy surely does love her, doesn't he?"

Declan nods and then glances at me. "Yes, he does. I almost stood in the way of that, and I'm really glad I didn't."

My cheeks flush because I know if I hadn't mentioned the love she shared with Liam, Declan wouldn't have seen it with his own eyes.

Caetlin sets her hand on mine, pulling me away from Declan's stare. "And how are you feeling, my dear?"

"I'm doing much better," I reply, and she squeezes my fingers.

"That is incredibly good to hear. Declan and Emily both speak so highly of you." My cheeks flush and I dip my chin to avoid her seeing the tears gathering in my eyes.

The rest of the night is full of laughter and stories of Declan's childhood. Caetlin didn't ask about mine, so I assume she's more than aware of my upbringing. After dinner, Declan and I walk to his old bedroom.

A bed sits to the right, centered against the wall, covered with black sheets. The walls have shelves with different photos of Declan and other men. I recognize a few of them with Rhys. He has a desk in the corner – closest to the windows. The ensuite has a large shower and a vanity with an oval mirror hanging on the wall. The walk-in closet sits adjacent to the bathroom and is empty, aside from some towels on the shelf.

"Ma wanted to fill the closet with some clothes for us, but I told her not to."

"Thank you. I don't know how many more clothes I can accept." I send him a look that makes him chuckle.

"What would you like to do while we're here?" He steps forward and pulls me into his arms. He presses his nose against my hair and breathes in deeply before his shoulders relax.

"I want to see historical castles."

He laughs loudly at that request. "Then I shall take you to every castle in Ireland mo ghrá."

We spend the next several weeks traveling to hundreds of different castles. Some were, without a doubt, scary as shit the moment they came into view, so I *know* they were haunted. Others were sad. It was astonishing to be able to *feel* the energy in the stones of the past lives that lived in those walls.

The history of this country is remarkable. I absorbed every word. We were told of the different kings and queens, princes, princesses and other people who lived in the castles. The areas that I struggled with exploring were the cells and dungeons. The air in them was suffocating with pain and suffering. Those were the nights I experienced nightmares. And every time, Declan would stroke my hair and whisper sweet, encouraging words. Reminding me that I was safe and with him.

Each day that passes, I feel pieces of myself that never previously existed make themselves known. Those pieces of myself are quiet and calm.

I look over the limitless view of green grasses and trees at the back of the mansion. Caetlin has many horses grazing, and it makes me miss the peace that Lily brings.

"Mind if I join you?" Caetlin asks from the doorway.

"Of course not." I gesture for her to sit next to me. The light tap of her shoes sounds on the stone.

"Declan says you like horses?" She sits admiring the same view as me.

"I wouldn't say *horses*, there is one particular horse – Lily – I developed a really strong bond with her when I went to live with Declan."

She nods. Facing me, the corner of her lip tips upward. "There is a Goddess that is believed to have been a Mother Goddess and a Warrior Goddess. Her name is Epona. She was a Goddess of horses. A very formidable woman, that one. When Declan had told me about your love for horses and the steps you've taken to eradicate what has haunted you, I immediately thought of Epona."

"Declan told you what I've done?" I croak.

Her eyes become mischievous. "Of course he did. And I am quite proud of you for even giving him the light of day."

I chuckle, "I'm very grateful for the love he gives me."

"The men in this family sure know how to love deeply. But the women in this family? That's what they write about in history books." She winks and pats my hand one more time before standing and leaving me outside.

The last few weeks in Ireland were magical. It felt like a dream being a part of a family and being surrounded by a mother figure that was loving and caring. Caetlin is a powerful woman who is running an empire all on her own and has men at her mercy.

"I have one thing I think I need to do," I tell Declan once we board the private plane.

"What is that, ghrá?"

I look out the window for a moment as the plane coasts down the tarmac. "I need to close a door that should have been locked a long time ago."

Turning my head to Declan, he studies my face, waiting for me to explain further.

"I need to speak to my mother."

I stand outside my childhood home. The peeling shit-colored paint remains, weeds have taken over the yard, and trash of all sorts is littered throughout the entire property. The atmosphere is thick with the neglect I sustained here. The pain I suffered.

And yet... I don't feel the suffocating weight of it. It hovers just outside of the protective fortress I've built around the life I'm building with Declan.

Declan's fingers intertwine with mine as I stare at the last piece of my past that I'm unchaining myself from. With a last deep breath, I walk up the chipped concrete steps. I knock on the weathered front door, and it groans in protest. The distant sound of things being put away and steps coming close comes from the other side and then the door swings open.

My mom stands in the doorway in a set of ripped pajamas and a faded robe draped over her shoulders. A cigarette hangs loosely from the corner of her mouth, smoke rising from the tip.

"Well, well, well. Look who decided to grace us with her ungrateful presence," her voice scratches my ears like metal scraping the floor.

"Watch your tone when you speak with my wife," Declan growls.

My mother's eyes snake down his body. Her eyes darken in lust and my hackles raise. When she notices the movement, her eyes flick back to mine and a smirk grows on her lips.

"Wife, you say?" She glances back at Declan, her voice changing to the purr she uses to grab the attention of men. My blood heats at her blatant attempts at trying to seduce Declan.

"I came to talk to you," I interrupt.

Her eyes fill with disdain when she turns her gaze on me. "What? Can't keep your man here satisfied?"

Declan takes a step forward, but I put my hand against his chest to prevent him from moving.

I take in her appearance more closely. Her hair has thinned out since the last time I saw her. Her skin is grayer, and her face is scabbed in multiple places from her picking it. Her frame is more skeletal than feminine. The more I study her, the more I pity her.

I breathe out a quick breath and shake my head as I look at her with a smirk on my lips.

"What the fuck are you smiling about? Think because you landed yourself a man with some money you're better than me? Did you forget that you're just like me? Washed up and dirty."

"You know what? You're not even worth it. You've been infected with poison for so long that you can't see anything different. I feel bad for you. I feel bad that you won't be anything more than the foul woman you are now. I feel bad that you are so miserable with your own existence that you need to ruin everything and everyone else around you, including your daughter, who you were meant to love and protect, but instead you allowed grown men to rape her while you stood by and listened to her cries for help."

I don't give her time to say anything. Instead, I turn around and walk away.

Thunder rumbles through my ears as we drive up the winding road back to the estate. The grassy field and the trees of the forest around us begin to transform into a deep emerald as water starts to fall from the sky.

Another boom of thunder reverberates through the sky. Ripping open the door, I jump out of the car and take off running through the field. My heart is pounding in my chest as I struggle to run through the wet grass. Declan calls out my name, but I don't stop. I continue running until I slip and fall to my hands and knees.

Tears fall from my eyes as I stare at the grass while trying to catch my breath.

Tipping my head back, I close my eyes, and feel the rain cleanse my body and soul of the evil that was forced upon me. Of the pain that was inflicted at the hands of monsters, I couldn't escape. The resentment I held for my mother and of the grief for the childhood I was robbed of.

Hair sticking to his forehead, clothes saturated and sticking to his body, Declan stands in front of me. I meet his Caribbean-blue eyes and he smiles warmly at me. My lip quivers and I sob into my hands. He kneels down and pulls me into his chest. His presence envelopes me in warmth despite the cold raining down on us.

His thumb and forefinger grip my chin and he tips my head to look at him. The thunder booms around us and the sky is lit up by lighting. The raindrops splash onto every surface of the earth and our skin.

"You're free," he whispers, and he kisses me.

Epilogue

Declan

5 years later

"Ah!" Paige's screams ring in my ears as doctors and nurses scramble to get her into the delivery room. She's clenching my hand so tightly that I've lost feeling in my fingers. The erratic beats of my heart fill my ears with the blood rushing through my body.

"Fuck! It hurts!" she squeals through her tears. Her pain-stricken face is red and sweaty. Her chest heaves with each rapid breath she takes.

A nurse begins helping Paige remove her clothes to be placed in a gown when she pauses. "We have a head!" she screams, and then the room is thrown into utter chaos as the doctor hurries to put some plastic blue covering over his chest and shoulders.

My hand remains tightly in Paige's grasp and the nurses work around me to get her legs propped up into position.

"Okay, Paige. When you're ready, we need you to push," the doctor says.

Paige shakes her head violently from side to side. "I can't, it hurts," she whimpers and then her face scrunches in pain as another contraction hits, and her body involuntarily begins to push.

"Fuck!" she screams and her other hand flies out to grip the bed's railing.

"You can do this, mo ghrá. I'm right here with you. I know you're in pain, but it will pass as soon as you bring our baby into this world." I push back her sweaty hair and kiss her forehead.

Her tears fall down her face as she looks at me and I wipe them away.

"You can do this," I whisper.

She whimpers again as another contraction hits and her stomach tightens as she pushes.

"Almost there!" the doctor encourages.

Nurses run around the room readying for the arrival of our first baby.

I watch as the strongest woman I've met, brings another life into this world.

Paige roars in pain with her eyes closed tightly and then slumps against the bed in exhaustion. The loud cries of our baby fill the room and my eyes fill with tears as the doctor lifts our tiny person and turns them to face us.

"Congratulations! You have a beautiful, healthy baby girl." Paige's hand squeezes mine and our eyes meet.

A girl... we have a baby girl.

She sobs and I lean in to kiss her forehead again. "You did it, my little phoenix," I whisper.

After our baby is checked and weighed, the nurse brings her over and places her just inside Paige's gown. Her cries immediately disappear the moment their skins touch. She has dark hair like her mother and her nose is shaped like mine. She's a perfect mix of us both.

My heart is an explosion of love and happiness. I never imagined this life in my future. I have the love of my life as a wife and now I'm a father to the most beautiful baby girl.

"What would you like to name her?" I whisper, watching the enchanting scene before me.

"Aileen," she says caressing her forefinger along our daughter's brow.

"Aileen," I parrot. "Our bright, shining light. It's perfect, just like her ma."

Paige's tired face smiles up at me.

We watch our baby girl as she starts to maneuver around on Paige's chest and then latches onto her breast to nurse.

A light knock comes from the door and then it opens. Rhys, Sarah, Emily, and Liam walk silently in. Sarah and Emily immediately start crying when they spot Paige and Aileen.

"Oh my God, Paige. You're a mom," Sarah whisper-cries through her palm on her mouth. Tears flow uncontrollably down her face.

"Is the baby a boy or a girl?" Emily asks.

"This is Aileen, our beautiful daughter." Paige peers down at her and a smile spreads over her face.

"Congratulations, brother," Rhys says with a slap to my back.

"Congratulations, Boss," Liam says.

I smirk at Liam. "You've been married to Emily for a year now, Liam. We're family. You really should stop calling me Boss."

He chuckles and lifts his shoulders in a shrug. "Habit."

"Are you ready for this?" I peek over at Rhys who is watching Sarah with soft eyes. Her small bump is on display in the figure-hugging sundress she is wearing today.

"Yeah, Dec... I think I am," he whispers.

After spending an hour with us, our family leaves.

"Want to hold her?" Paige whispers.

I nod and walk over to the bed. Paige lifts Aileen up and hands her over to me. "Mind her head."

I cradle her tiny body in the crook of my elbow and look down at her perfect face.

"Hello, little babe," I whisper and caress her fingers. Her small hand opens, and she grips my forefinger, unable to fully close her fist around it. Tears form in my eyes and slowly fall down my cheeks.

I look up to Paige, who is crying with a smile on her face. "Thank you," she says, with eyes full of tenderness and love.

"What for, mo ghrá?"

"Saving me."

Ready to follow Emily's journey?
Freeing Emily is coming Summer/Fall 2024!

Want to read more about Sarah?
Sarah and Rhys's story is coming Winter 2024- Spring 2025!

Acknowledgment

Ya'll…. I wrote a whole ass book…

I can't even begin to find the words to describe just how grateful I am that you took a chance on my debut novel. It truly means everything to me.

It's been an interesting journey. Saving Paige came to me during one of my many insomniac episodes and I wrote about 3 chapters in my head. The next day, she took form. The fact that it's out there in the world and people are actually reading and enjoying my writing is absolutely mind-blowing. I hope you fell in love with Paige and Declan as much as I love them.

To my husband, thank you for all your support during my deep dive into the romance world. I know I've talked your ear off many times from the stories I've fallen in love with. Thank you for being a life-line for me the lean on. Thank you for helping me stay motivated in all aspects of life. You are my rock. My life. I love you.

To my beautiful son, Brentley, I know you're still little but the fact that you would ask me how my book writing was doing melted my heart. Telling me how much you think people will like it despite having absolutely no idea what I am writing about meant more to me that I will ever be able to put into words. I love you with every fiber of my being.

To my sister, Chealsey, thank you so much for being an amazing support system. I am so blessed to have you as family. You mean so much to me and I am grateful for the relationship we have. Being able to share my ideas with you and having someone share the same excitement I feel is amazing. I love you.

To my new friend and fellow author, Jessi Hart, THANK YOU so much for helping me on my path to becoming an indie author. Without your constant help, I would have been completely lost. I appreciate you so much.

To Maggie! Thank you so much for being my editor! Your recommendations were so amazing and helped bring out my story in a way that made it that much better. I appreciate you helping me and I look forward to working with you on future books!

To my Beta readers, I don't think you understand how much it means to me that you were willing to help me see what parts of my story that could flow better with different changes. It really opened my eyes and made me a better writer. Thank you.

www.ingramcontent.com/pod-product-compliance
Lightning Source LLC
LaVergne TN
LVHW100509110826
845146LV00002B/574

* 9 7 9 8 9 9 0 6 0 3 9 1 2 *